Cover Copy

To love and protect…across worlds.

In a world divided by war, a princess meets her rival mate...

Epic fantasy for young adult readers. First love, magical skills, addictive reading.

Eighteen-year-old Hope Wincrest calls the Outback of Australia her home away from home. She is a princess of Dralion from the planet Magio, where the two leading nations are at war. While in the Outback, Hope is warned by her warrior father—who holds the prophetic ability of forethought—that she is about to meet an enemy protector. She doesn't expect him to be her soul-bound mate, a man she must now work with to piece together her unknown mother's lost heritage.

Peacio's Silas Carver follows the calling of his soul to Australia, only not all goes as planned. Discovering Hope is his mate has him demanding his release from their bond. She agrees, but only if he first helps her learn about her mother.

Hope must lay her life in Silas's hands during a journey which takes them deep into foreign lands. Waging a battle of the heart, and of the land, can the young mated pair find their place with each other?

Books by Joanne Wadsworth

The Matheson Brothers Series
Highlander's Desire, Book One
Highlander's Passion, Book Two
Highlander's Seduction, Book Three
Highlander's Kiss, Book Four
Highlander's Heart, Book Five
Highlander's Sword, Book Six
Highlander's Bride, Book Seven
Highlander's Caress, Book Eight
Highlander's Touch, Book Nine
Highlander's Shifter, Book Ten
Highlander's Claim, Book Eleven
Highlander's Courage, Book Twelve
Highlander's Mermaid, Book Thirteen

Highlander Heat Series
Highlander's Castle, Book One
Highlander's Magic, Book Two
Highlander's Charm, Book Three
Highlander's Guardian, Book Four
Highlander's Faerie, Book Five
Highlander's Champion, Book Six
Highlander's Captive (Short Story)

Billionaire Bodyguards Series
Billionaire Bodyguard Attraction, Book One
Billionaire Bodyguard Boss, Book Two
Billionaire Bodyguard Fling, Book Three

Books by Joanne Wadsworth

Regency Brides Series
The Duke's Bride, Book One
The Earl's Bride, Book Two
The Wartime Bride, Book Three
The Earl's Secret Bride, Book Four
The Prince's Bride, Book Five
Her Pirate Prince, Book Six
Chased by the Corsair, Book Seven

Princesses of Myth Series
Protector, Book One
Warrior, Book Two
Hunter (Short Story - Included in Warrior, Book Two)
Enchanter, Book Three
Healer, Book Four
Chaser, Book Five

Warrior

Princesses of Myth, Book Two

Joanne Wadsworth

Warrior
ISBN-13: 978-1-99-003416-9
Copyright © 2013, Joanne Wadsworth
Cover Art by Joanne Wadsworth
First electronic publication: September 2013

Joanne Wadsworth
http://www.joannewadsworth.com

AUTHOR'S NOTE:
This book is a work of fiction. The names, characters, places, and incidents are products of the writer's imagination or have been used fictitiously and are not to be construed as real. Any resemblance to persons, living or dead, actual events, locale or organizations is entirely coincidental. The author does not have any control over and does not assume any responsibility for third-party websites or their content.

Published in the United States of America

First digital publication: September 2013
First print publication: September 2013

Dedication

For my daughter, Marisa, who is growing up before my eyes. You are so precious. Hugs.

Acknowledgements

To my hubby, Jason, and kiddies, Marisa, Caleb, Cruise and Rocco, I love you all, and thank you for allowing me the time to write.

This book was so much fun to write, and even more fun to edit and sculpt, thanks to my amazing editor, Penny Barber.

For my readers, you rock. I received such a wonderful response after *Protector's* release, and this series lives because you joined me, taking the journey to where imagination and magic soar.

Chapter 1

"Hope, I know you're hurting." Goldwyn Wincrest, my aunt, strode beside me along the path to the horse corral.

I kicked at the red outback dust underfoot. "I can't stand my existence being kept from my own mother. All these years, she's believed me dead."

My father, Alexo Wincrest, was reuniting with my mother, Kate, right now, and had forbidden my return to Dralion.

"But Alexo's trying to fix things, to build a relationship with Kate after eighteen years of separation. We need to give him the time he's asked for." Argh, how could Goldie be so reasonable when, at nineteen, she was only a year older than me?

"My own mother's a mystery to me, as is the sister I've gained along with her. How on earth do I have a twin? I need answers." Even as I understood it, I detested Dad's request.

"Lieska's been scouting for us. She contacted me telepathically and said she has news. Let's wait on her."

"Alexo never taught me to sit idly by. I can't believe I must."

"It's what he's asked." Goldie kept stride beside me. "Alexo had to protect your mother and sister's whereabouts from Donaldo since the day he brought you home as a baby. It was not an easy task, but it was done."

I unclipped the gate and waited as she came through. "My

father has forethought and forewarning. Alexo should know I won't sit still."

"You must." She tipped her black Stetson back and eyed me. "He's asked you to wait before meeting your mother and sister. There'll be a good reason. He sees the bigger picture, Hope."

"What I wouldn't give to have his prophetic abilities, or any of the strength skills of our people."

"Just be glad Donaldo Wincrest doesn't have Alexo's skill of forethought and forewarning, because as much as I love my father, we'd all be in trouble if he did." Her breath whistled out.

Donaldo, my grandfather, ruled our home land of Dralion with precision and determination. My mother, Kate, had been of Earth, and even though she was Dad's soul-bound mate, she was not a skilled Magioling. Donaldo would never have allowed her for his son had the prince brought her home.

A shiver chased down my spine, even as the sun blazed high above. By leaving her behind on Earth, Dad had sought my mother's protection. She had remained safe, but at what expense?

A light breeze swirled. The displacement in the air had to be Lieska. I needed answers and Lieska was a warrior, close to our age. A trusted confidant.

Her form wavered into view and solidified a few feet away. Yes.

Lieska stepped forward, brushing the dust from her hip-hugging leather pants.

"What news do you bring?" I burned to know.

"I come from the trenches." She shoved her fingers underneath her dark hair and swished it. A smattering of dried nettles fluttered to the ground, one leaf catching in the spiked belt on her side, which held a curved dagger.

"Peacio?" I froze. Carlisio Loveria, along with his fighting force of protectors, ruled Peacio. "What's the land of our enemy got to do with finding out more about my mother and sister?"

"Kate Sol. That's your mother's name. Your sister's is Faith. Bad news, that one." She sighed raggedly. "I've seen Faith with Davio Loveria. In Peacio. Obviously not the place I expected to find her, but I tracked her from Dralion."

"What?" Dad would never allow such a thing. He had not hidden my mother and sister for eighteen years just to allow my sister to be with Carlisio's grandson. That would be like throwing her to the lions. "That's outrageous. Why would my sister be in Peacio with him?"

With a firm shake of her head, Lieska said, "Your sister is soul-bound to Davio Loveria. I've spied them together and can assure you I speak the truth. It is a complication your father has clearly foreseen."

"Tell me you lie. This can't be."

The mated bond was revered, but this had to be a cruel joke. We had not had a mated match between our people and theirs in forty years. Not since enchanter Gilles Moyer spelled the dome, the energy field over Dralion protecting our people from Peacians.

"It's true."

My heart lurched.

Goldie stared at me. "If that's the case, Donaldo can never know of this. To discover his newly returned granddaughter is mated to his enemy would take our war to new levels."

"You are right." Lieska nodded. "I've spoken to Alexo, and he protects this knowledge. It is one of the reasons he makes Hope wait. He has asked me to speak of his current needs with both of you."

I raised a brow. "Continue. Tell me all he's requested."

She stroked the polished hilt of her dagger. "Faith holds forethought and the battle skills as your father does. She is a telepathic and can 'port. She moves freely, as all warriors and Wincrests do through the dome room. Faith's rising is complete, and along with it came the ability of mind-merge, a skill we've no historical records of. Alexo has a specific request."

I inhaled, slowly. One of my passions was the study of our people's strength skills. I worked here on this outback station, and when on our home world of Magio, spent a great deal of time documenting all I could. "Mind-merge doesn't flow through the Wincrest line and my mother is an Earthling."

Lieska eyed me. "Unless she is not."

The wind picked up, swirling the dust at my feet. "What do you know?"

"Your sister's ability of mind-merge has come from your mother's line. Alexo has had forewarning. You'll soon get close to a protector, and when you do, find a way to piece together all you can on Kate Sol's line. You must do this without giving yourself away to your sister, as the protector in question knows her. It's imperative you and Faith not yet meet."

"That's all he gave you? The unknown skill of mind-merge and Kate Sol's full name?"

"You must discover the rest, for there is nothing more he can do from Dralion."

"Great." How was I to get close to a protector? "Did he have any advice, even a smidgeon more?"

"It's not advice. He said he loses sight of you for a few days, but it's what needs to happen. He told me you must rely on those around you. Not all is as it seems."

"What? Alexo never loses sight of me with his skill, unless I'm in the dark. How can I be in the dark?"

"He didn't like that piece of his forewarning either, but it's what needs to be. His words."

Goldie squeezed my arm. "I'm concerned, particularly about this protector you're going to get close to. We don't associate with our enemy, not unless there're swords and bloodshed involved."

Dad had seen more than he'd spoken of. "Obviously I'll

need to carry a weapon."

Lieska unstrapped a knife from a sheath on her calf. "Your father said you would not be harmed, but take it."

I lifted the cuff of my blue jeans, and strapped the band of warm leather above my ankle. Slotting the blade carefully into place, I resolved to see to his instructions. I would not let him down.

Goldie crossed her arms. "This is why the Wincrests rule Dralion. We do what we must."

Lieska fisted her hands. "Yes, and Alexo asked me to speak to Guy next. Our young enchanter has made his own arrangement with Faith since he spotted her in Peacio. Alexo needs Guy to know he's heard of his talk with Faith, and he expects him to keep quiet on all he's discovered about her being mated with Loveria. No word of any of this can get back to Donaldo. Faith's mated relationship took with Loveria before her ties to Alexo were known. Now their soul-bond cannot be undone. Even the Loveria family keeps quiet."

Horses whinnied from the corrals and Goldie checked over her shoulder. "Guy's here somewhere. Probably with Maslin in the stables. Give me any further updates the moment they come to hand. With Davio Loveria mated to my new niece, and a protector soon coming into contact with Hope, we need to take the utmost care."

"Certainly." Lieska turned to me and set her hands on my shoulders. "I told Alexo I would keep an eye on you, but he said you'll handle what's coming. Make sure you do. You do not have any strength skills."

"I promise I'll take care." My eighteenth birthday had passed a few short weeks ago, and no skills had come as I'd entered adulthood.

Her fingers pressed deeper, smearing dirt on my red-checked outback shirt. "I have confidence in you."

"Thank you, and for all the information you've given me."

"Do not thank me too soon. You are to meet a protector." With a nod, she stepped back, teleporting away.

"Argh." Goldie shivered. "I do not care for the thought of you coming into contact with one of the enemy, yet I can't argue against Alexo's forethought. Your father is a menace though, with his prophecies and allowing them to unravel as they should."

I smiled. "Perhaps I'm supposed to kill the protector once I've seen to this discovery of Kate Sol's line."

Goldie chuckled. "Make sure you do."

My grin widened and I set my thumbs into the loops of my jeans. "They are a thorn in our sides. If we had Carlisio Loveria's land, imagine how much more prosperous Dralion and our people would be."

As we passed under a towering stand of eucalyptus trees Goldie linked her arm through mine. A touch of shade relieved the oppressive heat for a second. Drought was killing this land.

"How I would love a slice of Peacio. We would actually have grass to feed our cattle. Even this off-world station suffers as our lands at home do."

Once the rains came, we'd return our stock numbers to full force on this massive Australian outback holding. "It's fortunate we have the mighty river bordering this land, and Maslin's water skill."

Maslin, a warrior two years older than me, had earned my respect. He moved large quantities of water during the river's release periods and sent it further infield. With just a flick of his fingers and a thought, it flowed and soaked into the ground, bringing life to the river pasture and sustaining it for our remaining stock.

Tucking one loose blue shirttail into her black jeans, Goldie eyed the red plains that ran forever into the distance. "I love this place. When it finally rains, I'm going to roll around in the fields. All of them."

"That won't be possible. There're eight-thousand square miles out there."

She flicked my arm. "It doesn't matter how long it takes me. So much space will make the task all the more enjoyable."

We walked alongside the high-railed wooden corral. Saunder, the thirteen-year-old nephew of two of our station's warriors, offered a treat to the stallion hitched to an inner holding post. Two years ago, Peacio's protectors had taken Saunder's father at the battle of Eventide. Without either of his parents, he'd chosen his uncles to raise him. The child was one of the few allowed outside Dralion who was not a Wincrest or a warrior.

Goldie opened the corral gate and grinned at Saunder. She crossed to him and ruffled his messy brown hair. "I see you've saddled our boy. Does he want a run?"

"I knew you'd be down soon." He gave her a lopsided smile, plucking his fingers through suspenders holding up his loose, long-legged pants. The boy adored Goldie.

Bumping my shoulder into Saunder's, I winked. "You should be doing your schoolwork. Your father would expect it if he were here." We adored our children, ensuring their immediate and extended family raised them, usually within Dralion's villages. Yet Saunder had asked to come here, and his wishes couldn't be denied.

"I have to help feed the mares first. My uncles asked me to."

"I'll take this one from you then." Goldie reached for the stallion's leads.

"Thanks." Saunder passed them across then raced out the gate.

Holding a hand to my chest, I wished for all the world Saunder had his father back. I'd never handle losing my own. I loved my dad, and I cherished our close bond. Which was why, deep down, his decision to keep my existence a secret hurt, no matter his reasoning.

"You're wanted, and loved." Goldie's gaze softened as she crooned to the huge chestnut stallion.

The wind tickled my hair about my face. "Are you talking to him or me?"

"Both of you." The stallion lifted his sleek head, pushing into Goldie's hand as she petted him. "Although he listens better."

Coming around in front, I dug into my pocket and pulled out a bite-sized treat, which I was never without. "Here, boy. Hope loves you more. Don't you forget that."

Dropping his nose into my palm, he gobbled the treat. I scratched between his silky ears. We had two-hundred breeding mares, and this stallion loved them all. "Maslin said you'll be seeing the girls tomorrow. I know you're looking forward to that."

Knocking his muzzle into my shoulder, the stallion let out a throaty snicker. Oh, he knew exactly of what I spoke.

Goldie laughed. "Now that we have Lieska's information, the facts surrounding Alexo's decision to bring your mother home to Dralion makes more sense."

I scuffed my boot along the dusty ground. "She's not an Earthling as he's always thought. That means I'm full-blooded." Donaldo had never held my Halfling status over my head, for in his eyes I was innocent of my birth. Yet we all knew what he expected of my father. For years Donaldo had demanded Alexo choose another. If my grandfather could have found my mother and removed her from the equation, he would have. My sister was highly skilled, which meant the mated bond had prevailed and the line continued. Knowing Kate was a Magioling must be the sweetest news for Donaldo.

I stroked the stallion's neck. Only half our people discovered they were soul-bound, but I wanted the strength of the commitment. Goldie did too. We'd spoken of it often. "I want the mated bond because I know how precious it is."

Goldie's gaze roamed the horizon where Rocky Ledge ascended. The Ledge, a massive red rock sitting on the plains, ran as far as the eye could see with a vivid blue, cloudless sky above. "You don't have feelings for any other. That's a good sign you're mated."

"My poor sister though." I set a shaky hand to my chest as I traced the scar I'd had since birth. I hated remembering that time and this mark was a firm reminder of the tragedy of my birth.

Of my death.

Of the doctor's scalpel which had cut my skin.

To protect my mother, Dad had said very little over the years. I'd gone into surgery, and the physician had done all he could to restart my heart, but my life had ended before it had even begun, right here on Earth.

Goldie hugged me, covering my hand. "Don't think about it. You're a survivor. You died the day you were born, but today you live. Give Alexo what he's asked for. His wife never expected to see him again, and when she finds out about you..."

Neither of us knew her, or how she would react, but going by Dad's request I remain away, more than just the discovery of Kate Sol's family line was afoot.

With a sigh, Goldie released me then set her booted foot in the stirrup. "I'll take this one for a run. While I do that, you check on Saunder and make sure he gets to his tutor." She hoisted herself into the saddle, the leather creaking as she settled. "I believe Maslin said he was going to take some of the men with him down to the river for today's flooding. He wants some of the cattle moved. We have a station to run. Let's get to it."

I stepped out of her way as the stallion pawed at the ground. She rode out the gate, and off.

Hanging over the top of the half-beamed railings, I studied the land. Wincrest Station grazed thirty-five thousand head of cattle, although we were somewhat shy of that with the current drought. Dralion meanwhile, several times the size of this nation, housed a massive desert, along with isolated snow-capped mountains and boggy rainforests. Great areas of inhospitable land forced us to build our villages only around the far reaches of the coastline. The cattle we reared and the horses we bred on this station provided for those back home.

Goldie and her horse soon became a speck in the distance and my thoughts returned to my sister, mated to Davio Loveria.

What I wouldn't give to have even one-tenth of Peacian soil under Wincrest control. It was rich and fertile land and always beyond our reach. Huh, insufferable Loverias.

I jumped down, and a small cloud of red dust plumed at my feet.

Endless red dirt.

It worked its way into every fiber of our clothing, our hair and our skin.

Still, I loved this land and work called. I walked to the long run of white weatherboard stables, and cupped my hands to my mouth. "Hey, Saunder."

Inside the wide central holding room, the area was clear. On one wall, hooks held saddles and tack. On the opposite, square bales of hay had been stacked to the ceiling. Nope, no Saunder here.

Out the back door, the fenced yard housed mares and their gangly-legged foals. They swished their tails, swatting at the buzzing flies.

Further along, a man stood with one leg hooked on the lowest railing. The sunshine highlighted short, red-gold twists of curls cut close to his head.

Who was that?

Sometimes warriors came who I didn't know. This one wore the dark leathers and belted side-sword of our highly battle-trained, his height matching our tallest men.

I licked my lips, my gaze traveling down his body. His worn, black leather vest stretched over broad shoulders. The tails of his loose white shirt fluttered from under his vest.

Wow. I fanned myself and plucked the front of my shirt away from my heated skin. He was one gorgeous specimen I'd like to get my hands on.

"Hello there. May I help you?" I certainly hoped I could.

He lifted his head, slowly turning to look my way. His eyes were to die for, a blue as deep as the ocean with softer specks intermingled. I could have drowned in those eyes.

"What are you doing here, Faith? Why are you not with Davio?" The paler flecks blinked out.

Drat. He couldn't be a warrior. This must be the protector Dad had warned me of, the one who knew my sister. He was here, already.

Every muscle in my body tightened. The dagger weighted my ankle.

He set one hand over his sword, and his nostrils flared. "No, you're not Faith." He stepped forward to tower over me, inspecting me from head to foot. "I feel—damn."

Yep, a spark of recognition lit his eyes.

"What's your name?" He circled me, his body only a breath away.

"Hope." Strangely, I felt calm. Heck, how was that possible?

Frustration flickered in his eyes. "I feel the pull of the mated bond. With you. You are the reason I'm here."

Oh no.

No. No. No.

Crap.

My fingernails scraped my palms. "You're on Wincrest Station."

A fast breath whistled out from between his lips. "Then we're in a world of trouble."

Shaking out my hands, I stamped my feet. I could deal with this. Dad had asked me to figure out where Kate Sol was from.

"What's your name?"

"Silas Carver and I don't intend to stay. You're a Wincrest, the last person I would ever wish to bond with."

I snorted. "I have no desire to join with a protector. You're safe from me."

"Perfect." His gaze drilled me to the spot. "Clearly your sister doesn't know about you. I would have heard about a twin."

"She doesn't, and mustn't."

His lips twitched. "That's a deal. This thing between us"—he motioned with his hand back and forth—"isn't going to work. I certainly have no intention of mentioning you."

"I agree."

"Good, so I think it's an easy call to say we give this up, right now."

"Absolutely." I gave him a firm nod then remembered Dad's wishes.

Stink.

"Um, no. Not right now."

He tapped one booted foot on the ground. "Would you care to explain why?"

A second passed. Two.

"My father is Alexo Wincrest."

"I know who your father is. I believe we've already covered my knowledge of Faith."

"Right." I glanced at the ground then back at him. "I've bad news. Alexo told me of your coming. He has forewarning."

A tic pulsed in his jaw. "He didn't tell you to run hard and fast? In the other direction? Because I have no intention of mating with a Wincrest. My cousin Davio has."

"Davio's your cousin?" Hmm, interesting.

"Not for long. I'm disowning him. He comes with too many problems, the worst, your sister." Contradiction lit his eyes.

"You're lying." Those mated to each other couldn't speak a falsehood without the other knowing. Neither could they hurt each other, not when their souls were bound.

He lifted his shoulders and let them drop. "I figure I'll be renouncing him fairly soon. That better?"

I smiled, seeing the truth. "I believe we can work together."

"We're going to end this now."

"Sorry, no can do."

"I'll start with the words of release."

I linked my hands behind my back. "I'm not going to agree to your release, yet."

"We'll wish each other well, and be on our way. You can find another man, and it'll be my pleasure to see you do so."

I frowned. "Your hearing is bad, Silas Carver."

"Give me your approval to do the same." Still not listening.

"That's not going to happen, not when I need your aid."

"Perhaps we speak a different language."

"Nope. I hear you just fine. My mother's name is Kate Sol. You know Faith, and I do not. Apparently, I need your help. You must tell me what you know and of my sister's newfound skill of mind-merge. Leave nothing out."

"Seriously?" The deepest lines marred his brow. "I don't agree, and this conversation is going in circles. To release each other, you must accept my words. You may find another man of your own choosing. In fact, I insist."

He was stubborn, but then so was I. "Nah-ah. You are my country's enemy, but as my mated one, not mine. Help me with my assigned task, and then I'll let you go."

"I would have to be an idiot to do so."

I slapped his shoulder. "Great. I can live with you being an idiot. It won't be for long."

"Why is it Wincrests do not listen? You are as bad as your sister."

"Oh, now tell me of her." I clapped. "Everything. Don't forget her ability of mind-merge."

"As long as we make this quick, but Alexo Wincrest knows

her existence is tied to Davio's. Twenty-four hours ago we discovered it's a deadly skill, one which is night-night for her if she's kept from my cousin for more than three days."

"Hell. I had no idea. Are you certain it's deadly? This is the worst news."

Bracing himself with a hand on the fence rail, he nodded. "We're certain. I'm sorry to be the one to tell you."

I stepped closer, the toes of my boots touching his. "Tell me more. Once I know all you do, I can release you from our bond. I wouldn't ask you to remain mated to me except for this. If my sister has a deadly skill, you mustn't hold back. I've been charged with discovering all I can."

He grabbed my shoulders and I shivered at the delicious contact. It was expected, even though unwanted. He was my mate, the one my soul was bound to.

"Your sister survived the ordeal by mere minutes upon her return to Davio. She was gone for three days to Dralion and suffered physically while she was away. She must be in the same room as him to mind-merge, and without this connection, her body shut down. I witnessed the deterioration myself." His blue gaze held mine, his hands warming my skin. "Her lungs filled with blood and she almost bled to death before my eyes. It was a gruesome sight. Once she merged, it took hours for her fast-healing ability to restore her. I would never wish to witness such a thing again."

"I can't imagine all you speak of, but I know it's true. Continue, please."

"When your sister mind-merges with my cousin, it's not something she can hold back. Other than this, there's nothing more I can tell you. You should go to your father for more. He is aware."

I focused on those words as they left his mouth. Dad would know all of this because of his forethought. His request was not all it seemed. "I need more time to hear what you have to say."

He stroked to the edges of my shoulders. "No. The mated bond builds fast and we can't allow that to happen."

"Hope."

It was Saunder. I spun around.

Silas withdrew his sword.

"No. He's just a boy." I stayed him with a hand on his chest. "Oh." I flushed. That was one hard chest. Like rock hard.

Saunder bounced out and raced across with a wide grin. "There's a mare in labor. One of the warriors is with her, but he told me to come and get you." He glanced at Silas. "I'm sorry, sir. I don't mean to interrupt, but the mare carries the strongest line."

Silas moved forward. "Hope is busy with me at present. You'll need to excuse her."

Yes, I had to focus on getting Silas to stay with me, or at least, not to leave me yet. I needed whatever information he held. I met Saunder's gaze. "I can't come right now, although I wish I could. Could you grab one of your uncles for me?"

"Sure thing."

"Great." I turned him by the shoulders and nudged him toward the stables. "Go now."

He hurried away.

Taking Silas's hand, I pulled him along the side of the building. We needed somewhere quiet to speak. I hadn't noticed at first glance he was a protector, but the warriors about likely would.

"Where are we going?"

I pointed to the sprawling earth-toned, brick homestead on the hill. It was a magnificent structure, one of Earth's designs with three floors and a wide wraparound porch. Darkened glass kept the harshest of the sun's rays at bay. "See the corner balcony on the top floor? That's my room. Can you zap us there?"

"Whoa, your bedroom?"

I patted his chest. "Ah, yes." Oh boy, such hard flesh he had there. "There'll be no distractions."

"No distractions in a bedroom?" He groaned. "Perhaps I do have idiot stamped across my forehead?"

"No." I smiled. "But that can be arranged if you'd like."

Rolling his eyes, he grasped my arms. "We keep our distance. This is going to be one fast conversation then I leave."

Everything darkened as he jumped through space, and a second later, we stood on the balcony outside my room. He reached for the glass door and slid it open.

White lace curtains blew out and I scooped up the folds and tucked them back as I entered. "Thanks for coming."

He snorted a laugh. "Yeah, funny." Striding across the snowy carpet to the far wall, he eyed my bed. Made of New Zealand rimu, the posts smooth and round rose to the ceiling. A white netting canopy trickled over the edges, ready to be drawn down at night. Turning toward me, he leaned one hip against the headboard, as far from me as the room allowed. "You wanted to talk. Let's get this over with."

I tapped my chin. Hmm.

"Why aren't you speaking?"

"I don't know what to say."

"Say see you later, Silas. I agree we never lay eyes on each other again." He rolled a hand in a continuing motion. "I can't wait to hear that."

"Silas." I crossed the room toward him and he sidestepped, knocking against my bedside table. A framed photograph of my first ride on this station tipped and he caught it as it fell.

In the picture, I'd been three years old, my short legs flapping over the sides of Dad's dark leather saddle. A far-too-big Stetson on my head had threatened to wobble off, although the grin on my face said it all.

"You like horses?" His gaze moved from the picture to me.

Unable to help myself, I crept closer. "I love them. Do

you?"

"Yes. I've been riding since I could walk. Even coming into my ability to 'port hasn't stopped me from riding every chance I get." He replaced the photo. "How'd you come to be with Wincrest when Faith was raised by her mother?"

"There's no easy way to say it." I teared up, because the memories had resurfaced today.

"Hey." He caressed my arm, making my skin tingle. "I make a great listener, even though it doesn't appear that way."

"I died at birth, is what happened. My father brought me home to bury me, and as he did, my heart restarted from the teleportation jump. He called the healers and notified Donaldo. My father would never jeopardize my mother's safety, so I remained with him. There's likely more to it, but I don't know the finer details. They've never been spoken of."

He pulled in a deep breath, his chest rising. "You look well now."

"The healers who saw to me were the best."

Sliding his hand around mine, he wrapped his fingers tight. "I can't push you to release me from our bond, but you must know it has to be done. Do you feel what I do?"

"Yes." I sighed, wanting to know more about him. "You're adamant then, you won't help me?"

"The bond builds." He stroked my palm with his thumb. "Fast. We can't allow it. I've told you all I know and I can't think of anything else."

I closed my eyes at the truth he'd uttered.

Think. Even I saw we had to end this if I had all his information. "There'll be one condition. I'd like one man's release for another's, Saunder's father."

"You mean the boy from the stables? His father?"

"Yes, Tawson Rivera was taken at the battle of Eventide two years ago. If you free him, I'll free you. That's my deal."

He gave a low growl, which made me jump. "If you agree,

I'll give you what you want. I do this for the child."

"I can see that." He dropped my hand. "Which is hard to argue with."

"Silas, I grew up without one of my parents and I understand how Saunder feels. If it's within my power to see his father returned, I have to. Those are my terms. They're quick and precise, and you'll have what you want from me in the end."

His gaze narrowed. "What about your request for my aid. We both understand no more will occur?"

"Of course, and I keep my word once given. I will release you."

He inhaled, deeply. "I'll go speak with Carlisio and return with his decision." Bending his head, he gave me a short bow. "Take care, my mate."

His mate? Not for much longer. "You too."

So fast, he flashed away.

Gone.

My mated one had left.

I swept my hand through the air where he'd been, my heart a heavy weight in my chest.

This moment hurt.

Chapter 2

I heaved myself over the gelding's silky back and into the saddle, my outback shirttails flying free behind me.

A new day had dawned and after having kept to myself for most of the previous one, repeating my conversation with Silas in my mind, I was finally ready to speak to Goldie.

She trotted in beside me on a bay mare, her blond hair breezing out underneath her black Stetson. She wore low-rise jeans and an emerald half-button shirt, the rich color stunning with her violet eyes.

"Let's go." She grinned, slapping the reins on her horse's rump.

I followed suit, giving my horse his head. Adrenaline pumped, blood flowed through my veins and invigorated me. This was life, riding free across the greatest plains of this world.

"I miss our races!" I yelled into the wind, digging my knees in to urge the horse to a faster speed. "Usually you cheat."

She wore a familiar wicked smirk. Yep, a second later, she and her ride disappeared, teleporting away.

"You don't change," I said, although she wasn't there to hear me.

I petted the horse's neck, my hair whipping around my face as I rode low and fast. "We'll catch her up."

A half hour later, the familiar cluster of bush trees

bordering the closest water source to our homestead came into view. Goldie crouched before the watering hole. Her mare munched on a small patch of dry grass growing along its shallow bank.

With a frown, I jumped down beside the dry creek bed. Our animals needed to drink when we passed through here. "The levels are low."

She ran her palms down her legs, and stood. "Maslin needs to see this. I wonder if he can drive the water further inland from the river during the controlled river releases. Some of his magic needs to be performed here."

I removed my Stetson, and the breeze lifted sweaty strands of hair from my forehead. Oooh, so nice. I shielded my eyes against the bright ball of raging sunlight. Not so nice.

The sun's rays baked the earth wherever one looked.

"I think if he could get any water this far from the river, he would have done so." Maslin's water skill was a rare one. I had studied what he did, but his ability didn't run at full strength since he hadn't been born of the mated bond, not as I now knew Faith had. I wish I was skilled, but not all were. At times, brothers and sisters born to the same parents differed. One might have multiple skills and the other some, or even none at all.

Plopping my hat on my head, I bent at the creek's dry edge. Deep cracks sucked at the remaining water.

My horse snickered, pushing his muzzle into my back and tipping me onto my knees. "I know, boy. I'll get you some water." I pulled him back and removed the water flask from my saddlebags. Setting my palm under his muzzle, I poured out a handful.

A whinny of pleasure, and he lapped at the clear drinking water.

"What about barrels of water, Goldie? We could get some of our warriors to set them under the trees at each hole. That might work."

She flapped her Stetson in front of her face. "Maybe. We could at least try."

I put the flask away. "There's something I need to tell you."

"Uh-huh." Holding out a handful, she gave her horse water.

Taking a deep breath, I came around to stand before her. "I met the protector."

"What? Why didn't you say?"

"I just did, but you're going to hate this." Best to get straight to it. "Silas Carver is my mate."

Plugging a finger in her ear, Goldie twisted it. "Ah, I must have heard you wrong. I thought you just said the protector was your mate."

"I did." I rolled my shoulders and a bead of sweat slithered down the center of my back. "He's also Davio Loveria's cousin, and as Dad said, he knows Faith."

"So, I'm not hearing things? Why did Alexo not tell us this?"

I blew out a breath. "I imagine you would have been on hand to kill him first, and ask questions later."

"He's a protector. Of course, I'd kill him. Alexo needn't have been so vague."

I rubbed my forehead. "Silas said Faith's ability to mind-merge means her life is tied to Loveria's. They'd just discovered her skill is a deadly one if she's kept from his cousin for more than three days. He told me she only survived the ordeal by mere minutes upon her return to Loveria from Dralion. Without the mind-merge, her body shut down. Her lungs filled with blood and she almost bled to death before his eyes. I've never heard of such a deathly skill."

Pacing, Goldie rubbed her chin with her thumb. "This puts a new spin on things. Did the protector speak of anything else?"

"He knew no more."

She stopped in front of me. "Perhaps this information is all you'll need from him."

"I hope so, because he insisted we end things, but I've struck a deal with him first. He wants me to release him from the bond and I said I would, provided he returns Tawson Rivera to us."

"Oh." Her gaze lit. "Will it be done?"

"He speaks to Carlisio. It'll be one man's release for another's."

She took her horse's leads. "Perfect. Let's hope you have all the information you need to seek what you must." She hoisted herself into her saddle. "Let's head to the river. We'll speak to Maslin about the barrels."

I mounted and we rode, our conversation of Silas not set from my mind.

He was my mated one, the man soul-bound to me, and he'd told me to find another, that it'd be his pleasure to see me do so. My heartbeat thumped, heavy and hard. Once I gave him my acceptance, our lives would forever change. No more would he be mine.

What was I thinking? Huh, stupid bond.

Even though we could walk away from each other—it was rarely done—my soul would still call to his because the bond couldn't be broken. Still, that's what we'd chosen. What I'd live with.

I turned my mind from Silas, focusing on the land as we neared the river. Glorious fields of green, the mighty river rippling in between it all, pulsed with life. Ducks and birds took flight along the waterway, sweeping low into the rushes either side with a cacophony. Thousands of head of cattle grazed into the distance.

My heart lifted at the sight, giving me a sense of freedom from my desolate thoughts.

We strived to provide for our people back home when they could not. And for Saunder to have his father back meant I could live with any decision I now made.

Goldie pointed north. "Maslin's coming." She lifted her Stetson and waved it. "Why don't you talk to him of your idea for the water barrels? I'll check out the river levels and take a depth recording."

"Sure." Pressing my knees into the horse, I rode toward him.

Maslin galloped on his horse with a freedom born of his love of this land, and it was impossible not to grin at his enjoyment. Riding free across plains untouched by civilization was sheer magic. Dralion was of a similar landscape. No highrises or cities of concrete there. Our people simply didn't harbor technology as those on Earth did. Instead, we adhered to the older ways, where everyone in the village raised our children. Our people didn't physically age past our eighteenth year and we lived easily to one-hundred and twenty. Our lives were simpler, yet fuller and enjoyed with more youthfulness.

Sitting in his saddle, Maslin lifted his stone-colored hat and whooped it up, his bold copper hair blowing in the breeze as he rode in beside me. Breathing fast, he pointed out the new area he'd flooded. "That field will be sprouting strong in two weeks. It will be a beautiful sight. The waterway system is cranking all the way north of here too. The cattle are in heaven." He slapped his well-worn blue jeans.

I beamed. "It's wonderful."

The systems were in place to flood the lower fields, but Maslin used his skill to send precious water further inland than what was physically possible. Because of him we'd managed to keep at least eighty percent of the cattle on the station.

"I should tell you the watering holes are low." I sat higher in my saddle. "Goldie and I spoke about some of the warriors 'porting in water barrels. Perhaps we could talk more about that strategy tonight at dinner. Will you come?"

He stared, the freckles on his nose prominent. Then he smiled. "I'll be there. I'd like to talk to you too."

"Sure."

He cleared his throat and continued, "I saw Lieska this morning in her search for Guy. I heard about your mother, Kate Sol, and your sister, Faith, as well as the protector foretold to come. That's not an easy task Alexo's set you, so if you need help or to talk, come to me."

"I will." Maslin was loyal to Goldie and me. Working together on this station had cemented our bonds. "In that case..."

My stomach tightened into a tight knot, my thoughts returning to Silas. "I met my mate. He's the protector."

His eyes widened. "Shoot. Keep going."

"He spoke of what he knew then he released me from our bond, only before I can accept I made a deal. I'll let him go, provided he returns Saunder's father."

"Whoa, I don't know what to say, but you can't be mated to one of them. Donaldo will never allow it."

The wind lifted, blowing blades of green grass in a rippling wave. It was beauty in its purest form, calming my mind a little.

"Think of the positives." He wore a small smile. "Imagine Saunder having his father back. That's a sight I long to see."

His words made me smile. "Me too, and I will focus my energy on the job Alexo's left me. My sister has the ability of mind-merge and Silas told me what he knows. I have to piece together what I can of my mother's Sol line."

"Sol is a common name. That will not be easy." He glanced toward the river and with two fingers between his lips, sent out a hearty whistle to Goldie. "I've measured there, Goldie."

Stepping away from the bank, she acknowledged his words with a wave. Back on her horse, she let loose, riding along the bank's edge. Ducks hidden within the reeds cackled and took flight, their wings brushing the glistening surface as they swept across the river to the other side.

Her horse's hooves pounded over the earth as she rode in. "I love this spot." Her eyes shimmered brightly. "I took the secondary recording down further."

"Great. That was the one I missed." Maslin prodded the horse with his heels and turned his mount. "Back to the homestead."

With a nudge to my horse's flanks, I followed them, my thoughts on Silas. Always on him. When would he return with Carlisio's decision? Would he bring our warrior with him?

I picked up speed as Goldie and Maslin edged further ahead.

Why couldn't I get Silas off my mind?

I had to think of someone or something else.

Maslin. He loved this land as I did. He would be a far better match for me than Silas.

I'd known Maslin for two years. He was dependable and strong. He was a warrior and my friend.

We would suit, and Silas had told me to find another.

I pressed a hand over my heart. That thought hurt.

The soul-bond was revered. Silas had dismissed me so quickly. Such a jerk.

Gripping the reins, I urged the horse to a faster speed.

By the time evening came and I'd showered, my thoughts were still jumbled about in a tangled heap.

Leaning in, I wiped steam from the mirror in my white tiled bathroom as I held the bath-towel I'd wrapped around me in place. My blond hair was a mess, and my skin overly pink from the bright sunshine. I picked up a brush and worked it through the knots then dried the long strands and set a clip at each side, silver with a small amethyst stone to match my Wincrest violet eyes.

And being mated sucked. Or at least, being cast aside did.

"Hope."

I froze. Silas.

"Coming." I tripped over my towel as I grabbed the doorknob and yanked.

I stared at him. Gawked really. Oh wow. He looked deliciously edible in tailored black pants and a pressed white shirt, his sword belted low on his hips. His damp hair lay in tight curls and I itched to run my fingers through it. Bad thought.

Tugging the collar of his shirt, he stretched his shoulders. "How about we talk after you've dressed? I can wait. Take as long as you need. Lots of fabric. Cover yourself up."

Too cute.

"Wait here. I won't be a moment." I picked up the hem of my towel and crossed to my dressing room. With a shuddering breath, I shut myself in and pressed my back to the door. This was it. He was here with Carlisio's answer.

It would be yes. How could it not be?

I snatched a short blue dress from the rack and pulled it over my head. Crisscrossed panels at the back drew the soft cotton snug around my waist. I added a pair of nude-colored heels then left the dressing room.

Standing in the same place, his hands now pressed behind his back, he inclined his head. "Are you going somewhere?"

"To dinner."

A tic pulsed in his jaw. "With whom?"

"My aunt. Her name is Goldie. Some of the warriors on this station as well."

"You hang out with the wrong crowd."

I smiled and sashayed toward him. "Sorry. Can't change that. Tell me what Carlisio said."

"He granted your request. Your warrior's freedom for mine. The deal is, you speak your acceptance and I'll deliver."

Oh my goodness. Saunder was going to get his father back. He spoke the truth, but still I asked, "Are you certain?"

"You know I don't lie. Speak the—" His gaze shot to the door as if he sensed a presence.

A knock sounded then Maslin called, "Are you there, Hope?"

Silas slid his blade from its sheath and drew me toward the door, a finger pressed to his lips. "Who's he?"

"Maslin Sol," I whispered. "One of our finest warriors."

He snorted. "You have another man coming to your door? Already?"

"I invited him to dinner." I stuck both hands on my hips. "We're releasing each other. Let's not forget that."

His jaw locked tight. "I know, and now get rid of him so we can finish this thing."

I reached for the brass knob. Opening the door wide, I flattened Silas to the wall behind so he couldn't be seen. "Hey, Maslin."

Wearing navy pants and a shimmery gray shirt, he held out a snow-white rose, its petals in a tight bud. "It's from the rose garden at the palace. I know you like these. I snuck back for it so you'd have a little home away from home since you can't travel there because of Alexo's request."

It was a sweet gesture. I took it from him and breathed in the delicate fragrance. "This is my favorite color. I've read white roses signify the beginning of time."

"Me too. Yellow roses are for the gift of friendship."

"I've heard that." I gave him a smile. "And red, the oblivion of love."

He leaned against the doorjamb and chuckled. "My father gives my mother red roses all the time. Too sappy. Are you ready for dinner?"

Silas raised his blade, which meant no.

"Not yet." I pushed Maslin and backed him into the hallway. "I promise I'll be down shortly. Wait for me there."

"Are you sure?"

"Yes." I reversed into my room and shut the door, releasing a deep sigh. "That was close."

Silas sheathed his sword. "This residence is filled with warriors."

"Ah, yeah, that kind of happens in a Wincrest home. Not much I can do about that." I fingered the rose in my hand.

Silas took it. "Does he bring you flowers all the time?"

"No." I snatched it back. "No one's given me a flower before, unless you count my father and the gardener at the palace."

Leaning in, he speared me with a narrowed look. "You want to explain why Maslin Sol did?"

I shoved one hip to the side. "Yeah, I think he said it's a little bit of home away from home. You truly do have a hearing problem."

He blew a breath into my face. "No, I have a mated-bond problem. You."

"I'm not a problem." I stared him in the eyes.

His nose touched mine, his gaze fixed. "I want to kiss you so bad."

"What?" I froze.

"Do you have a hearing problem?"

I dragged air into my lungs. "I think I have a mated-bond problem. You."

His nostrils flared and he backed up. "Give me your acceptance we end our relationship now. I need to walk away."

I touched my lips. "Um, I'm liking the kissing idea. Do you think we could do that? You know, kiss. Just this once?"

"Hell, no." He paced, clicking his fingers. "I'm waiting."

"For my acceptance?"

"Bingo, Miss Bright-spark."

I smirked. "Right, Mr. Hot-head."

"Are you being smart?"

With a silly grin, I crossed to him. "Absolutely. Now, your acceptance." It was best to get on with it. "Silas, I wish for you to live and to love...to find the woman of your dreams." I reached out and tweaked his nose. "For her to be completely nosy and anyone other than me. Okay, how's that for our agreed release?"

"Damn near perfect."

"Okay, you have your freedom. Go and be happy." My vision swam. Oh no, I was not going to cry. This was good he was going.

Wiping his thumb across my cheek, he drew away a tear. "You're crying."

"Tears of happiness." I plastered a smile on my face.

He searched my gaze. "Your sister will be my constant reminder of you."

I clutched the rose tight. "I hope she takes a blade to you, and sets you in your place. After she does, know I wish it were me."

He laughed. "Jeez, she would slice me up quick-smart if she could. But at least I will be safe from you."

Squeezing my eyes shut, I breathed out. "Goodbye, Silas."

His lips pressed to my forehead then a soft breeze fluttered.

He was gone.

A knock sounded on my door.

"Just a second." I set the white rose on my bedside table. It was time to live. Without my mate.

Maslin offered his arm and I took it. "I was in the hallway. Sorry, I couldn't leave, not when I thought I sensed another in your room. I was worried it was the protector, and I'm afraid I heard parts of the conversation. Do you need to talk?"

"I don't want to talk about him. Ever. Talk about something else. Anything else."

He directed me down the stairs. "I was there the day Goldie moved through her rising. You have the same strength she does, though you hold no skills. Your decision to absolve the bond was right."

At Goldie's rising a massive crowd had gathered and packed the spectator's seating, eager to see what level of strength Donaldo's daughter held. Down on the sandy-floored arena,

Goldie had worn her skin-tight black combat leathers and knee-high boots. With one's rising came three-times the strength, and her power that day had been phenomenal.

One's rising was the most spectacular event to watch, and Goldie's just so, as she'd drawn her sword around in an arc of precise movements. Dad, the best, had trained her.

"Hope, the choice you just made will return Saunder's father to him."

I dropped my chin as we walked. "I need some time to get over Silas."

"I'll give you a day."

My gaze darted to his. "Huh? A day?"

"That's right."

We entered the wide-open foyer on the first floor, my heels tapping on diagonal tiles of midnight blue. Recessed lighting showcased rich burgundy walls filled with breathtaking landscapes of Dralion. I always slowed to admire them, and Maslin did the same. I stopped before my favorite.

"The black granite cliffs of home." Maslin studied the fine piece of work. The cliffs, an impenetrable force and a natural wonder beside the ocean, stood like sentinels and ran unbroken for ninety miles either side of the palace. "During training, we practiced on the edge of those cliffs. I love being near water."

"Tell me about your water skill. Something I don't know."

He set his hand over mine. "My family came from No-Man's Land forty years ago."

The thin band of shifting sands lay between Peacio and Dralion, effectively dividing the two warring nations.

"You've never said how they made the move to Dralion before the dome was created." For now, no one could enter unless they had the teleporting image, one strictly reserved for Wincrests and warriors.

"My father was a young man when the dome was created. He was one of the few who volunteered his services to the warriors to confirm the field was impassable. When they returned from scouting the border between No-Man's Land and Dralion, they discovered what we call the gray area on Sol land."

"What's a gray area?"

"There are certain parts of No-Man's Land the Sol tribe can't access. Or I should say, we can but our skills are ineffective there. I'm still learning about my Sol—" He scrunched up his neck, his eyes rolling until the whites showed, and he slithered to the floor.

"Maslin." I reached for him as Silas jumped over his prone body out of nowhere and whipped a hand over my mouth.

"Shh. Don't scream."

Not a chance. I bit his palm and he released me. I glared. "What do you think you're doing?"

He blew on his hand, running his thumb over his palm. "You have sharp teeth, and don't go drawing attention to me, to us."

I looked in all directions. "There's no one around but us."

"There're others on the other side of this homestead. I checked." He crouched and pressed two fingers to Maslin's neck.

"Did you kill him?" I dropped to my knees then pressed an ear to Maslin's chest, checking for a heartbeat.

"No," he said, pulling me back to his side. "But I wish I had."

Another warrior lay across the floor of the sitting room's entrance a bare five feet away.

I gasped. "That's Saunder's father. Did you kill him too?"

He followed my gaze with his. "I had to knock him out to bring him here. Neither of your warriors are dead."

Kneeling, I tilted Tawson's face toward me. "Oh my." I touched the man's bristly beard. His skin was sallow, his jeans and shirt torn, ragged and hanging from his gaunt frame. But he was back. "Don't you feed your prisoners?"

Silas drew me to my feet. "We have to keep them weak."

"I can certainly see that." My gaze bounced between Tawson and Maslin.

"Look at me." Silas caught my face between his hands. "I've kept my end of our bargain."

"I knew you would." A strange heaviness invaded my mind. Weird.

"Hey." Silas brought my attention back to him. "Maslin Sol is not to touch you again. I heard you both speaking and came to investigate. He has intentions toward you."

"You released me."

He rubbed his thumbs over my cheeks. "I'm asking this of you because I can't have a visual in my mind of the man you choose. Surely you..."

His words were lost to me. My head felt like lead.

"Did you hear me?"

"Maslin's considerate and kind. He's my friend. Because of our bond, you hold my soul. I can never have more than a friendship with him, but I will take what I can."

"As you hold my soul." His blue eyes made my heart ache for what couldn't be.

My mind splintered, pushing outward. I clutched my head at the burst of pain. My mind reached for his and connected.

Mind-merge, Faith's skill, the one Dad had spoken of, the one which ran through the Sol line.

Oh hell.

Chapter 3

"What did you just do?" Silas stumbled back.

"Ah, I couldn't stop it. My mind wanted to merge."

He scrubbed both hands over his face, mumbling under his breath, "That didn't just happen. No, it didn't." He marched from one side of the wide entranceway to the other. "Damn it. I should have left the prisoner in your room and not come searching for you."

"Obviously." Although right now this mind-merge didn't feel deadly like he'd said. Merging within his mind felt sweetly calm, quite at odds with his current state of being.

He snorted. "There has to be a way out of this. I can't have your life tied to mine. This is your skill, not mine."

"I know so little about it. Can we undo what's been done?"

"We'll speak to Davio. He's mated to your sister and used to her mind-merge. He'll know more."

My legs wobbled. "I have a skill." I should have been elated, only I sighed. "I have a crappy skill."

"The worst possible one."

My mind stirred and stretched within his, wanting to deepen its hold. "This can't be real."

He groaned. "I think it is. I can certainly feel you merged within my mind."

"I can't believe I'm going to ask you to take me to Loveria, but we should go and seek more answers."

"He'll be in the castle's rec room at this time of the evening. Or if not, he won't be far away." He gripped my arm. "Are you ready?"

"Yes." Dark encompassed us then we were there. Loveria Castle, the last place in the world I'd ever thought to be.

The rec room, around fifty feet long and wide, housed a pool table set with colorful balls and an assortment of pool cues hung in a wooden frame on the wall. The polished floor gave way to thick cream carpet and four white leather couches faced each other. Centered between them was a chunky wooden coffee table.

Silas backed away. "I'm not sure it's wise for you to continue to be merged and to deepen our connection. Since Faith can't hold the mind-merge over the distance of this room, I'll head over there."

My mind clutched his. "I don't know. I feel like I need more time." I held onto the pool table, and didn't dare grab him. He moved farther away, and as he did, my mind pressed outward, needing to maintain the hold.

I dug my fingernails into the green felt on the table. "Slow down."

My mind couldn't stretch the distance as he continued. The connection broke like an elastic band snapping. I staggered back. My head throbbed and the loss of his mind sent an ache to the depths of my soul.

"Hope?" A questioning look darkened his eyes. "Breathe through it." His fists clenched then un-clenched at his sides.

With my chin down, I shot him a narrowed glare. "I did not like that. How long does Faith merge for?"

"Five minutes and then she's good to go."

"Out of every three days, right?"

"That's the maximum. Faith merges more than that, usually whenever she and Davio are together. Her skill is like an addiction. She can't withhold her mind from his when she's in his vicinity."

My head throbbed to reconnect and I could well imagine the need. "I merged for a minute, maybe two. I think I need the five you spoke—"

The solid oak door swung open, and in strode one of the Loverias. I'd seen images of the three men, who all appeared alike, because I'd been told to know my enemy.

This was Carlisio's grandson. Davio Loveria slanted his head to one side, brown hair wisped with golden strands falling to his shoulders. His dark eyes drew into tight slits as his gaze moved over me. Close to six foot four, he matched Silas in height.

The hairs on the back of my neck zoomed up. My blood heated. Wincrest and Loveria blood warred. On Magio, only our two lines held the rare forethought skill. Combined with our history, it meant their direct line and ours couldn't come within five feet of each other or the aggression between us rose to fierce levels.

Loveria, in an impeccably fitted black silk shirt and dark pants, breached the five-foot mark, stirring my blood. I stared him down. "Keep your distance, Loveria. You know our past." A thousand years of battle was impossible to lay aside.

Circling me with slow steps, he set his hand on his side-sword and tapped it. "Carlisio agreed to the release of your warrior. I was there with Silas at the meeting. And I'll stand where I please since my ancestors won the war and this is my land." He shot a look at Silas. "Why is she here?"

"Hope has mind-merge so I brought her. It's thrown up a problem." Silas crossed his arms with a hard slap. "You better have some good advice. Right now, I could use it."

Loveria frowned and muttered, "She is a Wincrest and Donaldo is determined to eliminate my line in full. Bringing her here was wrong."

"You know the bond, Davio. I cannot allow any harm to come to her, and she is your mate's sister. What can you tell me of mind-merge?"

Loveria's gaze slashed into me. "Are you sure you have it?"

"Yes, and how does my sister stand your company?" I had not considered the thought of her blood warring with his before, but this close, my Wincrest blood bubbled through my veins like a riot of fire. She must suffer the same as only the two lines of Loveria and Wincrest did.

"She mind-merges. The moment we touch skin-to-skin, the aggression and pain disappear because of the mind to body connection."

Chills chased across my skin. "She has to merge and touch you? That's despicable."

"She has no issues with it." He planted his feet wide and crossed his arms. "Step back if you can't handle the heat. Five feet and the tension will dissolve."

My chest tightened. Loveria was too close, and Silas too far away. I needed to merge with my mate since my head thumped as if horses stampeded within. "I'd rather swallow nails, thanks all the same."

He cocked an eyebrow. "I can't believe my cousin is mated to you."

I blew a hostile breath, right in his face. "It happened, but not for long. Why don't you leave since you're not helpful?"

"Whose castle is this?" He gave me a cocky grin. "You are much like Faith, temperament-wise."

I kicked his shin. I couldn't help myself.

"Ow." He hopped about, holding his leg.

"I can't believe I'm even related to her. Why has she not slit your throat?"

"She loves how I frustrate her."

Why was he still grinning?

I glared at Silas. "We need to leave, and I need to mind-merge with you."

He held his position, remaining too far away for me to connect. "We've released each other, and now you're leaving me with no choice."

I saw his point. He'd made his decision clear from the start and had kept his end of our bargain. What was I doing? "Give me the time I need to mind-merge then take me home." My mind cried out for those precious five minutes. I'd take that and deal with the rest.

"I'm coming." He crossed the room "We'll sort something out."

As he did, my mind released, connecting and burrowing deep into his.

Oh, the wonder. It was a moment I would never forget. The second I joined with him, every muscle in my body loosened and relaxed, and my mind bedded down in its own sweet little spot. Perfect.

He caressed my arms. "Better?"

I smiled, weakly. "I have a skill."

He pulled in a deep breath. "A deadly one."

"Your mind is blocked. I'm just resting within, but not able to see any thoughts."

"C'mon. You don't expect me to share?" An incredulous look crossed his face.

"No." He was a protector. I was a Wincrest. Of course, he blocked.

His fingers dug in. "It feels warm and soothing with you merged. I didn't expect that." His nails pricked my flesh. "I don't like it either."

Davio cleared his throat. "Remember, it's only her skill, Silas." He crossed to the long bank of square-cut wooden edged windows. Outside, moonlight touched on the green garden in front. "What does it matter if she dies?"

Silas peered into my eyes. "It matters to me, Davio. She

must live.”

Unable to help myself, I snuggled deeper into Silas’s mind. “My life is not your concern. Alexo watches over me, and always will. I will find a way to bypass this mind-merge.” How, I had no idea, but I’d find a way if it existed.

Silas drew me closer. “Faith has forethought. If she brings up her mate’s image, she’ll catch sight of you in her vision since it’s very strong. She sees images as if she were there in person. I doubt you want her seeing you here with Davio, and if that’s the case, you and I need to leave.”

“I need another few minutes with you. It really does take five to recharge. I can feel it.”

“We’ll go to my room. Yours might have angry warriors within. Later,” he said to Loveria.

Darkness enclosed me, and he ’ported.

We arrived where he’d said. A massive bed pressed against one wall, an ocean-blue comforter with the swirling colors of the sea, spread on top. Four plump white pillows rested against a headboard made of dark wood with an *SC* delicately engraved along it. Beside the bed, a black leather jacket lay as if tossed carelessly on top of a wooden chest with the same insignia on the front.

“Take a seat.”

I crossed the room to a padded couch of beige, with floor length curtains of the same velvety fabric tucked in behind. I smoothed my hands over its softness. “I know this mind-merge is unexpected, but would you permit giving me five minutes every three days to deal with it?” I was at his mercy. “I’d quite like to live, and so far it doesn’t sound like there’s a way around this need for the merge.”

“Our souls are bound even though we’ve released each other. You know I’m driven to give you whatever you ask.” Heaving a deep breath, he eased onto the couch beside me. “That being the case, yes. Although we’ll designate a place to meet, and I'll zap in and out. The less time we're in each other's company, the better."

"Thank you." I clutched his hand. "I mean that."

He stared at our joined hands then tore his gaze away. "Faith said your mother, Kate Sol, was left at an orphanage in New Zealand at three days of age. Are you aware of this?"

"No." I sat straighter. "What can you tell me?"

"The nuns who ran the home said your grandmother's name was Katerin Sol, and they named your mother after her. Katerin promised to return, but never did, and your mother grew up with no family, no knowledge of her Magioling ancestry."

"I've studied the skills of my people since my early teens. You can be sure I'll focus my attentions on this ability to mind-merge. There has to be someone who knows something, and I'll find them."

Katerin Sol. Sol was a common family name, as was the given name Katerin. It wouldn't be easy to track Katerin Sol's heritage based on her name. But this mind-merge skill was unheard of, so likely quite rare. I might discover more if I combined the two and followed that track.

Easing back into the thick cushioning, he sighed. "Why does Alexo's request to delay meeting Faith matter so much? Don't you wish to know your sister? I can't imagine not knowing mine."

"You have a sister?"

"A twin. Her name is Silvie." He said her name softly.

"You're close to her?"

"Yes."

I shouldn't ask such personal questions, only I ached to know more about him.

"But we were talking of your sister, not mine." He squeezed my hand.

"I do want to meet her, particularly now we share the ability of mind-merge. But she's been through so much. She's come from Earth and discovered she has a father she never knew about, along with receiving strength skills, and then a rising to complete and above all else, she's had to contend with Loveria as her mate. You said she nearly died. And Alexo is trying to forge bonds with her and my mother." I inhaled, ever so slowly. "He always sees the bigger picture. Do not forget he has forethought."

"Faith would want to meet you."

"You can't know that."

"I do. My sister and yours are close and she told me Faith longed for family. It was only ever her mother and her."

I gave him a small smile. "You sound as if you care about her."

"Like I'd care about a stone under my shoe."

I laughed. "Then stop concerning yourself over her."

"She attends high school in New Zealand, in Te Puke. It's a town near the coast. She's also a couple of months shy of her final exams. Wouldn't you like to know more?"

"Yes." I edged forward.

"She's stubbornly feisty. In an aggravating way."

"Oh, she sounds just like a Wincrest." Perfect.

A roll of his eyes made my smile widen. "Hell, yes. She's one, through and through. I can't believe we're now dealing with two of you, which means twice the aggravation."

I knocked my shoulder against his. "Hey, five minutes is hardly having to deal with me. And on that note"—I stretched out my legs and stood—"you can take me home. Our five minutes is up." I pulled him to his feet.

"Yeah. Where should we make that safe location to meet?"

"My bedroom. That would be best." Well, not best, but I had little choice.

"We'll make it every other night. Faith's headaches begin on the second day. You don't need to deal with them if you don't wish to."

"Headaches?"

"Bad ones, which is why I'm offering."

Ah, the bond was at play. He couldn't see me harmed.

"As you wish."

"I do." He bent over me, the moonlight filtering through the windows grazing his cheeks. "What of Maslin Sol? I won't tolerate you having any close involvement with him. I don't like him, and that stands."

I laughed, and then as he shook his head, realized he was quite serious. "I'm pretty certain it's only me who has to like him. I told you he's a friend."

"Your need to mind-merge only works with me, your mate."

"I understand that."

It went without question that most mated men got incredibly possessive over their women. That was part of the bond. Yet we had both accepted we walk away from it. Unless...

I couldn't help myself. He didn't wish for descriptions of men, so I pushed to see what his reaction would be. "There's the enchanter, Guy Moyer. Coal-black hair and pale blue eyes tinged with swirling silver. He's not with anyone. Or Killian might be interested in me. He's one of Dralion's leading eight. Massive man, who carries around a metal mallet and kills just for the sheer pleasure of it. Although, I wouldn't be able to hide from him the fact I needed to form this mind-merge. It's not a secret I'm prepared to keep from my future"—I let the end hang—"you know."

He gripped my arms. "I said no visuals. You did that on purpose. They're out."

"Are—"

"No." He shook his head then I lost all breath as he 'ported us away.

We arrived in the dark and it wasn't my bedroom.

The air smelt musty and damp. "I think you have your

coordinates screwed up, Silas. Where are we?"

"An out of the way place. Wait here. I'll light a lamp." Something rustled as he walked away then a rattle came as if he fumbled with something. "Got it."

A flickering flame came to life within an oil lamp he held. The light cast our surroundings in a gentle glow, revealing one window with greasy panes and a dozen wooden crates stacked against the walls. We were in an old hut. I curled my toes inside my shoes and rubbed my bare arms because of the chill in the air. "Nice digs."

"This is the best location for protectors to 'port into. Three cabins surround this hut. They've got the basics for a short stay, but this one is for storage."

"What are you saying? What short stay?"

He snorted. "Your talk of other men made me think *kidnap*. We need to speak more about us before I take you home." He stalked to the door and yanked it open. "Give me a couple of minutes to go check out a cabin."

"We're adults. We could've talked in your room." And what did he mean, we needed to speak more about us? There wasn't an "us."

He looked at me. "Your mind is resting in mine and I damn well like it. It's frustrating the hell out of me, so you're not going anywhere until we sort this out. We need to chat."

"About?"

"All our options." He left.

As I followed him to the raggedy-planked front steps, his silhouette blended into the dark outline of the trees beyond and with his continuing distance, my mind-merge fell away. The disconnection made my heart heave within my chest. What a silly, needful skill.

So...options? Hmm. I tipped my heels off and grabbed the straps as I stepped off the porch. I gasped, landing barefoot in the thickest grass ever.

Nooo way.

This had to be a dream.

Squeezing my eyes shut, I counted to ten and flung them open.

Nope. Blades of the deepest green grass still reached my knees.

I brushed my fingertips through the vision of paradise. Wow.

Oh yee-ahh.

Down I went. Onto my stomach, rolling around, I clutched handfuls of grass, tore it free and threw it high, giggling as it sprinkled on top of me.

What a dream.

I loved this place for the grass alone. Yay to being kidnapped!

Inhaling the richness of the soil, I stretched, arms and legs flapping as I made a grass-angel and dug my own little hollow in paradise.

"What are you doing?" From overtop, Silas frowned, the lamp swinging in his hand.

"Ah, duh, I'm having a moment. You want to join me?"

"On the ground? No." He extended his hand. "I realize the outback is experiencing a drought, but surely you've seen grass before."

Swatting his hand away, I snorted. "Not like this. The drought's been going on for years and if you didn't realize, I'm there half the time. Nah-ah. I'm not moving. It's not every day a girl gets to play in the grass."

"I see." His blue eyes crinkled at the corners. "Although, I can guarantee this grass isn't going anywhere. You can come outside and play in the morning, if you wish."

Wagging one finger at him, I moaned. "Don't try and be funny. The morning is too far away. Oooh, I just had a thought. Since this kidnapping was your idea, mine is that I'm sleeping outside under the—" A big fat drop of water landed on my cheek. Then another on my arm. Next, my forehead. I grinned from ear to ear. "No way."

Heavy drops of glorious water splattered all over me. I lifted my hands to the sky to grab at the flurry. "Oh yee-yee-yes."

Silas chuckled. "I've never in my life seen anyone so happy about getting wet."

"It's grass, and I'm getting wet. What a day." I laughed, and was about to resume rolling when Silas plucked me from the ground. "Hey."

He took my hand and led me toward the trees. "When it rains, it pours in these hills. We need shelter."

"But—" I looked back at my slice of heaven. "There's grass, and now there's rain." I growled as he drew me away. "Oh, you can't be this cruel."

Grinning far too smugly, he said, "Our cabin is right this way."

I kicked at the small puddles in the grass as I tramped through it. "You are so lucky to live on this land."

He tugged me. "Once we get inside, I'll pop to the castle's kitchens and pick up some food. I know you haven't eaten, and neither have I."

"Oh, I'm definitely hungry." Continuing along the grassy path between towering pine trees, I swore water gushed somewhere not too far away. I tapped my ear. "That's not a river is it?"

Bringing my hand to his chest, he kept a firm hold. "Yes, it is. A fast-moving one."

I squealed. "Let me see." I tried to heave free. "Silas, this kidnapping is no fun."

"The river is swift and dangerous. We'll go when it's daylight and you can see for yourself."

I let out a loud sigh. "I wasn't thinking of swimming in it."

At least, I hadn't until he'd mentioned it. That would be great. I'd love a midnight swim. It wasn't as if he couldn't teleport us out of trouble if something happened.

"The morning." Two words, stubbornly stated. "Here we are."

A small clearing sprinkled in moonlight led to a little log cabin with a front porch and overhanging roof of wooden shingles. Silas pushed open the front door. "We're the only ones here. Inside with you."

"No fun at all." I groaned and grumped as I stomped in. Water pooled at my feet as I halted on the rough wooden floorboards. I tickled my toes in it.

He shut the door, setting the lamp on a dresser beside it. "You're shivering."

"I don't care." I dragged the hem of my blue dress to the side and wrung it out. Water dripped to the floor, so mesmerizing.

"You're soaked through. I'll go rustle you up some jeans and a t-shirt with that meal. You and Silvie are the same size. That sound good to you?"

"Sure." Water dribbled down my back from my hair. Nice.

"In the dresser there're towels and blankets. Don't catch a cold while I'm gone." He 'ported.

With his leaving, I peered around the room. A bed was tucked against the wall, the double mattress covered by a thick gray blanket. Opposite was a small window with lace netting across it, and underneath a round wooden table and two chairs layered with dust.

I opened the top drawer of the dresser and heaved out a quilt of stitch-work squares in a multitude of blues and greens. I flapped it out and spread it over the bed.

Searching the next drawer, I found green towels neatly stacked beside pillowcases. I wrapped myself in a scratchy but clean towel and used a second one to dry my hair.

With the damp towel, I wiped the dust from the tabletop.

"The little woman is making the place a home."

I spun around at Silas's cheeky tone. Throwing the towel at him, I tut-tutted. "Where's the food, honey?"

He set a wicker basket on the table, and passed me a bundle of clothing. "I half expected to return and find you outside, back in the rain."

"Then next time, that's where I'll be." I set jeans and a white shirt with a yellow embroidered hem on the bed. "This is perfect. Thank you."

Silas laid food on the table, clattering dishes and cutlery. "I'll keep my back turned while you change. This is the only room and I don't care to get wet outside."

"If you look, I'll throw my knife at you."

He chuckled. "What knife?"

"The one I left at home." I scrambled, pulling the jeans on, the denim sticking as I hopped about. "Have you stayed here before?"

"A bit. I like the river."

Dressed, I patted my chest and took a deep breath. "I'm done. You can move now."

He turned, ever so slowly. "You're my first kidnap victim."

"I better be." I sat at the table. "People get locked up for this sort of thing in Dralion. I know you have certain sway with your King Carlisio, but certainly not mine. Donaldo would slice your head from your shoulders."

He pried the lid off the first dish, and the scent of chicken floated into the air. "What about Alexo? Will he come?"

"I doubt it. It's not as if I'm in danger from you. His forewarning only activates if I am. Although, he could check on me with his forethought, but he's busy with my mother, so I'd say even that's a no. You should be safe."

Yum-yum. My mouth watered for the golden-fried chicken drumsticks and roasted sweet potato with buttery corn. "Oh, you did well. The little woman is pleased."

He passed me a fork and a flask of water. "I love a good steak, but chicken is my next favorite meal. I was worried about my choice from the servery. I had no idea of your tastes."

I speared a cube of crispy-skinned potato and popped it into my mouth. "I'll eat anything, except tomatoes. For some reason they make me feel sick, but not tomato sauce. That, I love all over my meat."

"I see. No tomatoes. I'll remember that in the future."

"What future? This kidnapping is a one-deal thing, right?"

His blue gaze darkened. "We'll see."

I forked up corn and chewed, arching an eyebrow. "Then for the next round of kidnapping, I'd like to go for a swim. Taking me to a fast-moving river would be perfect."

He caught my hand and lifted it to his lips. "There shall be no swim, as I've said."

I merged my mind solidly with his, unable to hold back with him this close. "You're not very adventurous, are you?"

"The river is dangerous. Your life means something to me."

I pulled my hand free and took one of the drumsticks of chicken from the dish. "I'm not holding you to anything."

"We'll have to sleep in the same bed. I'm not prepared to leave you tonight."

"You're truly serious about keeping me here?" He really hadn't cared for my talk of other men, and we were soul-bound. Regardless of our earlier decision to end what we had, that was near impossible to do now. We would always have this tie of mind-merge, pulling us together for at least a few minutes every other day.

"Yes." Easing back in his chair, he scrubbed a hand along his thigh. "I was up before dawn, and you've been on my mind all day. I returned your warrior and now I sit with you because you have the skill of mind-merge. Things have changed. I need more time to think about our options."

"You can't have Saunder's father back." That was a given.

"I understand. Tell me more of what your father's requested you do. I see I have no choice but to be a part of this, for now."

"He said once I met you, to find a way to piece things together. He needs to know everything about my mother's Sol family line. And I must also discover what I can about this new skill of mine."

"Alexo Wincrest must have seen more than he originally told you. It'll be why he never warned you off me, particularly if he knew your life would be tied to mine. That makes sense."

"Yes." What would have happened if after I'd met Silas, I'd sent him immediately on his way? My agreement would have come much quicker if it were not for Dad's request. And my skill of mind-merge would still have come in, only I wouldn't have had Silas to merge with. Would death have come within three days?

Returning one of the empty dishes to the basket, he murmured, "We'll do this research of yours together."

"Wait." I grabbed his arm. "I've asked so much of you today. Are you sure?"

He pulled me to my feet. "My wishes do not count with the bond in play. What further information were you made aware of?"

"My father advised he loses sight of me for a few days. Somehow I go dark, but I have no idea how or why."

"A few days?" He removed his sword belt and set it against the corner of the headboard then kicked his black boots off and sat on the bed. He tugged me down beside him. "That doesn't sound good."

"My father has no fear of my disappearance. I mustn't be gone long."

Underneath the thin down mattress, the ridges of the base's wooden slats poked through.

"Let's sleep on this information. In the morning we'll have

clearer heads." He raised my legs and tipped me under the covers then joined me. "I still don't like the idea of you disappearing for a few days. We'll stay close."

"I have no idea when I go dark. He didn't exactly say."

He extinguished the lamp, and moonlight filtered through the tiny square window. He rolled to his side, facing me. "We'll stay close. I can't dismiss the mated bond. Our souls call to one another and it's strong."

I felt it too.

"I can't keep my distance from you, Hope. That would result in your death."

"Yeah, but yours would result if my grandfather, Donaldo, ever found out about you. The need to protect goes both ways."

A low growl rumbled from his throat. "It sounds like you're arguing with me."

"I'm pointing out the facts. Alexo keeps the knowledge of Faith's relationship with Loveria a secret."

"We don't have their kind of relationship."

"So this is a non-relationship?" I smiled. That actually suited me.

"Yes."

"Okay, honey. I got it."

He pulled me to him. "I have no idea why, but I like you. You have a smart mouth."

I snuggled closer, resting my cheek against his chest. "Mmm-hmm. So do you."

He let out a slow breath and it fanned over the top of my head. "I still want to kiss you."

"Hell, no." I grinned to myself.

"Are you repeating my earlier words?"

"Yes, I am." He rolled me, coming up over top. My heart raced. "Don't—"

His kiss was potent as he claimed my mouth.

I had no response. I was lost, hypnotized as we shared

breath and a moment more special than any in time.

He cupped my face in his hands and stroked my cheeks, his thoughts escaping for the first time.

I read them so clearly within the merge.

He wanted this moment to last.

My heart soared and my soul called to his on the deepest level. "We are in a world of trouble," I murmured against his lips.

His hold tightened, intoxicating me. Then he eased away an inch, maybe two. "You have the most beautiful spun-gold hair. It catches even the moonlight and glows like silk."

I cleared my throat. "I know I just said trouble. You should stick to your side of the bed in this non-relationship."

A wicked grin widened his mouth. "I could drown in the brilliant violet of your eyes."

"Do I need to slap your face?"

He laughed. "Yes."

I pushed him away, trying to get my heartbeat to slow. "Go away."

He rolled into me, held me close. "I'll be good. Just keeping you warm. It's my right."

I curled up, squeezing my eyes shut. "I can't believe I'm sharing a bed with you. Do you snore?"

"Terribly. I'm also a bed-hog."

I heard the partial lie, but to which half of that statement? "Hmm, since I'm squished between you and the wall, I'm picking you're a bed-hog."

"You feel all warm and soft. I'm not going anywhere." He nuzzled my hair and yawned. "Go to sleep. You'll need your rest if you want to be on your toes tomorrow."

I didn't doubt it. The minutes ticked by, and I slowly relaxed. My soul-bound mate lay beside me. For one night, or perhaps for more? I had no idea.

Chapter 4

I awoke to light tracking through the small square window, one that was now barely visible because Silas's broad shoulders blocked the way. It had rained off and on during the night with a *tap-tapping* against the wood-shingled roof. Each time I'd stirred as it had.

Stretching my legs, I rubbed them against Silas's socked ones. Oooh, toasty-warm.

His lips touched my cheek as he tucked me in closer. "It's too early. I need another half an hour."

"I didn't say anything." I ran my fingers along his shadowed jaw, smiling at the prickly sensation. "Do you like sleep-ins?"

"Yes." He dragged his eyelids open then pressed the small light switch on his modern Earth watch. "Ah, it's already seven. Unbelievable. I can hear your stomach rumbling."

Butterflies abounded as he placed his hand over my belly. "That's because I'm hungry, Mr. Sleuth."

"So I wasn't imagining your sharp tongue."

"I do not have a sharp tongue. I have a sharp mind."

He groaned, swung his legs out of bed then reached for his boots. He laced them, peering over his shoulder at me. "I'll be back. I'll go raid the castle's kitchens, again."

I crawled to him. "I see you're not a morning person."

"Nope." He picked up his sword and belted it around his hips. "Not when I was lost in a nice dream."

"About?"

He leaned in and kissed me. "Don't wander too far from the cabin. The outhouse is around the back."

I released my mind-merge, feeling the ache of withdrawal inside my head as I did. I looked into his eyes. "Gosh, it's like I'm not supposed to leave your mind. I can't believe how heavily one with this skill relies on the other. Could you bring some paper and ink? I need to start recording this." I slid my hands underneath my knees to prevent myself from reaching for him.

"Sure I can. What do you usually eat for breakfast?"

"You choose." I squeezed the thin feather mattress as he stepped back and 'ported.

Right, the outhouse.

I strolled outside and gawked as the rain fell. Large, fat drops splattered into my palm as I held it out from under the eaves of the small porch.

Oh, amazing.

Fresh water.

I sipped it. Across the small clearing, two other closed-up cabins sat, surrounded by giant pines.

Above, a lush green canopy drooped under the weight of the night's rainfall and tree trunks glistened as water streamed down their sides. Everywhere, so much water.

In the distance, the river roared.

As I jumped off the top step, water splashed over the bottoms of my jeans and toes.

I was away, twirling around and skipping toward the river so close.

Dirt and grass squished around my feet, and I grinned as I came out from under the trees. White water tumbled over wide gray boulders and rocks. Oh, this was not the idle outback river I was used to. No. This was an art form in motion, nature at its most chaotic, singing of life.

I scrambled over the slick rocks at the sides and stood on the highest point, mesmerized by the pounding water and the spray coating my bare arms.

The water pebbled as I tickled my fingers over my skin. More. I wanted more.

Beaming, I looked over the rapids. Dad would be experiencing a forewarning if I shouldn't be here. I'd always had an affinity for water, despairing over the outback's drought, yet I took every opportunity to swim wherever possible in Dralion. "Dad, you know I'm a super strong swimmer, and I can't miss this."

I waited, jiggling about.

No one appeared, not Dad to forestall me, nor a warrior he'd sent.

I was good to go.

I dove, and the current shot me to the surface. Water dumped over my head then swelled under and tossed me back up. Over and over, I was volleyed about.

I giggled whenever I broke for air, and my squeals echoed all around. It was bliss. Goldie should be here to enjoy the fun. She would love this.

I gulped rain-scented air while the scenery rushed past. An occasional deer flashed by, prancing along the bank, drinking from the surging water. The rumbling, gushing river raced me down the valley. As the forest vanished, cattle grazed in glistening pastures below a blue sky dotted with gray bubbling clouds.

What a sight. If only this stormy weather would hit the station.

The station? Heck, I had work and I should be there.

I eyed the river ahead. An area pooled to one side. I had to make that. Kicking out, I headed away from the center. Finally, I made the shallows. I splashed about as I found my feet, the rocky bed sharp. "Ouch." I jumped as the stones cut the underside of my foot.

I dragged myself onto the sandy shore and flopped onto my back. My jeans clung to my legs, and the borrowed shirt had been stretched beyond repair.

"There. You. Are."

Goldie's tone was low and her gaze intimidating as she stood over me. Next to her Dad stood, his arms crossed and his thick black leather coat flapping heavily around his ankles.

"Hey." Okay, I was in trouble.

Two sets of violet eyes, the exact shade as mine, mirrored frustration. Dad stepped forward and lent me a hand. "I watched."

He drew me up, and I wobbled as I kept off my sore foot. "Is the protector, Silas Carver, the one you want?" he asked.

Goldie hissed in a sharp breath. "No, Hope. The plan was to get Saunder's father then go your separate ways. What happened to the plan?"

"It's gotten a little lost." I glanced between the two of them. "Neither of you can hurt Silas. He's the other half of my soul and you know how deep the—"

"No, no, no," Goldie snapped. "You said you were ending it."

Dad grunted. "It's not possible, Goldie. Hope holds the skill of mind-merge as her sister does. I had forewarning days ago which I couldn't speak of, and as we've now discovered, Faith can't survive more than three days without merging her mind with Loveria's. The same goes for Hope. Death follows, and damn it, both my daughters now hold this rare skill."

Goldie paced. "Argh, so that's why you allowed her to meet the protector."

Well, wasn't this a lovely family reunion. "Ah, perhaps I should point out there is some good news in all of this."

"And that would be?" Goldie kicked at the pebbles lining

the river's edge.

"I have a skill, which means there might be more to come. I will also document all I'm learning on mind-merge. Which is now firsthand. It can't all be doom and gloom. I won't allow it."

Dad tilted his blond head. "I do feel you hold the key. That emotion came through strongly during my first forewarning. Obviously, we can do nothing about the protector. I would never stand in your way as Donaldo stood between your mother and me. We'll have to hide your relationship with Carver, as we do for Faith."

Goldie gritted her teeth. "This is such a mess, Alexo."

"I know." He shoved his hands in his pockets. "But we are keeping the news contained to just a few. Maslin, Lieska and Guy Moyer. Faith searches for Guy's father and our other captured warriors as she can, provided Guy keeps quiet. Which he will. I too have spoken to him since Lieska did."

Goldie nodded. "They are all loyal."

"Although, the less who know, the better." Dad regarded me. "I would dearly love to know where you disappear to soon, but my forewarning only shows I lose sight of you, along with the strong feeling that it must happen." He pulled me into his arms. "Take the utmost care."

"I will," I said, my words muffled by his shirt.

He eased back, taking my arms. "I see Carver searching for you now, but before I go, you should know your mother still adapts to our world and I can't be far from her side."

"Why do you wait to tell her of me?" There must be more, and it frustrated me that I didn't know.

He exhaled, ever so slowly. "She has gone through so much since her arrival in Dralion. She's been spellbound and can never return to Earth. Then there's all that's happened to Faith, with your sister's mated bond to Loveria and near death because we were unaware her skill could kill. Kate now knows her mother, Katerin Sol, took her to Earth, abandoning her so far away from her Magioling people. The news shook her." He paused, rubbing his jaw. "When I first found Kate on Earth she'd just spent eighteen years in an orphanage. All she wanted was a family of her own to love, and I longed to give her that, no matter the length of time we had together."

"Did you always know it wouldn't be long?"

He squeezed his eyes shut then opened them again. "I cannot have visions of myself, and I made the mistake of telling Donaldo about Kate. From that moment, the risks to her became obvious. Donaldo would never allow me to have an Earthling for a wife and weaken our skilled line. He'd never harm a child of mine, although your mother's death was a certainty in order to see me married to another. He wanted full-blooded heirs, which is why I hid my comings and goings to Earth. Except, your grandfather caught on."

"Oh." I understood.

"I couldn't expose Kate's whereabouts to Donaldo. As my soul-bound mate, her protection came first. I also had to take care not to activate the blood-bond between you girls and me. That link is as strong as the mated relationship except your bound one holds your soul. I held off, deciding to leave the moment you were born, and I watched your birth with my forethought from close by."

He pushed a hand deep into his hair. "Only I did not see your death until it was too late. You were so tiny, so cold, and I had to take you with me. I chose that moment to bring you home and to bury you somewhere close to me."

Arms shaking, I hugged him. "You saved my life by doing so. I've always known that."

"I should have returned you to your mother when you took your first breath. Except your heart was so weak, and I wasn't sure what another teleport jump would do."

"I know, and my mother had Faith. She did not need us both." The depth of our blood-bond drove my need to ease his pain now. Dad had loved and raised me by his own hand.

"Faith was born with a minor form of the blockage you had. The doctors operated on your sister after your death. They did not want to see Kate lose both her babies."

I gasped. "Tell me everything."

He looked skyward. "Carver is searching, but I will speak of what I can. After Faith's eighteenth, when her forethought developed, I knew I'd been given a highly skilled child. I've always believed you girls to be Halflings and I had not expected such a thing. But the mated bond had prevailed and given me a child with full-strength. Donaldo would accept that, because our line would continue strongly. When Faith came into her skill of mind-merge, one that's not carried within our Wincrest line, we knew Kate was not of Earth."

"I see." My mother had been abandoned, left in an orphanage on a foreign world, never knowing where her family had come from. "How did Faith come to be with Loveria?"

"He tracked her through their mated bond, and before I knew she held the highest strength skills. At the time, I still kept my distance. Within days, he'd laid claim to her. I couldn't reverse what was already done."

"Their bond had taken."

"Yes, it develops fast, as you're discovering. Even Carver cannot set your mated relationship aside. He hunts for you now."

I rubbed my chest. "He said we have a non-relationship. I can't push him for more. I don't even want to."

"Davio Loveria hides Faith's true identity. He cleared Peacio of Donaldo's spies to ensure Faith could safely travel here, but Faith stays low. She doesn't venture too far from the castle or from Loveria, and she heeds my warnings. It's imperative you do the same. Never take your safety for granted here. Donaldo has sent more spies into the lower ranks of our enemy protectors. Right now they seek acceptance where they can."

It could take months or upward to a year for them to gain access. I'd entered a battlefield. "I'll be careful."

"Good." He squeezed my arms as he stepped back. "Carver's pursuit is closing in. Goldie and I must leave."

Goldie groaned as she hugged me. "With these changes, I'll need to talk to Maslin and Lieska. Guy too. I expect you at the station soon."

"Yes, I'll be there." I shivered as the wind picked up and my sodden clothing clung to my skin.

Her lips flattened into a tight white line as she glanced toward the forest upstream. "I hear horses. Carver must have bought reinforcements."

"Go. Silas and I need to talk." Three horses galloped free of the trees two-hundred feet away, two men and a woman riding. "I'll be fine."

Dad held Goldie's arm. "Carver will watch over Hope." To me, he said, "We will talk soon. By the way, there is a mess in your hair."

They flashed away.

I felt my head, my fingers catching in a mass of tangles. Oh, so now he tells me. With a low growl, I plucked out bits of leaves and pine needles. Yuck. No girl wanted to look her worst. As the female rider closed in, I flicked the debris to the ground.

Dark brown hair blew over her shoulders, inky, skintight pants encased her legs and a leather vest covered a ruffled white shirt. She wore knee-high, black leather boots and a sword belted at her side. She pulled her horse up in front of me. "Silas told the truth. Faith does have a twin. An identical one."

"Apparently." I eyed her. She was a protector and I was the enemy. That I would never forget.

The second horseman rode in, his animal snorting. This protector was huge, broad-shouldered and dressed as most of their battle-hardened were in dark leathers. He gripped his horse's reins, stilling him with one simple command as he glowered at me then the woman at his side. "Another Wincrest, Viv. We should kill this one before Silas gets here."

They drew their swords.

"Put your weapons away!" Silas bellowed as he thundered in. He slid to the ground then stood firmly in front of me as he faced the others. "Zac, Wincrest or not, she is still the other half of my soul. You will never harm a hair on her head."

The protector grunted. "She is a true Wincrest. Unlike Faith, this one grew up in Dralion."

"I get that."

I stepped in beside Silas, spearing him a look. "Why'd you bring them?"

Waving a torn piece of cloth, he said, "I found this from your t-shirt upstream, snagged around a rock. I thought the worst and needed reinforcements to search for you. Zac and Viv are loyal friends." He pulled off his dark leather jacket and wrapped it around my shoulders then zipped it up. "You shouldn't have moved from the cabin. It's my job to keep you safe."

Encased in warmth all the way to my knees, I sucked in a deep breath. "I'm not a job." I found the armholes from within my leather cocoon and shoved my hands through. The sleeves swamped me.

"You feel like one." He rolled one cuff to the wrist, and then the other. "Zac and Viv know who Faith is."

"I got that part." While hauling my damp hair free of the collar, I found another small twig and flicked it to the ground. "You still didn't have to search for me."

"I had no choice. You were missing when I returned. Anything could have happened."

"Like what?"

"You could have drowned."

"Huh, with a father who has forewarning? That's so unlikely as to be impossible."

He took the edges of my collar and brought us nose to nose.

"Your father never warned you off me. So far, in my opinion, he's not of the right mind."

"I think we both remember I have mind-merge, which is why we're together. He's not so dumb after all now, huh?"

Viv laughed. "Oh, she's good. She has a bite to her tongue. Faith will like her."

"Will those two truly keep our secret? I don't trust protectors."

"They are loyal, without a doubt."

Zac cleared his throat. "I will accept your presence because you are his mate. That is the only reason."

Viv jumped to the ground and crossed to me. "Silas told us of your ability to mind-merge. We understand a little of your skill because Faith holds it."

Zac groaned, rather loudly. "I can't believe we have to deal with two Wincrests now. What did we do to deserve this?"

"Excuse Zac," Viv said to me. "My mate is barely used to Faith. It will take him some time to adapt to you as well."

"No one needs to get used to me. I am a Wincrest, after all."

Silas caught me around the waist, and drew me toward his horse. "Let's get you back." He caged me between the animal and him then bent to my ear. "Merge your mind with mine."

Merging, I sank deep into my space, finding more comfort than I could have imagined. It was bliss in his mind. "I like swimming. The water calls to me."

"I see you're fascinated by it." He pressed a kiss to my forehead as he reached past me and grabbed his horse's reins. "Let's return to the castle rather than the cabin. Faith was there last night but left for school this morning, so all is clear." He swung up into his saddle and offered his hand.

I put my hand in his and he drew me up in front of him. The breeze stirred my drying hair, and I raised my face to the sunshine streaming through the broken layer of clouds. "This is a lovely spot."

Arms wrapped around me, he held the reins. "It's one of my favorite places." He called to Zac and Viv. "My mate needs to warm up. We'll meet you at the castle." He nudged the horse's flanks and snapped the reins. We were off, heading across the grassy green field dotted with tiny yellow flowers.

The cattle bawled as we skirted in and around them.

Sinking deeper into his mind, I smiled as the wind rushed at me. "Alexo and Goldie came to the river."

"You were in trouble then?" His question was demanding, his voice raspy.

"No, not in the way you mean." Turning, I glanced at him. "Alexo fully explained what happened at the time of my birth. His words reassured me and gave me a deeper understanding of what he went through, of why he still needs more time before speaking to my mother."

Silas pushed me down in the saddle then wrapped his arms around me and the horse's neck. "I see. Speak to me after I 'port us back. You don't fast-heal and I won't have you getting a cold."

He made the leap, galloping smoothly from one grassy meadow to another, the blast of added speed from the horse making my pulse jump. "I love that. I wish I could 'port."

The castle loomed high on the hill, puffy cotton-ball clouds breezing overtop a massive, gray, stone wall. Loveria Castle spread over several acres, and Silas urged his horse toward the northern end, where a twin-towered gatehouse stood three-stories high.

Underneath the curved archway we rode, and into an inner courtyard. He slowed as we neared a tidy run of stone stables. Zac and Viv rode in beside us, having also 'ported.

Silas eased back and slid from the saddle as he brought his horse to a halt. He passed the reins to a young stable hand and thanked him. "The gravel is sharp and you're not wearing any footwear. I'll help you down."

"I can handle it."

"Don't argue." He lifted me off.

"I like arguing." I tapped his nose.

"Silas," Zac called out. "Viv and I are heading to the arena for training. We'll catch up with you later."

"Sure thing." Silas waved to them as he led me to a side entrance. To me, he said, "Don't speak to anyone I don't authorize you to, particularly the sentry guards."

Stationed at the base of the stone steps to the castle, a protector stood, military-still. His dark hair was clipped close to his scalp and a scrolled engraving of the letter *P* was tattooed down the side of his neck, the tail end of the letter disappearing beneath the neckline of his vested white shirt. Over both biceps, throwing knives were strapped, and poking from his right boot a polished dagger gleamed. He nodded at Silas as he guided me inside.

"Why not 'port us?"

"I want you to know the way in and out since you can't."

We continued down a long passageway with textured silvery-white walls, the ceiling twelve feet high with silver filaments inlaid into the plaster corner scrolls.

I wanted to stop and admire the stunning landscapes gracing the walls every ten feet, but Silas pressed forward. "There isn't time."

"Why not?"

"The guards have pin-prick hearing, and I need to warn Carlisio I've claimed my mate."

"Hold on. Claimed? When did this happen in our non-relationship?"

"I have no choice. You have mind-merge and your welfare is my responsibility. Your sister is equally as dependent on Davio."

Never had the thought of being bound to Silas annoyed me more than at this moment. I let out a loud sigh. "I'm not anyone's responsibility, let alone yours."

"Yes, you are. I see it more clearly now." He snagged my arm as we reached a set of gray marble stairs with a smooth banister curving upward. "My rooms are on the second floor of the north terrace."

"Tell me more about Faith?" I asked since he'd brought her dependency on Loveria up.

"She's a rebel."

I ran to keep up. "A rebel is one I can respect."

"Spoken like another rebel."

I stopped, right in the center of the passageway where white roses bloomed in a vase. "You're angry? You can't tell me it's only because I went for a swim."

He turned on his heel, staring at me. "Down a fast-moving river. After a storm. With you on enemy soil."

"So. So. And so?" I crossed my arms.

"I didn't expect to be so worried about you. The feelings have come quickly."

He ushered me backward into an alcove with a life-sized statue of a fearsome looking protector. Chiseled from smooth green stone, holding a battle-axe in one hand and a sword in the other, it looked as intimidating as Silas now did.

"That's the way of the bond." I poked him in the chest. "Argh, how are we supposed to make this work? If you ever turn up at Wincrest Station, a warrior is bound to take your head off. No one will ask why you're there. You can't just say you've claimed me. We need to talk about it."

He leaned in, pushing me against the statue's cold stone. "We are mated. I cannot turn away from you any more than you can turn from me."

Pressing a hand to his chest, I held him at bay. "What woman would you wish for, if you could choose exactly who she was?"

His gaze searched mine, and an image of a faceless woman

slipped through his mind-merge shield. She could fight alongside him, like a fellow protector, definitely not me.

"I see."

"Our soul-bond draws me to you. I cannot undo the fact you are a Wincrest. I will come to accept it."

Damn, I couldn't take from him what he wouldn't freely give. Which left me with little choice. "We need to take a break." My chest tightened as I issued the words, because it was the last thing I truly wanted. Stupid bond.

"That's not a wise choice. I must accept what is. So should you."

He pressed my palms flat to his chest. The heavy beat of his heart pounded against my flesh, my hands heated and pulse jumped then vaulted a second time and beat in time with his. He'd aligned our heartbeats as our mated men did in order to strengthen the bond. If I were ever in any distress, he'd know because our hearts would beat in sync. "How could you?"

"It was my choice."

"More like your fate." My chest throbbed. "I would never have asked this of you."

"I know you wouldn't have." He dipped his head to mine. "I must be able to feel what you do, to know when you need me. If I'd done this earlier, I would have caught your increased heart rate at jumping in the river and known to come. It is done."

"I spend half my time in Dralion. Our hearts beating in sync will only add to your frustration."

"You will not do anything dangerous where I can't reach you."

"Swimming in a river is not dangerous."

"So you've said, and so I've disagreed." He drew me into the passageway. "We should go before someone comes. These halls are never so quiet. My bedroom's close." Four doors down, he opened a dark wood door and guided me through. He gestured toward the bathroom. "Clean up. I'll return to the cabin for the clothing I left there. I must also speak to Carlisio and update him."

I unzipped his leather jacket and passed it to him. "Thanks for this."

He tossed it onto the wooden chest at the end of his bed. "I want you here. You must know that."

I saw the truth in his words, yet I'd also seen his true desire. I could never stand and fight beside him, not when our countries were at war. "You go speak to Carlisio Loveria."

He kissed me, stroking my cheek with his fingers. "I don't care to leave you, not after what you saw in my mind."

"I would rather know the truth than ever have any mistrust between us. Truly, go." I walked to the bathroom and shut the door. Oh boy, what was I going to do with him? I wanted my bonded mate, but to what extent? My mind-merge dropped away. He'd left.

Searching the vanity cupboard, I found a towel, and then set it on the white-gray speckled surface. Drat, my reflection in the mirror over the basin showed a fright. Leaves stuck out of my hair. I plucked free what I could then shucked my clothes and stepped into the shower. After flicking the water lever, I tipped my head back under the spray and worked shampoo through to the ends of my hair, getting rid of the rest of the mess.

Clean and dry twenty minutes later, I found the clothing Silas had left outside the door and dressed in a pair of snug jeans and a fitted violet t-shirt with a low V-neck. I looked for a pair of shoes.

Nope, nothing. Oh well, I had cut my foot earlier and maybe it was best I go bare—

Whoa. My foot had not hurt since—

I grabbed my left foot and hopped about as I tried to find the cut.

Jeez, maybe it had been the right one.

Skipping to the other foot, I checked it out.

Where was the cut?

My hands shook, because no matter how often I checked each foot, the outcome was still the same.

I'd fast-healed. No cut. Not even the trace of a pink line.

Nothing. Nada. Zilch.

I swayed and toppled onto the bed.

"Dad," I called out, not sure if this warranted his forewarning to activate since I wasn't in danger.

A blast of air from behind tossed damp hair into my face and gave me my answer.

"Let's go. I saw what happened."

"I can fast-heal."

He pulled me to my feet. "I know, honey. I'm taking you with me right now. You will have the skill of telepathy in mere seconds and if you're not with Goldie, she turns up, outside this castle, completely uninvited. The forewarning was strong."

Everything darkened then we jolted down in the middle of the battle-training yard before the homestead, the red dust of the outback swirling at my feet.

"*Goldie. Goldie. Goldie.*" My mind kept calling telepathically to her, unable to stop.

Dad shook me. "Relax. The threaded link is building. Stay calm. She'll answer you."

"*Hope? Is that you?*" Goldie's frantic voice rang crystal clear in my mind.

"*Goldie, I can fast-heal. I can hear you.*" I trembled as our threaded connection tightened.

"*I know it's scary when your telepathy first kicks in. Wow. And how do you know you can fast-heal?*" She sounded excited.

I needed to see her.

"*No, don't answer that. I'm coming to you. Even if I have to storm Loveria Castle.*"

"*No.*" Goldie wouldn't have let me go through this alone. "*I'm not there. I'm in the battle-training yard. Outside. Dad brought me home.*" I fidgeted.

Wind rushed then with an ear-piercing squeal, Goldie plowed into me and smothered me in her arms. "This is amazing. I knew you would have more skills than that stupid mind-merge. Now, fast-healing and telepathy I understand." She pulled me with her in a dizzying circle. "Lieska's coming. I just told her."

Air swirled, and Lieska laughed. "This is wonderful." She withdrew her short dagger. "Let me confirm you fast-heal."

Alexo snatched her arm. "Lieska, behave."

Goldie grinned. "She won't even bear a scar, Alexo. A small nick is all part of the initiation."

Dad growled and Lieska sheathed her dagger, her green eyes glinting. "All right, you win." To me she snuck a look. "*Later. Do you hear me?*"

I bubbled with joy as her voice bounced around inside my head. "*Yes, loud and clear.*" My heart lifted as those dearest to me were now closer than ever before. I hugged Lieska, squeezing so hard she actually groaned.

"We have to celebrate." Goldie beamed.

I jumped about, my excitement endless. "Yes, but I need some boots." I was still barefoot and the outback ground was hot.

"I'll get them." Lieska 'ported to my room.

Dad took my chin in his hand. "Take the utmost care. Even though you fast-heal, I will not allow you to get hurt. Now, I must go. I left in the middle of a conversation with Kate."

I grinned. "Sure. Say hi from me."

"You know I can't." He pinched my cheeks. With a chuckle, he released me and flashed away.

Lieska returned and passed me my riding boots. "Here you go."

"Thanks." Leaning against Goldie, I pulled them on. "So we're all good on not killing Silas if he pops by, right?" I sent Lieska a look. "You heard about my mind-merge?"

"Of course, Goldie told me. The skill that kills."

Goldie tightened her ponytail with a yank. "I told Maslin, her and Guy no killing. The three of them weren't happy about it, but they'll do as they're told."

"I've already sharpened my sword." Lieska slid the blade from her side and angled it so it glinted in the sun. "And I'm looking forward to Carver's first visit. No killing doesn't mean I can't harm."

I moaned. "You can't be serious."

Raising her own side-belted sword, Goldie tapped it against Lieska's. "Practice with me, my friend. Show me what you can do."

I backed up. They trained hard and without mercy.

"Come and talk to me while those two fight." Maslin scaled the wooden railing of the training area and perched on top. He wore a blue-checked shirt and tan jeans, his Stetson low on his head.

"Hey."

"I heard about your mind-merge with Carver." He did not look happy.

Lieska laughed as her sword came down over Goldie's. The heavy ringing of metal on metal made me scamper up the railing. I might fast-heal, but I truly didn't care to get hurt. "I need to keep the news quiet, obviously."

"Yes, I was told. You can count on me."

"Maslin, you should get down here," Lieska called, her dark hair whipping about her face as she countered Goldie's next strike. "You're the one who let a protector disable you. Bad-bad."

Goldie chuckled and jumped forward, advancing on Lieska. "I second that."

I straddled the top beam, facing Maslin. "I'm sorry. I didn't see him coming, and I would have warned you if I had."

With his gaze narrowed to slits, he rubbed his thighs. "He'll never get the chance to take me by surprise again." He touched two fingers below his eyes. "I'll have these open. You are my princess, not his."

So serious. Um, time to change the subject. "I have telepathy and fast-healing. It just happened."

A smile tugged at his lips, lightening his stern expression. "Excellent, although I'm not surprised." He scanned the area, from the stables to the right, to the feed sheds on the left. "You're a Wincrest, and there isn't one in history who hasn't held skills."

"Silas isn't here, if you're looking for him."

"Just keeping my eyes open." He leaned in to talk over the din of the clashing swords. "Come with me to the Rocky Ledge's watering hole. I'd like to talk to you. Away from here."

"About?"

He eased over the top railing and jumped, bent his knees and landed with a soft thud. "Everything." His gaze veered to Goldie's where she held her position against Lieska in their fight. "Goldie, I'm taking Hope out riding. We'll catch you later."

"Gotcha."

I took hold of his arm and he 'ported us to the stables. Guy tinkered with a silver stirrup at his workbench, his unruly, coal-black hair falling over his brow.

I hadn't seen the young enchanter in days. "There you are."

Since his father's capture at the battle of Eventide two years ago, Guy and I had studied under the same tutor.

"Hey." He grinned.

Maslin stepped past me. "Guy wished to see you after hearing about your skill of mind-merge from Goldie. She told us together."

"Your sister looks just like you, by the way." Silver, which displayed his strongly skilled line, swirled around the edges of Guy's pale blue enchanter eyes. "Although, I knew she was not you the moment I saw her."

Maslin snatched two saddles from the rack and headed for the outer door, calling over his shoulder, "Hope, I'll grab some food for lunch and see to the horses. I won't be long."

"Sure." I crossed to Guy. "I can't believe you've met Faith before I even have." I checked out the melted portion at the base of a stirrup he was working on. "Oh, well done, the spell of heat without fire. That's the closest I've seen you get to melting metal."

He gave a lazy shrug. "I'm getting there." Guy passed the stirrup to me. "I think the ditty needs to be longer to keep the heat generating. I'll master it and when he's released, prove to my father I didn't slack in my studies. Not once."

Running my fingers over the warm metal, I smiled. "I know you haven't slacked." Oh boy, what must he think of me, bound to a protector? "So, you heard about Silas?"

"Yeah, you're bonded to one of them, like Faith." He sighed. "Your life is tied to Carver's, as hers is with Loveria's. I'm sorry."

I leaned against his workbench. "Me too, but there is a benefit."

"Impossible. Although, this I'd like to hear."

"Now I'm mated to a protector, I'll do everything in my power to find your father and our other captured warriors. Alexo mentioned your agreement with Faith."

"I would have told you as soon as I saw you. It was only a few days ago I spotted Faith with Loveria on Peacian soil and struck the deal."

"I'm glad she agreed to your request. It shows she thinks of our warriors even though she is mated to the enemy. It's a good sign she's loyal to us." I set the stirrup next to his opened notebook filled with his scrawl. "Ah, how am I meant to read this? I can't document your skill when this is what you give me."

Looking sly, he nudged my shoulder with his. "Just ask and

I'll repeat what I've written for you."

"Or you could write with a tidier hand. Oh my goodness." I grabbed his arm. "I haven't told you yet. I have telepathy and fast-healing. It just happened."

"Congratulations. Alexo must be pleased."

"Yes, and tell me, you sensed a firming toward the location of yours when we last spoke. Do you have any more news?"

Men always felt the call, the insistent burn to locate their soul-bound one, and Guy had spoken to me of his desire, the pull at times coming from Earth, and alternately from Magio. He worried greatly since he had searched for her from among his fellow warriors and not discovered his match.

"She moves around too much. If she is a Peacian as you have discovered yours is, I will not travel down that road. I'll steer clear of her and ensure the bond doesn't activate."

Even Silas's true desire of a woman, a protector who'd fight by his side, was one I couldn't fault. Our countries were at war, our relationship—no, non-relationship—a secret we must keep. Things would have been easier had he never come and activated the bond. Although where would my mind-merge have led me? To death because he had not? I shuddered at the thought.

No, what was done was done. Now I needed answers about my ability of mind-merge. Someone must know it. Or about Katerin Sol. Who was she and where had she come from?

"What are you thinking, that has that deep frown on your face?"

"Katerin Sol, my mother's mother. I must find her or her people. That is where I will discover what I need to know about my mind-merge. Or at least I hope I will."

"Hmm." He tapped his chin and glanced over his shoulder to the door Maslin had left by. "The surname of Sol is referenced to the sun, and many of the desert families hold it. Have you spoken to Maslin about this? His Sol ancestors are from a compound in No-Man's Land. His grandparents are still there and their tribe is remote."

Maslin was a Sol. I should have spoken to him. "I'll get onto that."

"Hope, the horses are ready." Maslin patted the doorjamb as he peered around the corner. "Guy, we're heading to the Rocky Ledge's watering hole. The horses need a run."

"Sure." Guy saluted. "You two have a nice lunch."

I approached Maslin. "Could we talk more about the Sol compound?"

"Ah yeah, but let's wait until we get to the Ledge." He ran his hand over my horse's saddle, yanking and checking the buckle. "I'll give you a foot-up." He clasped his hands and I set my foot into his palm-hold.

I jumped and slid into place.

Maslin passed me a hat. "Check your saddlebags. Make sure you're happy with what I packed."

A flask of water, snacks and sandwiches. "Yep, that's good."

After hoisting up into his saddle, he rode out and I followed.

Maslin grinned at me, clicking his tongue to encourage his horse into a gallop.

I joined him and picked up speed as we let our horses have their heads. "I love this place," I yelled into the wind as we raced.

"Me too," he shouted.

We rode, our surroundings still beautiful in spite of the harsh drought.

Brilliant colors shimmered around us, red the predominant, with the dusty landscape broken by the towering gum trees. Beyond the rocky hills, the ridge rose steeply to meet the rich blue of the sky. The sight enthralled, because the Ledge was like a slab of stone appearing out of nowhere.

An hour passed and we neared our destination. What must

Donaldo be thinking with Saunder's father now returned? He would have heard and I should have asked one of the warriors, only with all I'd been through, I'd forgotten.

"Hey, Maslin, what happened with Tawson Rivera?"

"Lieska took him to Dralion when he woke. She informed Donaldo she'd found him in Peacio, making up quite the tale. Tawson was groggy and unresponsive, his recollection of those hours before and after he woke hazy. Saunder's with him, and as far as I've heard, Lieska's word stands."

Hmm, Silas should know what had occurred since I'd left him.

Telepathy.

Trust between mates was a given, and those who had the telepathic skill always connected in order to maintain closer contact. I only hoped with him being a protector, I still had that level of trust to create the threaded link.

Focusing directly on him, I sent out the call. "*Silas. Please hear me.*"

The horse underneath me pounded across the hard-packed earth.

No word from Silas, not a flicker.

"*Answer me, please. We need to talk.*"

"*Hope?*" His voice was a stunned whisper.

I grabbed hold of the link and locked it down. "*Oh my, guess what?*"

"*Hell, you have telepathy. Brilliant. Wait there. I've been detained. It took a while to find Carlisio, but I've finished speaking with him.*"

"*Um, I'm not in Peacio. Alexo collected me when he saw I fast-healed.*"

"*What?*" His voice rebounded around inside my head. "*Damn it. I leave and he comes and takes you. Where are you? Your bedroom?*"

"*No, I'm out riding.*"

"Where?"

"On my horse."

"Don't be smart."

I groaned. *"I'm with Maslin and I doubt the two of you would get along."*

"Where are you riding to? You and I shouldn't be separated right now. We spoke about this."

My saddlebags held a meal, one he wasn't invited to. *"Ah, none of your business."* I didn't need him turning up, not that he had the image for the Ledge to 'port to.

A furious snort traveled down our link. *"I'll kill him if—"*

I snapped it shut, blocking him from reconnecting. Laying out the groundwork was important. He couldn't tell me what to do.

Gripping the reins, I shoved all thought of him aside and soaked in the beauty of tumbleweeds blowing across the land.

Running my hands down the gelding's sweaty neck, I settled lower. The ride lengthened, and we passed several half-dried watering holes before Maslin angled off toward the one we'd aptly named the Rocky Ledge. The Ledge's watering hole descended deep inside a rock-strewn basin, one the cattle found impossible to reach. This hole held the most water of all of them.

As we drew up to the side, we slowed our mounts. I slid my leg over the saddle and jumped to the ground.

Maslin took my horse's reins, slung them over a low branch and tethered our rides to the same tree. He grabbed the supplies from his saddlebags and mine and inclined his head toward the rocks which rimmed the basin. "We'll eat down by the water."

"Sounds good."

He looped a blanket over his arm and led the way.

I followed over the rough boulders, scrambling in some places until we reached the heart of the watering hole. This was one of my favorite locations, an oasis with towering trees along the perimeter offering delectable shade. The water invited one to swim, and the soft patch of green grass to sit.

Maslin flapped out the gray saddle blanket and spread it over the ground. He dropped his pack, lay down and clasped his hands behind his head. "I love this spot. It's so peaceful."

"Thanks for thinking of this." The outback had many secrets, and this location was one of them. I plopped down and settled on my back with my ankles crossed. I peered through the dappled leaves above. Blue sky dominated, with not even a wisp of cloud in sight. So serene.

"I understand you need to mind-merge with Carver every third day."

"For five minutes when I do." I rolled to my side and leaned toward him on one elbow. "I didn't know this would happen with Silas. Although he and I should take things slow. There are too many factors for me not to make that call."

"The slower, the better," he added.

I wanted to be honest with Maslin. "With the mind-merge I saw what Silas desired, and it's not to have his enemy as his mate."

"He should want one of his own."

"I need to keep an open mind, but being here reminds me of the world of difference between him and me. I spend half my life here, and the other half in Dralion. I'd have to find a way to factor Peacio into it, and I'm not sure I can do that."

"I don't envy the position you're in, only do not eliminate me from the equation." He passed me a flask of water, one of the cut sandwiches and some fresh fruit. "Now, no more talk of him when I'd like to talk to you about my grandparents."

"I'd like that as well. It's your father's parents who are from No-Man's Land, right?"

"Yes. For my father's efforts with the warriors many years ago, he accepted the relocation they offered him to Dralion. My grandparents though, still live in the Sol compound, and one of the benefits of serving as a warrior is gaining access out. I travel to No-Man's Land whenever it's possible, although our relationship is new and I'm still getting to know them."

"It must be awful for your family, particularly with your father losing contact with his own parents." I unwrapped then bit into one of the sandwiches he'd brought.

"It's difficult, but we're immensely grateful I can visit and take home news to my family. I'd like to take you to the compound. And now I know of your mind-merge, I've had niggling thoughts. I've heard a little about it, or at least I'm sure I have."

"Oh my goodness. You might have heard of mind-merge? No way."

"Only a touch, because I've not paid a great deal of attention, and my trips to No-Man's Land have been about meeting my family and rebuilding lost bonds. I didn't want to excite you too soon if I wasn't correct."

I jiggled about, unable to sit still. "Tell me more. Don't miss a thing."

"When Goldie told us everything, it seemed too much of a coincidence. I've heard the odd bits and pieces about the merging of one's mind to another's from within the Sol compound. We should investigate."

I bounded to my feet and skipped in a circle. "No-Man's Land experiences the disruption of the energy field." How had I not paid more attention to the fact Dad lost sight of me for a few days? I had to be in the dark for that to happen, or of course, in a gray area. The only gray area was within No-Man's Land near the border to Dralion where one's skills faded in and out because of the dome's energy field so close by. I reached down and grabbed Maslin by the hands. "We have to go. Now."

He squeezed my fingers. "We may find your Sol ancestry is linked to mine. I've always felt certain ties binding us, and we could be remotely blood-bonded through familial ties. It would make sense."

Our friendship had always been a given, and a blood-bond would certainly have aided in that. "How many Sols live within this compound?"

"A few hundred, but the compound moves as each season changes. The gravitational pull on the planet causes the gray area to fluctuate, but the tribe is never more than thirty miles from the old stone church's base. They've been there for three months, and they're not due to move until the next full moon."

Because of such a seasonal fluctuation, and if some of the Sols held mind-merge as I did, then they surely couldn't be without their skill. "The full moon is tomorrow night. We need to go before they move."

"Yes, or it'll take longer to locate them if we hold off. Let me contact Goldie and let her know what we're doing." He was silent, and then shook his head. "She's not answering. I'll inform Guy instead. He knows the location of the stone church. I've taken him there once or twice." He paced away then returned with a grin. "We can go. Guy said he'll collect the horses from here for us. Are you ready?"

"Like, yesterday." We were leaving, now, for the Sol compound. I couldn't wait. Only Dad had said he would lose sight of me for a few days. Had the fluctuation in the gray area come early?

Maslin 'ported us.

Damn, too late.

We had arrived.

Chapter 5

"I'm an idiot." I uttered the words to Maslin as my boots sank into coarse orange sand. Lifting my arms to hold my balance, I blinked against the added brightness after the pitch-black of his teleportation. My feet had settled an inch down, and everywhere a lifeless sea of sand spread out. "They've moved."

Twisting around, I found the old stone church Maslin had spoken about. Oh, it looked nothing like a church. Squat, square, and constructed of thick slabs of orange stone, it held a flat roof made of the same. It blended in with the desert sands.

I opened my telepathic link with Goldie, but found nothing. We'd arrived, and our skills were useless. Getting here was easy. Leaving was not.

I tried Silas too, but no response.

Oh boy, not good.

Now I was here, I didn't like the idea of being without him for the next few days.

I slapped my thighs. "I am too impulsive."

"Sorry, I didn't think, but the tribe never travels more than thirty miles from this base. Don't worry. We'll sort this. We can walk thirty miles. It should only take a day."

"Grrreat."

"Hey, we always have supplies at this church. This is nothing we can't deal with."

"I'd rather you be able to 'port." I looked at the sand-hills surrounding us, at the bare expanse of desert. No signs of civilization. Talk about a dummy.

With his hand on the front door knob of the church, Maslin shoved his shoulder into it. The dark wood scraped open over the sand gathered underneath its bottom edge. I gritted my teeth. "Yuck. It's like fingernails on a chalkboard. How old is this place?"

"The church has stood for hundreds of years. It's said in the beginning members of the Sol clan were married here, which was how it came by its name. Although now it's primarily used as a storage location and teleportation point during the season, the Sols set up camp here. We'll go inside and find out where the caravan has moved to."

I followed him into the windowless interior where it was cooler compared to the heat outside.

Oil lamps hung near the door, and Maslin lit one and passed it to me. "Watch your step."

Six wooden pews were stacked one on top of the other at the far end. In front of them, several mattresses had been piled in a wonky arrangement, and to the side, wooden storage crates abounded. "This feels like a bunker, except it's not underground."

"Yeah, that gear is stowed here for when the worst of the sandstorms blow in. There'll be plenty of dried food and clean clothing in the crates. The tribe only takes what's necessary since their teleporters can renew supplies once they set up their new camp."

I rubbed my arms. The walls flickered orange in the lamplight and the flooring was made of the same stone, but blasted smooth. Such solid construction.

Maslin lit another lamp and held it high near the wall next to him. He tapped a chart tacked to it. "Check this out. They've moved due west of here, closer to the Peacian border. If we head out first thing in the morning then we'll get there by nightfall."

"Okay, that'll be two days away from Silas. I can handle that. So, we should set up for the night?"

"Yes. The sun sets here at five and rises in the morning at the same time. We should pull some of those mattresses over to sleep on, check through the supplies and pack a bag to take."

"What will happen once we get to the compound?"

"I'll have the image and coordinates needed for teleporting. At that point, you can speak to the Sols with ease because I'll be able to 'port you as you wish."

"I can't wait." Yet I had to for another day. That sucked.

"I'll get you to Carver so you can mind-merge in plenty of time. No harm will ever come to you in my care."

Silas. I wished he were here. I was an independent woman, but merging my mind with his had increased my dependency on him. Not that great.

"I meant what I said. Nothing bad ever."

The depth of Maslin's vow had me barely holding back tears. I trusted him. "I know you won't."

"There's nothing we can't deal with. I've promised to look after you, and I always keep my—"

The sharp clang of steel on steel beyond the door had me swinging around. My heart pumped faster. What the...

Swords? What was going on?

Maslin stepped in front of me, obliterating my view of the door as he withdrew a short dagger from a sheath along the inside of his arm. He passed me his oil lamp. "Stay here," he whispered, and slunk to the side of the door.

"Damn it, Carver. Stop fighting with Guy. I had him bring us here, as you demanded. And you, Loveria, let go of me. My arms are killing me, pinned to my back."

It was Goldie. Guy had brought her? Silas and Loveria were here too?

I slid in beside Maslin and set the lamps on the floor.

Silas stood in a fighter's position, his sword raised against Guy's. This was unexpected.

"Your enchanter drew his sword on Silas first." Loveria had Goldie restrained to one side. He continued, "I'll let you go, Wincrest, when Moyer lowers his weapon. We both agreed to no blood being spilt while we searched for Silas's mate."

"Hope isn't lost, you dimwit." Goldie cranked her head around and glared at him. "Maslin told Guy he was bringing her here. Here is where they'll be."

Silas shot Loveria a quick look. "There's no tribe here as they said there would be. They lied."

"Warriors do not lie." I stepped into the doorway.

Goldie harrumphed. "See, I told you she'd be here. Let go, you imbecile."

Loveria pushed her away and wiped his hands on his buff leather pants. "Gladly."

"Are you hurt?" Silas's gaze moved over me.

"No. I'm among my own, remember?"

Guy pounced on him and Silas heaved to the side, barely bringing his blade up in time to deflect the attack.

I wagged my finger at him. "My mate, you need to be more worried about yourself. And, Guy, if you draw blood and he can't walk, you'll carry him out of here."

"I'm not carrying him." Guy tapped the flat of his blade. "Damn, you being bound to a protector is all kinds of wrong."

Silas grumbled as he joined Loveria. "Hope, come here."

I leaned a hip against the doorway. "No, I'm good, thanks."

He glared. "Get. Here. Now."

I crossed my arms. "No. I'm. Good. Thanks."

"You cut me off during our telepathic connection."

"Tough. Sometimes I get moody when someone says they are going to kill someone else. Who I know."

"What do you expect me to say? You told me you were with him." He shot a daggered look at Maslin.

"Puh-lease." Goldie let out the mother of all sighs. "As much as I want to hear you two fight, we're losing daylight. I gather we're sleeping here." She clamped one hand on Maslin and the other on Guy, hauling them past me.

Silas advanced. "I promised your aunt no blood would be shed if Moyer brought us here, but if I see Sol even breathe on you, all deals are off."

I looked into his eyes and the truth blazed back at me. "Maslin knows you're my mate. I made that clear, not that you and I are fully committed to each other."

"Trust me, we're committed." He pulled me to him and bent his head. "You are a difficult mate, disappearing constantly from my sight. I couldn't focus on my work with the way you left."

"Too bad. I can't teleport, so I'm at the whim of others."

His lips brushed my cheek. "I—" His lashes fluttered down as he drew in a haggard breath.

"You?"

His mouth came down on mine, his kiss taking my breath away.

I held onto the rear loop of his black jeans. Wow, my mate could kiss like there was no tomorrow.

Oh yes, he felt so good this close. Such a sensory overload. If only I could merge my mind with his...

A small sigh escaped me. What was I doing? I didn't need him thinking he had to watch over me every second of every day. I had a life, so separate from his.

A low groan rumbled from him. "This is not the place, or the time."

"My thoughts exactly, and we've a thirty mile walk ahead of us tomorrow so we can reach the new Sol compound. That's why Maslin brought me. He's heard of my skill of mind-merge and believes we'll find answers there. This could be where Katerin Sol's family came from."

"I never considered No-Man's Land as where Katerin Sol's ancestry might come from. There are so few who live here, and this desert isn't a part of Dralion or Peacio. Is Sol certain he's heard of mind-merge from within this clan?"

"He's heard the odd bits and pieces, although his trips here have been more about meeting his family and rebuilding lost bonds. Maslin's grandparents remained here forty years ago when the dome was created, but his father took the opportunity to relocate to Dralion when it was offered. We must have had tight ties with No-Man's Land back then."

"You hear that, Davio?" Silas called to him.

Loveria swung to face us. "Yes, and so should Faith. She needs to know about this."

"No, she can't. My father said he loses sight of me. She won't know where you are with her forethought, any more than my father knows where I am. Being in this gray area is the same as being in the dark. Visually they can't see us, just as we don't have the skills to reach them, either by 'porting or telepathic communication. We're on our own out here."

He swiped a hand through his golden-brown hair. "If she checks on me, which she will before the day is out, she won't see me and she'll worry."

"Did you not warn anyone of where you were headed?"

"Zac and Viv know." A firm statement as he eyed me. "They were the only ones I contacted before we followed Moyer's 'porting airstream to this location."

Silas ran his boot back and forth, scuffing up the sand underfoot. "They'll tell Faith when we don't turn up before nightfall and likely guess we're in the gray area."

"That'll be what Zac and Viv will suspect." Loveria came closer, breaching the five foot mark, which had my blood bubbling in confrontation to his. "Hope, why do you keep holding off from meeting your sister?"

I battled to keep my warring emotions under check. Being

this close to Loveria was the pits. In fact, anywhere in his vicinity was. And to think my sister had to merge her mind with his and physically touch him, skin-to-skin to cease the pain which now beat at me. It was a shame this was not a skill and lost within the gray area. Instead it was embedded in my DNA.

Setting my hands on my hips, I huffed. "I've already told Silas why. Kate still adapts to Dralion. She's gone through too much since her arrival and Alexo is waiting to 'see' the right moment to tell her of me. He has not asked for long, so I will wait. And if Faith knew of my existence, would she keep it to herself? Would she speak to Kate?"

Loveria cocked a brow. "Faith has always longed for family, so I can only say she will kill me for what I've withheld. She will want to meet you."

Silas snorted. "Faith will kill me first before she ever lays a hand on you. I am the one mated to her sister and have known the longest. That will not pass her notice."

I glared at them both. "Then it's best she not know right now. This is Alexo's problem and one he should have to deal with. Not me."

Silas gripped my shoulders and maneuvered me back two steps. "You have to remember the five foot mark, and to restrain your temper around Davio."

"I don't have to restrain anything. I like fighting with him. It does my soul good."

His lips twitched. "Yes, so I see. By all means, ignore my request."

"I will, and Loveria and I wouldn't even be fighting if you hadn't have brought him here, or come yourself. You didn't need to."

"I came because I am driven to see to your welfare. We are soul-bound, and it appears I detest having you out of my sight."

"Well, get used to it. I am from Dralion."

Loveria coughed. "Right, since you two are back to

fighting, I'll head inside and set up somewhere for us to sleep, as far away from the warriors as possible. We'll need our rest for tomorrow. That's if we can get any." He walked to the door and edged inside, fisting his hand over the hilt of his sword.

I doubted anyone would sleep well this night.

"We'll join him." Silas snagged my hand.

"Hey." I bumped into his back as he stopped in the doorway. Around the perimeter of the room, four lamps glowed softly, just enough to cast a little light into each darkened corner.

Guy, in his brown rawhide pants and midnight-black shirt, heaved four mattresses toward one wall, and tossed a green woolen blanket over each. Maslin and Goldie stood, quietly conversing. Goldie raised a hand and beckoned me.

"I need to talk to Goldie."

"As long as you understand you're sleeping with me."

"We'll see."

I joined Goldie and Maslin as Silas and Loveria shoved three mattresses against the wall where they'd have the greatest distance from the others.

"I can't believe what's happened," I said to Goldie.

She rolled her eyes. "What's unbelievable is that I'm going to sleep under the same roof as a Loveria."

"I'd say it's a day in history which will forever go unspoken of," Guy said as he trudged across.

"Hell yes, to that," Maslin concurred.

"It's an awful situation, but we don't have any choice. We're here, so we're going to have to deal with it." Goldie eyed Maslin. "You know your way around, so you're in charge of organizing all we need for this hike tomorrow."

"No problem. The Sols always ensure this place is well provisioned." He and Guy left to search the crates.

"Are you all right?" Goldie leaned in, her tone low as she continued, "Maslin updated me. Interesting to hear what he has to say about the Sols and mind-merge. We need the truth. I'm glad I'm here."

"Me too. I hope I find the answers I'm seeking at the compound." I slanted a look toward Silas. "I'm going to have to sleep over there. Silas is strong-willed and his decision about our sleeping arrangements made."

"And you're going to just toe the line?"

"For tonight. I hardly need an all-out war to start because I slept thirty feet away from where he would have preferred."

"He's out of his mind if he thinks he can snatch you away whenever he pleases. Stand your ground and ensure he knows what you will and won't accept."

"Oh, I will. I'll go help Guy and Maslin." I squeezed Goldie's arm and headed to them. I crouched next to the supplies they'd laid out and took one of the backpacks and loaded it with a compass, flasks of water, snacks and loose fitting, hooded white shirts. "Is there food here for us to eat later tonight?"

"The crate to your right has plenty of dried food. Grab what you need." Guy jerked his fisted hand over his thigh. "Being this close to those two is difficult. They hold my father behind steel, and I just want to kill them."

"You can't. My sister and I need them, and they won't have your father for long." My words rang with promise, even as quiet as they were. "None of our captured warriors should be imprisoned. We don't take Peacians and lock them away."

"Why would we want to?" Guy muttered. "Dralion is safe from their sort and we'll keep it that way."

I reached across and set my hand over his. "This isn't where you want to be, but neither protector can be harmed. You're my friend. I know how much you miss your father. I'll find Gerritt." I rose and slung three of the packs over my shoulders." Guy adored his father and missed him terribly. This was the worst situation for him to be in.

Dropping the packs at Silas's feet, I stared at him. "I'm going to sleep."

I lay down with the longest sigh and faced the partially opened door. It was close to dark outside, and I had the whole night ahead of me, smack in the middle of a bunch of sparring protectors and warriors.

How had I gotten myself into this predicament?

Or better yet, how did I get myself out of it?

I closed my eyes, breathing slowly in, and then out. Nope, that didn't help. I was as tense as could be.

Someone pulled on my ankle, and one boot popped free. I peeked, and Silas set it on the floor. He removed my other boot and sat beside me, his back to the cold stone wall. "Can we talk?"

I eyed Loveria, who hauled his mattress farther away and then strode to the door. He leaned against it and shuddered.

"He looks..."

"Davio's bond with Faith is tight. He doesn't care to be parted from her, but that is not what I wanted to speak to you of."

I glanced at the others. No one was within hearing distance and the room was fairly dark except for the gentle glow of the lit lamps. This was as private as it got, if we kept our voices low. "Go ahead."

"We left on bad terms. I don't believe I convinced you of my true wishes, and we have only fought since."

"I understood your wishes just fine."

"Not how I wanted for you to. I couldn't stay away once you cut our telepathic link. My worry increased ten-fold."

"It needn't have. I'm always among my own."

"That's what worries me. Maslin Sol has intentions toward you. The way he looks—"

I clapped a hand over his mouth. "He knows you're my mate and my life is tied to yours. You do not have the right to tell me who I may or may not have as friends."

He let out a huff of breath, which burst into my palm. He

plucked my fingers free and said, "You are impossible."

"You are worse."

"I missed you today."

"Because you like arguing with me so much?"

"That's right. No one can quarrel with me like a Wincrest. It's all rather refreshing, knowing you and Faith."

I almost laughed. "Are you trying to be funny?"

"I apologize if I said things I shouldn't have."

I tapped my ears. "Now, I know I didn't just hear an apology."

"You heard fine." He brought my hand to his chest as he slid in closer. "Carlisio has accepted my decision."

"I'm not anyone's decision. We are soul-bound, and that is a relationship. I mean a non-relationship, in our case. The fact I have mind-merge is just an added problem." I wanted to tug my hand back, yet that would only cause a scene. Goldie had now extinguished her corner lamp and settled for sleep. Guy and Maslin stood like sentries.

"Hope." My name was a bare whisper on his lips. "This is all because of that damn image you saw in my mind."

"We're mated and yet you wish for another. It hurts."

"I do not desire another woman, only the concept of who she would be."

"You were against us being together at the start and released me, requesting I do the same. After I merged my mind with yours, it threw what was between us up in the air."

"No, I kidnapped you because I desired to see more of you."

"Nah-ah, you saw red and that's all."

"I aligned our hearts because I wanted our relationship to gain in strength."

"Only after I saw that image in your mind."

"You formed a telepathic link of trust with me. We connected. You needed me, and I will always come."

"Ha, I did not ask you to come. You did that on your own."

He raised my fingers to his lips, kissing them one by one. "Exactly. I cannot stay away from you. Set that image aside, for me."

"I'll set it aside when I know it's me you want." What? Oh drat. I hadn't just said that out loud? Nooo, I couldn't have. My cheeks heated and I hauled my hand free. "I-I need a minute."

I was stronger than this. I didn't need a man to want me because I asked it of him.

Reaching over me, he flicked off the lamp and plunged our little area into dark. "Every hour we are together, strengthens our bond." With his lips near my ear, he murmured softly, "Thank you for coming and sleeping over here."

"Move to your own mattress."

"I need a minute." He nuzzled my neck.

I sighed. He did not need a minute. The lout was impossible. Which meant I wouldn't be able to move him if he didn't want to go.

What an insufferable bond.

Chapter 6

I walked outside into the eerie stillness of the desert. Dawn had yet to break as I slogged through the sand around the side of the church with a flask of water and bar of soap in hand. "Catch up, Silas. One would think you're nervous."

"I am, considering what's about to happen. I can shave without your help."

No, he couldn't. Loveria had returned from the washroom with nicks all over his face and without his fast-healing they would remain there for the day to come. "Loveria said there's no mirror. Since that's the case, I'm shaving you. I won't see you bleed unnecessarily."

He came alongside me. "There's the door, right where Davio said it would be." He turned the knob and shoved it open. As he stepped through the doorway, he swung his lamp about. "There's barely enough space in here for one, let alone two of us. How about—"

"Let me in." I pushed past him. Oh, the room was tiny, maybe seven foot square.

Setting his lamp on the stone counter, he peered into a bowl carved into it. "There's no plumbing."

"This is the desert. We should be grateful there's a washroom at all." The basin was plugged with a chain stoppered to a smooth round stone, and underneath the countertop, a grate had been cut into the floor. "Oh, that's very clever."

Silas removed a small towel from over his shoulder and dropped it beside his lamp. "I'm not sure about this."

"I'll do a good job." I angled his head to the left as I inspected the sharp red-gold stubble. "We'll need lots of soapy water." I uncapped the water flask and poured a little into the plugged basin then dipped the bar of soap in and lathered it up. Nice. I smoothed the froth over his jaw. "Dagger, please."

"Have you ever done this before?" He slid it free from the sheath on the inside of his wrist and passed it across to me.

"Sit."

He perched on the edge of the bench, bringing him closer to my height. "You didn't answer the question."

Turning his cheek with one finger, I held the blade nice and close to his skin and ran it in a smooth line down. "Nope, but I'm a quick learner, and if I make a mistake, I'll see it."

"My blood's red, by the way." He gripped my waist, keeping me still. "And take your time. No need for speed."

I grinned as I drew the blade along the next portion from his ear to his chin. "Don't be a spoilsport."

"Is that lamp providing enough light?" His gaze darted toward it.

"I wouldn't move, if I were you. I like this mouth of yours and I don't want to cut it up, no matter how smart it is." I ran the blade right under his nose.

"You like my mouth?"

"Don't speak."

"Can't help it."

I set the knife to the other side of his face. "There is nothing you can say that I won't guess at. Zip the lips."

His fingers curled into my sides. "Right now, I'm wishing I wasn't so fastidious with keeping my blade so sharp. I think I felt a nick."

"I told you to be quiet." I tapped his jaw shut and slid the blade along his neck. I inspected my work, dabbing along his skin with the towel as I cleared the last of the suds away. "Okay, I think I've got it all."

Taking the blade, he sheathed it. "I think I wet my pants."

I chuckled. "You did not."

"I like seeing you laugh." He pulled me back to him. "So, how's your head? This is the start of the second day without your mind-merge. Faith usually gets a headache around about now."

"There's no headache, unless I count you." I slid my arms around his neck and rubbed my nose against his.

"The second day is when she begins to suffer. You're not supposed to be parted from me for too long. That's the way of your skill."

"I can handle a headache when it comes. Stop worrying."

He stroked my back. "As the second day ends and the third begins, you'll feel worse. The headache is not one Faith can fast-heal. She has to mind-merge with Davio. One time she got so dizzy on her second day, she passed out. I thought she'd over-imbibed on the drink. Her headache was that bad."

"I said stop worrying."

"I watched her body shut down. There was blood everywhere. Her lungs filled and she coughed it out. She survived the ordeal by mere minutes after she mind-merged with Davio."

"You are here."

"I will never watch that happen to you." He pressed a hand to my forehead. "You already feel a little hot." He snatched up the lamp and supplies and spun me toward the door.

"Ah yeah, we're in the desert, Mr. Observant."

"Which means we should hurry since we've a long way to travel. Davio also needs to return to Faith before the day is out."

"The sun isn't up yet." Although along the horizon a hint of light gave evidence sunrise was close. "Hey, why did Loveria risk coming with you when he should have stayed with my sister?"

With one hand on my elbow, he guided me back the way we'd come. "Davio would never place Faith's life in danger. Carlisio would have had forewarning, and Davio would not have come if that were the case."

Carlisio Loveria held the same skill as my father, although a weaker strain, as only those children born of the mated bond could hold the full strength. His parents had not been soulbound.

"Alexo's forewarning never indicated any harm coming to me, only that I'd be missing."

"Which means we shouldn't chance that future." Silas extinguished the lamp as the sun peeked over the sand-hills. He increased his stride, tugging me along. "We were raised together, Davio and I. We are as close as brothers. He came because of me. I see the others. Everyone appears ready."

Loveria stood further away, holding out two packs. "No nicks, cousin. Lucky."

"More than you know." Silas shrugged one of the packs on and slipped the other over my shoulders.

"You do not sound grateful, and I couldn't harm you even if I wanted. Sheesh, you have a thick head." I yanked the soft white hood of my cotton shirt over my head. Long fluttery sleeves and a loose style allowed whatever breeze blew to cool my skin. Everyone had dressed in them, because the hoods gave plenty of protection.

Goldie, Guy and Maslin had their packs on and Goldie raised a hand and motioned me toward her.

I headed her way. "Hey, it looks like everyone's ready."

"Yes. Maslin's going to lead the team. We're heading due west. You can follow with"—she rolled her eyes and coughed—"ah, them."

Well, at least Goldie was a touch more accepting today. "Thank you for keeping your blade at bay." I glanced at Guy and

Maslin. "All of you. I appreciate it."

Goldie squeezed my arm. "Yeah, we only do it because we happen to love you a touch more than we hate them."

"Thank you. I think."

"Right, let's go, Maslin." Goldie tapped his back and they headed out, Guy following one-step behind her.

Loveria grumbled as he strode past me. "I can't believe I have to follow in the footsteps of warriors. What is this world coming to?"

"Just keep some space." I barely held back a smirk.

"You don't even have to ask."

"Hope." Silas encircled my waist with his arms from behind then brushed his cheek against mine. "Stay close to me."

I leaned into him. "I know I haven't told you—and I probably shouldn't—but I guess I'm glad you're here."

He nipped at my ear. "We are finally getting somewhere. Say that again."

Turning, I kissed his chin. "I was upset when you arrived, but I'm getting over it."

"More, and I meant the kisses."

"To give you an inch would not be—"

He kissed me, deeply, and I kissed him back, overwhelmed by the new emotions stirring within me. I couldn't get enough of his kisses.

As he broke away, his head came up. "I'm glad I came, if for no other reason than this moment and that declaration. Now, let's move out before we lose the others." He gave me a gentle push forward.

I followed in Loveria's footprints. Sand crept inside my boots, rubbing and chafing my feet from within. Oh boy, this was going to be one long day.

I wasn't wrong.

Seven hours later, I'd officially seen enough sand to last me a lifetime. And the heat, it blazed hotter and heavier than the outback's sun ever had.

The sand sweltered, a vapor rising like steam from the endless orange grains.

I blinked, attempting to keep Loveria in focus. If I could just keep my eyes on him and that layer of white cloth covering his back, I could keep moving.

That worked, for now.

My head throbbed as midday arrived.

Hell. It was awful.

Would this trek ever end?

I sipped water from my flask, which had never left my hand.

"We can stop for a five minute break if you need to." Silas's voice floated to me from somewhere behind.

"I'm fine." My head swam. Come on. Push on. Left foot. Right foot. Keep moving.

I lifted my arms as I swayed, grasping at air.

"I've got you." Silas scooped me up.

"Dizzy." I clutched his face, but several images of it still circled each other. "Ah, you shouldn't be able to do that."

"Do what?" Half a dozen rotating frowns came with his words.

My eyelids were too heavy and slid shut.

I didn't hear his answer. It came from too far away.

Blissfully in the dark.

Yet heat surrounded me. So much.

"Hope, talk to me."

A stinging slap on my butt had me dragging my eyelids open. What? Footprints dotted the sand. I squeezed my eyes shut and opened them again. I dangled down a man's back and when I pressed my fingertips together, they were all tingly and numb.

"I can't stand your silence." As he walked, his steps jolted my belly into his shoulder.

"Ouch. I'm not a sack of potatoes, and your shoulder feels

like a rock.”

“This was the best...” His words trailed away as the foggy haze returned and clouded my vision. My head shattered with pain, and then nothing.

* * * *

“You can see the encampment from the top ridge of the sand-hill we’re on. At that point, the gray area clears.”

Loveria’s voice swirled around inside my dizzy head. It was his, because he was too close and firing my blood.

“Silas, the warriors teleported to the compound after I said I’d come and get you. Wincrest, though, wants to see her niece in the next ten minutes, or else she’ll slice and dice you.” He sounded wheezy, like he’d run.

“Thanks for keeping quiet about Hope, Davio. She flaked out, and apart from her heart beating too fast, she’s breathing fine.” Silas’s deep voice curled around my senses, even as my head thumped like a drum. I needed to mind-merge.

Open your mouth. Tell him.

“Sure thing, but I’ve got to head off the moment we hit the ridge and check on Faith. My mate better not be suffering as this one is.”

What was Loveria saying? We were almost there?

“You go be with Faith.” A hand smoothed down my calf. Was Silas still carrying me over his shoulder?

I winced as my stomach bumped into bone. Ow. Yes, definitely his shoulder. I scraped one eye open.

“Yes, I can feel my skills returning.” Loveria let out an elated sigh. “I’ll see you later.”

“Take care.”

My mind fully awakened and targeted on Silas’s, connecting with the precision needed for the merge. Oh yes, I adored my mate’s mind right now. So deliciously all mine. “Yes. Yes. Yes.”

He slid me over his shoulder and propped me on my feet.

"About time you woke up."

"Sorry, I couldn't help the nap."

"Missed you. Really missed you." He kissed me, so fiercely I almost fainted again. He pulled back, a bare inch, his gaze darting all over me. "How do you feel? Your heart's finally beating right. I've been so worried. You won't ever do that to me again. Do you hear me?"

I flicked out my hands as they tingled, as blood raced through and returned to them. Even the red patches of sunburn on the backs of my hands healed with my restored skill. I sighed and wrapped my arms around his neck. "Righto, but you deserve some more lip action, and not the telling-off sort."

No sooner were the words out than he took my breath away with a soul-claiming kiss. So hot. His need swirled through me as I dug my mind deeper into my sweet spot.

Oh, I was not leaving his mind, or his mouth.

He stroked along my shoulders, down my sides and over my hips.

My heart raced.

"Hope." He murmured my name. "I can't ensure your safety unless I'm with you."

I snuggled closer, wanting those soft lips back on mine. "I want to neck some more."

He exhaled, the sound so sweet as his breath stuttered a little. "Say that again."

"I want to—"

"Hope Wincrest."

Damn. Goldie.

She stood on the highest ridge of the sand-hill, her blond hair whipping about her shoulders. "Your ten minutes is up, Carver. Get over here now."

I snagged Silas's hand and trudged toward her. "We're here?" Oh, of course we were. Duh. Where was my head? Kissing Silas had certainly scattered my thoughts.

Silas's fingers firmed around mine. "Davio said the Sols are just over the hill."

I slogged to the top of the rise. Below, on a stretch of long, flat sand, hundreds of brightly colored tents with striped awnings rippled in the wind. A four-post-high corral with horses and a three-post-high holding pen with cattle was closest. The animals' bawling carried on the breeze. "I can't believe it."

"Look at the children," Silas said.

At least a dozen small children scurried in and around the tents playing tag, their flowing white tunics covering them from their necks to their knees. A boy with black hair chased a girl with blond ponytails. She skipped around a market stall, an open-air tent which held baskets of fresh fruit. Oh my. The sight of apples and oranges made my mouth water.

"There." Silas pointed. "A line of people are waiting."

It was as he'd said, and then two dark-haired men wavered into sight not far from the line of people. They appeared out of nowhere, carrying a wooden pail in each hand. A small amount of water sloshed over the rims as they passed them to those in the crowd. On their heels, two more arrived and others within the crowd surged forward to take the water.

I smiled as the teleporters promptly disappeared. "They're bringing water for the others." My fingers curled so tightly into Silas's palm, I was sure to leave a mark. "Tell me this isn't a mirage?"

"It's not. Food and shelter awaits."

"Some of them could be my mother's family and related to me." I was eager to get there. "Where are Maslin and Guy? I don't see them."

Goldie answered, saying, "Maslin went straight to his grandparents' tent. Guy teleported home, but he has the image and can return with ease. So can I."

"Are you leaving?"

"Of course not. I'll stay for as long as you need me." She

patted my arm, her gaze narrowed on Silas. "Although you can leave. I'm sure you've had your allotted five minutes. I know I've seen enough of you today."

He sent her a sharp look. "Your niece and I are mated. I have accepted the bond, if you had not heard."

"Huh, there is accepting the bond, and then there is desiring the bond. Perhaps you should leave since you don't yet know the difference." She eyed me. "If he doesn't treat you right, I'll hurt him."

She would. And I loved her for it.

Silas stroked the hilt of his ever-present sword. "I will stay."

"Figures." Goldie slammed her hands on her hips.

"Um, can we have a minute, Goldie? I'll meet you at the Sol camp." Best to separate the two of them as quick as I could.

"I'll scout around."

"Thanks." She flashed away and I faced Silas. "My headache has gone and I feel strong again. You don't have to stay. You must have work you've set aside." Of that, I was certain.

"There are several projects I'm overseeing." He tightened his hold on my hand. "I can't leave you right now. Don't ask me again."

I rubbed my cheek against his shoulder. "I should be down there."

"I'll 'port us to the area near the stalls. That's where the most people are."

I burrowed deeper into his mind as everything darkened. We reappeared a foot from a basket of gorgeous red-skinned apples. This was real. I was here. "Where do we start?"

"There's a crowd coming. Maslin Sol brings them. Damn, it's impossible to tell who the elders are when we don't physically age."

Yes, all looked young, and now a dozen people dressed in

light colored tunics encircled us, the girl with the blond ponytails dashing in and around them all.

Sweat dampened my palms.

Silas eased in behind me, covering my back as those surrounding us murmured softly between them.

Maslin broke through the crowd, drawing two people along with him. "Hope, I told my grandparents of your skill." He extended one hand toward a man with bright copper hair and brown eyes, and were it not for the slightly darker tone of his skin, I wouldn't have been able to tell grandfather and grandson apart. "This is Menalew Sol."

His grandfather smiled. "Welcome to the compound. I look forward to getting to know you."

"It's nice to meet you too." I dipped my head respectfully.

Maslin set his arm around the shoulders of the woman who stood at his other side. "My grandmother, Merie."

The petite woman had a dash of freckles across her smooth skinned nose and long auburn hair coiled into a braid that dangled to her hips. "Maslin has spoken of you. Welcome."

"Thank you. I'm truly glad to be here."

More people arrived, including Goldie, who reappeared at my side.

Menalew cleared his throat. "Maslin told us of your plight and your skill of mind-merge. We have one of the elders searching for Elizara Sol. She is the youngest sister of Katerin, who left our clan thirty-six years ago. I knew your grandmother. We played together as children."

I clutched at my chest, my heartbeat fluttering all over the place.

"*Relax,*" Silas snapped along our telepathic link. "*Our hearts beat in tandem. It's incredibly uncomfortable when yours doesn't keep good time.*"

"*You're the one who aligned our hearts. Deal with it.*" I reached for Goldie and pulled her closer. "This is Goldie, my aunt, and behind me is Silas."

Menalew welcomed Goldie.

Silas groaned. *"What kind of introduction is that? Behind me is Silas?"*

"What would you have preferred?" I itched to move. *"This is real, isn't it?"*

"Yes. You're nervous. I'm not surprised."

"Pinch me now so I know I'm not dreaming."

"Gladly."

I jumped as his fingers nipped my waist.

Goldie nudged my arm, her gaze moving beyond the crowd. "Look, I think that's Elizara Sol."

I was up on my toes, searching as all hushed.

A woman clutching the folds of her white robes dashed forward. She had golden hair, silky and long, pinned with a jeweled clip, which sparkled in the last rays of the day. Chestnut-brown eyes, the edges rimmed with a lighter shade of milk chocolate met mine.

My chest tightened and Silas mumbled something, his words lost to me as I blinked back tears.

"Don't cry." Elizara's voice wobbled as she stepped up to me. "I'm overjoyed. They said you are Hope, my sister's grandchild." She clasped my face between her shaky hands. "Katerin was outlawed from here, but I can come to her. Where is she?" She peered over my head.

Trembling, I gripped her hands. "I'm sorry. I've never met Katerin, and I don't know where she is. My father raised me in Dralion. I live on the same station in the outback as Maslin." She must not know where Katerin was either.

"Oh, I had hoped. The elder who came for me said you had mind-merge." She closed her eyes and the lightest of touches brushed my mind then drew away. "I feel a link from you to the one behind you." She scrutinized Silas. "You are connected strongly to him. Good. You cannot be without him."

"How did you do that?" She'd tracked my merge to Silas, somehow, although she hadn't intruded.

Her lips tipped upward at the corners, a small smile forming. "You have much to learn and I will gladly teach you. Within this desert clan, some have mind-merge, although that knowledge is kept close to home. We cannot have outsiders know of the greatest weakness of these few, because reliance is the way of the skill."

"I want to know everything."

"Then you will need to stay, but to begin, Katerin was exiled. Her mate, Nathwer, left with her thirty-six years ago. What of you?"

"My mother was abandoned in an orphanage on Earth when she was three days old. The nuns named her after her mother. Her name is Kate."

"Your mother is well?"

"Yes, and she recently returned to live in Dralion with my father. I have a twin too, but my mother raised Faith in New Zealand."

A murmur came from those assembled, their collective voices whispering, "Her mother mustn't have mind-merge."

"No." I answered them. "Kate also never knew Katerin Sol. Her mother never returned for her."

Heavy gasps. Lots of them. Our children were adored above all else, being raised within villages by their immediate and extended family. None was ever abandoned as I had just described.

"If we'd known of your mother's whereabouts, one of us would have retrieved her from Earth and brought her here. I'm so sorry." Large tears slipped from Elizara's eyes.

"No, it's okay. You didn't know." Her pain quickly became mine as our blood-bond cemented. She was family, without a doubt.

"How many in your compound hold this ability of mind-merge?" Silas wound his arm around my waist.

"Four, including me. Over the years, we've lost many from it. Our soul-bound one holds our life in their hands. Although those who have that skill and of telepathy are far more fortunate."

"Why?" Anything that could shine good will on my skill was an answer I needed.

"If we hold telepathy, and our mate does too, then we can use that connection to weave the mind-merge along. Once this weaving is learned, it releases the strict three-day rule. Have you heard of that?"

"Of the three-day rule, yes. But not the weaving along the telepathic connection." My chest swelled and my heartbeat nearly bounded from it. "So there is a way around the death sentence?" This was the best news.

"That's correct. Of the four of us here with mind-merge, two have telepathy, as do our mates. Our lives are much easier."

Silas cleared his throat. "Hope and I have a telepathic connection."

Elizara clapped, beaming at us. "Wonderful. I will teach you how to weave the merge along the link, Hope. It takes a little practice to perfect for there is an intricacy to the method. The twin you spoke of, is she telepathic?"

I slid my hand into Silas's. I had to take care not to expose who Silas and Loveria truly were. The Sols knew Maslin was a warrior, and warriors and protectors did not mix. Silas was here, but I had not said he was from Peacio. Davio, though, was a different matter. He was a prince and his name known, the chance of a connection being made far greater if I spoke of him.

Silas threaded his fingers through mine. *"We cannot speak Davio's name. It is one passed down through the Loveria line. We must keep quiet. As yet we don't know these people."*

"That's what I just thought."

To Elizara, Silas said, "Faith and her mate are both

telepathic, but neither have successfully forged a link with the other. I know it's unusual, but it's what's happened."

"Oh." She pressed her hands to her mouth. "They must keep trying."

"After hearing this news, I'm sure they will." He squeezed my hand. "*A Wincrest and a Loveria mating is unheard of. Their blood wars too greatly, and even though they trust each other because of their mated bond, fundamentally their blood continues to fight. Davio believes this is what's halting the formation of his telepathic link with Faith.*"

"*We fight.*"

"*Not like they do. I am a Carver. My mother and Davio's are sisters. There is no direct Loveria blood flowing through my veins. It is only Loveria and Wincrest blood which battles in close contact.*"

Goldie rubbed my arm, her solid presence firm at my side. "Elizara," she said, "why was Katerin exiled? That's a harsh penalty."

"Katerin used her skill of mind-merge in an offense which had to be punished."

"An offense?" I asked. "How exactly?"

"I can speak of it, but only between you and your mate." Elizara looked at all those assembled, and without another word they slowly dispersed, the girl skipping away after the others.

"May I stay?" Goldie asked.

"I apologize, but the answer Hope seeks truly must be kept between the mated ones."

"This sounds worrisome."

"A little, but it is private and that is understood, even by those in this compound."

"Are you sure?" Goldie didn't appear convinced.

"I'll be fine." I gave her a hug. "I'm sure I can deal with whatever Elizara tells me. Nothing could be worse than the three-day deal."

She squeezed me in return, whispering in my ear, "The moment you call me telepathically, I'll 'port back. In the meantime, I'll go check in with Alexo and update him. That's if he's not watching you now. Are you sure you're happy for me to go?"

"Yes. I'll see you later."

"Take care." She shimmered and disappeared.

I scratched my head, my mind buzzing with all the possibilities of Katerin Sol's banishment.

Silas breathed heavily. "I fear your news too, Elizara."

"Even though the one with the skill merges only with their mated one, if we wish we can merge with another." She edged closer, lowering her tone. "It is so uncommon we rarely speak of it, but Katerin did this, taking over another man's mind, and in doing so, she directed his actions while holding that control. We considered what she did an offense of the greatest order, its punishment equally as harsh."

"Are you saying I can control Silas's mind?" Oh no, he wouldn't stand for that, nor would I consider merging my mind with any man other than him. "That isn't something I can even contemplate."

"Merging our mind with any other than our soul-bound one is detestable. But the taking of our mate's mind and holding it in our control happens without their consent."

"How? Silas blocks. All the time. How on earth would I take over his mind?"

"Ah, there is a moment of weakness for our mate, and that comes during the time when we join emotionally and physically. Because of the bond though, we cannot harm our mate. We hand back the control soon after it is given."

"You, ah, mean..." My tongue stuck to the roof of my mouth.

"Yes, when we make love our emotions overrule us," Elizara continued. "Our mate's mind becomes ours to control."

Silas coughed, quite haggardly. "You're saying Hope will see what I don't wish her to?"

"Yes, it's impossible for you to block at this point, which means there is a level of trust you have to prepare yourself for. Hope would have access to all you know, but she would return the control because to keep it against your will makes your mind susceptible to damage. With the bond we cannot harm our mated one."

"Hell," Silas whispered, his hand going icy in mine.

"I would return it." Not that I intended for us being together to go that far. Most of our people waited until marriage for such things and our relationship was so uncertain. Although, access to all he knew? Oh, like where Dralion's captured warriors were contained? Most definitely, Peacio's battle strategy against my country. Silas wouldn't want me to know any of that, and I would. Could I go that far at taking information with the bond at play?

He focused on Elizara. "Is there anything else?"

"Katerin suffered from a terrible mental illness, just months after she and Nathwer discovered they were mated. Nathwer kept a close eye on her, but her recovery was slow due to her first pregnancy. And during a short trip away, he returned to find her hallucinating. She'd slept with another thinking him Nathwer. Since the man was not her mated one, she did not have the protective desires which would have compelled her to release the control of his mind. This man ended up without sense, and he died minutes after Nathwer forced Katerin to release his mind." She paused, her breath shuddering out. "This is difficult to speak of, but the elders saw no other action than complete banishment. Katerin was exiled and Nathwer was charged with policing her. She was pregnant with his child, and it was his choice to go with her. No matter what she'd done, he still loved her deeply, and he didn't believe the child should have to suffer for her actions."

A soft sigh, one loaded with sadness. "I am sorry that it

must be I who tells you this, but there are also good things which come from the skill of mind-merge."

Silas groaned, his hands twitching. "At the moment I can't see them."

"You will in time. There is no bond stronger than that of the soul-bound one. Add mind-merge to that, and the pledge between the two deepens."

His hand dropped away from mine. "Or becomes more aggravating."

"This is frustrating for you?"

"Yes, but less so now I know Hope can merge through our link."

"Then come. I will teach Hope what she needs to know now so I can ease some of your worry." She turned, her robes fluttering around her ankles. "It's getting late and the sun sets quickly in the desert. You must stay the night so we may talk more. I also wish to know my niece."

We walked side by side as the sun sank over the horizon, yellow melding into dusky pink then inky-blue. Between the colorfully striped tents, we weaved our way to the outskirts of the compound.

"Silas, if you need some time out, I understand."

"I must stay. You need to learn how to mind-merge through our telepathic connection, and I need to know you can do it."

"Yes, you do," Elizara raised the bright yellow canvas flap of the tent outside of which she'd stopped. "This is my home, and it will be yours too while you are here. There are three sections, or separate rooms if you will. You two can have this one. Mine is at the rear. There is another entrance around the far side."

I ducked and stepped inside. The floor was made entirely of durable matting, a multitude of earth-toned colors streaming together. Elizara lit a lamp and hung it from a metal hook in the center of the tent. In the corner, a pile of pelts ranging from beige to dark brown were stacked beside a wooden crate three feet wide and two feet high. Plump pillows were scattered around the sides of the room, looking sumptuous to sit on.

"Take a pillow. We live rather nomadically, and our belongings can be rolled up and packed within an hour or two."

I followed her lead, taking a bright red pillow and sitting opposite her. Silas snagged a blue one and joined our circle.

"Good. Face each other, but keep a short distance between you," she said. "Let's begin with you, Hope. Open your telepathic link to Silas and ensure you're connected."

Crossing my legs in front of me, I set my hands in my lap and looked deep into Silas's eyes. *"I'm sorry for the bad news about me being able to take control of your mind."* Well, bad for him, but not for me. Silas had the ear of Carlisio Loveria and Davio was his cousin. What I could learn... Oh, I desired that, but drat, there was still the bond. I couldn't harm him.

"Somehow I'll deal with it. I can't have a Wincrest knowing the sensitive knowledge I hold and using it against Peacio."

"I take it you're linked?" Elizara asked me. "Once the link is created, look at the individual threads which make it up. Tell me what you see."

"There's a red thread intertwined with a violet one, and both tighten around a filament of gold."

"Ah, good. The gold is the thread you're after. It's the part of the telepathic link which signifies you're speaking with your mate. All other connections will have a silvery central thread. Focus on the golden one and weave your mind-merge through it, beginning right at the point where the connection forms. Don't allow your skill to veer off toward the other threads. No touching the red or violet."

"Okay, the starting point." I pushed my mind toward the tiny beaded opening. "Hold on. There's a crusting over the threads."

"Yes, but you can still isolate the central one. Just take

care."

"The crusting looks like glue." But there, a pinprick of gold. I arrowed my mind toward it, pierced the merge through the fissure and isolated only the rich-toned golden mated thread.

Keeping it on the straight and narrow, I followed the prized filament, grinning as I burst through on Silas's end and burrowed deeply into his mind.

Oh yeah, my sweet little spot.

I was there.

Rolling my head back, I moaned, "I did it."

A tinkle of laughter came from Elizara. "Wonderful. It feels amazing, doesn't it?"

"Yes."

Silas ran a hand over his brow. "I can feel Hope's mind-merge, but when I try to speak to her telepathically, nothing happens."

I straightened, my gaze jolting to his. "I didn't feel you try."

Elizara chuckled, and then gave my arm a squeeze. "He is anxious. Our mated males always are when there is uncertainly involved." She looked to Silas. "You cannot use the threaded link for both the merge and the telepathic connection at the same time. It is one or the other." To me, she said, "I need to see you can withdraw the merge as well. My only instructions are to take as much care in reversing as you did in traveling along it."

Pulling back along the threaded link of gold, I gave it all my focus.

"Elizara," Silas said. "Does she still need only five minutes to reconnect?"

"Yes. The same requirement applies as if she were in your company. Five minutes every third day, but once she's recharged as such, she can pull out."

I continued reversing along the telepathic link and removed myself with a soft plop into my own mind as I got to the end. I flashed her a smile. "Done."

"Perfect." She grinned in return. "I find there are times when I'm separated from my mate, like I am at present, and instead of suffering the painful headache which begins on the second day, I merge through the link and become restored. One with this skill could effectively survive indefinitely this way. I have something else to show you." She clambered to her feet and pried open the lid on the wooden crate. Returning, she passed me a leather-bound album. "This is a treasured family heirloom. On our eighteenth, we sit for an artist. There is a sketch of Katerin on the first page. I like to keep her image close by. Do you want to—"

"Yes." I grabbed it as Silas skimmed across on his butt and looked over my shoulder. I opened the front flap. A thin film of paper protected the first drawing, hiding it from my view.

"She and Nathwer sat for a portrait after their mated bond took." Elizara spread her white robes over her crossed legs and pulled a green pillow into her lap. "Their birthdays were just days apart, and they married quickly."

That was not unusual. Mated pairs generally wed within six months, a year at the most. Being soul-bound, their commitment would've been etched in stone.

Turning the thin film of paper over, I stared at the first image. The woman had pale blond hair, and brown eyes as Elizara did. Katerin's face angled toward Nathwer's, her adoration obvious in her wishful expression. Nathwer had dark brown hair and blue eyes, a slim build with wide shoulders. "Was Nathwer a Sol?"

"We are all Sols in this compound. Any who join us, becomes a Sol."

I smiled, tilting my head toward Silas. "Silas Sol."

His look said *not on your life*. "My father will not tolerate me changing my last name."

I chuckled and leaned in to kiss him. "You can call me Hope Sol."

Elizara let out a soft sigh. "Ahh, it is wonderful to see two young ones in love."

"Oh no, you have it wrong. We are—um..."

She turned the page. "Don't worry. Look, this is a portrait taken of Samania and Sarahiah. They are my nephew's twin daughters. Twins run in the Sol bloodline. Quite strongly."

"They also run in mine," Silas stated. "My sister is my twin."

"How wonderful. Maybe you two will, well, you know."

Elizara was headed toward issues Silas and I had never discussed. It was all too soon.

"All right, do you have any particular questions?" she asked.

I barely needed to consider it. "What do you believe has become of Katerin and Nathwer?"

"I don't know. I only hope Nathwer and her still live, that she recovered from her illness. She was not a telepathic though, so needed to stay close to him."

"Why do you think she wouldn't have returned to collect her daughter from the orphanage?"

Her smile dropped away at my question. "She was very ill, mentally. More so a few months after her marriage than at any earlier time. Although she always loved children, and longed for her first to arrive. To hear she abandoned your mother three days after her birth goes against what I would have ever considered." She tapped the sides of her legs. "Thirty-six years have already passed. What happened to Katerin and Nathwer may never be solved."

I squeezed my eyes shut. Katerin's story wrenched at my heart. Did I have grandparents out there, somewhere? And Katerin and Nathwer's images were right here. One with forethought would be able to track them. It was a start, a good one. "I will do all I can to search for her."

Elizara continued to frown, and I lifted the page showing

her nieces. "Tell me more about them. They weren't in the crowd."

"They celebrated their eighteenth birthday last week, and now they are away for a few days. The girls have taken time to travel the desert, following our border with Peacio's to the northern coast. It is a sacred journey undertaken by our young ones as they enter adulthood."

"Why is it sacred?"

"The land north of here belongs to our people, and we must know where each oasis is. We cannot survive without water, and as wonderful as it is to have teleporters within our family, we do not take them for granted. All our people must have the life-survival skills they'll need for their future. Their father has gone with them, as has my mate. They remain within the area where I can connect telepathically to them. It was a rough trip, and we have only just set up camp here. I'm glad I stayed, otherwise I wouldn't have been here to meet you."

"Me too. I wouldn't have wished to wait."

"One-half of your roots belong to the desert. You are home." She leaned in and hugged me, enveloping me in the scents of sunshine and sand. "These are your people. No matter where you live, you will always have a home here, with me." She slowly stood. "Now, I must go. I need to see to our evening meal with the other ladies. Come to the center of the camp when you are ready. They'll be an open fire pit which we all eat around."

"Okay." With Silas leaning over my shoulder, I continued to gaze through the portraits so carefully drawn. When I was done, I clutched it to my chest. "My family. I have more than I ever thought possible."

"You do, and it's getting late. How about I set up the pelts as a mattress to sleep on, and then we'll be able to rest as soon as we've eaten?"

"Great. I love that idea." I scrambled to my feet and tucked the album away in the crate. Silas made a neat stack, four thick in the center of the room. I tossed two of the pillows we'd sat on to the head of the makeshift bed. "I feel hot and sticky. I'd love a change of clothes."

He scratched his nose. "I'll have to pillage some more from Silvie."

"Please." I pressed my hands to his chest and kissed him.

"If my sister finds out I've raided her wardrobe, she's going to believe I've taken up cross-dressing."

"Then don't let her catch you." I stepped back, and he gave me a devilish grin before he flashed away, one that may have matched mine.

Shoving the tent flap aside, I stared out. All was quiet, most of the tribe likely helping with the meal as Elizara did. This compound would have to run smoothly with so many living here.

"Here you go." To one side of the tent, Silas positioned a small metal tub half-filled with warm water. He passed me a towel tied around a bundle of clothing. "I'll return again soon. Unlike you, I'm happy to clean up at home." He promptly disappeared.

I tugged off my gritty clothes and tossed them aside. In the tub, I stood with just enough room to cup the water and drizzle it over me. Not the best, but it would do. After I dressed in the white miniskirt and soft-pleated cream blouse with silver buttons he'd brought, I tipped my toes into Silvie's flat leather sandals. It was lucky we were the same size.

Waiting for him, I perched on the pelts, running my hands over their furry surface. My thoughts turned to all I'd learnt, and the predominant one that I could now merge with Silas from a distance raced through my mind.

This changed things between us. Being with me because he'd accepted that as his only alternative was no longer the case.

I could survive without him. Indefinitely, as Elizara had said.

A swirl of air lifted the strands of my hair and fluttered over my skin. Looking as delectable as ever, Silas wavered into sight. His hair was damp, and he'd changed into tan pants and a short-sleeved, white-collared shirt.

"While you've been gone, I've thought about this mind-merge through our telepathic link." I stood.

"Me too."

"What do you think of this?" Nervousness made my stomach clench, and I clasped my hands. Because of our bond, I was driven to give him what he truly desired. He still had to come first.

"Hey, just tell me." He took my hands, pulled them apart and held them firmly within his.

"You drew the short straw." My heart thumped so loudly he must hear it. He'd definitely feel it.

"No, I don't wish to speak of that. Not this soon." He tugged me outside where it was dark, the night sky twinkling with a million diamond-like stars. Oil lamps swung high from metal rods pushed deep into the ground. The beaming light provided just enough coverage to guide our way.

Silas led me toward the center of camp, where the sounds of others carried on the breeze.

"You still need to listen." I kept pace with him.

"No, I don't want to talk about it."

"We need to discuss what's happened tonight. You never had a choice, and now you do."

"I said no." One full-on glare.

"Silas, stop."

He swiveled around, hands on his hips. "Katerin Sol merged with another and took control of his mind. The man died. Do you want to merge with someone other than me?"

"No, and I'm not suffering from a mental illness as she did. I can control my reactions. I'll never take over another's mind because I have no desire to merge. That only comes with you."

His lips thinned into a tight line.

"We need to consider our new options, Silas. I can connect through our telepathic link and we need never even speak. You've already released me, and I you. That decision can still stand. Ours is a non-relationship, remember?"

Arms crossed, he stared at me, his eyes deepened to the darkest blue. "You want me to leave?"

To make sure I wouldn't reach for him, I shoved my hands behind my back. "I want to give you the chance to change the course of your life. It doesn't have to be with me. You could make that faceless image of the woman real."

He was stone-cold quiet.

A pin could have dropped in the sand, and I swear I would have heard it.

He pointed over my shoulder, and I turned to find we were the center of attention. At least two-hundred people gathered in the large clearing around a roaring fire thirty feet away, a fat pig turning on a metal spit in the center, watched us.

Whoa. How had I missed that?

"If you still want me to go, I will." His fists clenched and un-clenched at his sides.

I slowly nodded. I had to see this through. "I want you to have this choice." It was the honest truth, and he couldn't miss seeing that.

"Then let's try this. Perhaps I've even been waiting for just such an opportunity." Giving me a curt bow, he clipped his heels together. "Goodbye, Hope. A long life to you."

His form wavered and blinked away.

I stared at where he should have been. Was he really gone?

Ice crawled through my veins, freezing me in place.

He'd really left? Just like that?

My chest ached, the center deepening to such a throbbing ball of pain I wasn't sure I could stand it.

I shuddered as someone's arm came around my shoulders.

Elizara.

"He'll return. That man looks at you in a way even he doesn't understand. You gave him a choice, and not many would. I'm proud of you for that."

"W-we've not had an easy time since we met."

"Not all mated couples do. The bond is a given, but we must work at the relationship." She led me to the closest group, and motioned for me to sit between Maslin and his grandmother, Merie.

"You heard?" Tears welled in my eyes and Maslin's image blurred.

He bumped his shoulder into mine. "Hard not to, but you did the right thing."

I wanted to curl up and cry. "I had to set him free. I think it's what he's always wanted."

"You're better off among your own."

Tears leaked out and I swiped at them. I was. I must never forget.

The fire crackled, and a few of the men dressed in desert robes of white moved to bank the edges of the roaring flames and taper them inward. Further away from the fire, mothers led their children to a wide mat and handed them plates.

"Wait here. I'll get you some food."

I wasn't up for moving, or even talking, so I did.

Maslin returned and set the plate in my lap. I stared at it, although a watery film obscured the food. I would stop crying. Right now.

Tears dripped onto the pork and dribbled down the mound of potato. Letting Silas go was the only way. I just wish it didn't have to hurt so much.

Where was he? Had he returned home?

A mumble of words came from far away, and Maslin took my plate from me. I blinked to bring him into focus. "Did you say something?"

"Yes. You're obviously not going to eat, and you're clearly not up for company. I'll walk you to your tent."

"You will?"

"Up." He stood, pulling me to my feet. "You need to rest. It's been a long day."

"The longest ever."

With a hand at the small of my back, he guided me through the maze of tents to Elizara's. At the entrance, he dipped his head. "I'll see you in the morning. Goldie requested I stay, and I will."

He disappeared into the dark, and I raised the flap and trudged inside.

Bone weary, I fell over the pelts in the dark, right into the middle of them.

I lay where I fell, my chest heavy, as if a rock was wedged between my lungs, preventing me from drawing a decent breath.

Such a wretched burn.

For him.

I wanted Silas here.

That was impossible, now.

Argh, protectors. I hated them.

Chapter 7

"I cannot believe you loaned me such a skimpy string-bikini." I fanned my exposed middle.

"It's just us women. Come and help me with the lamps," Elizara called from near the ladies bathing in the compound's oasis. "Anyway, the bikini suits you."

"Yeah, it's lily-white, like I am." The next evening had settled and at least the deep basin of water surrounded by palm trees kept out prying eyes, a definite bonus.

"I'll come," someone said. Four women helped her string a line around the perimeter of the spring. Young girls sat at the edge, dipping their toes in the water, and in the distance, a trail of lights bobbed as more women made the short trek from camp.

Several teens dropped their towels into a pile as I negotiated around them. One by one, they waded into the water and dove into the deepest center.

Oh, now that's where I wanted to be.

My mouth watered at the thought of a swim.

"Don't worry." Elizara waved me away. "I know that look when the water calls. Go and enjoy yourself."

"Are you sure?"

"Absolutely."

I splashed in then dove. With arms outstretched, I kicked until I ran out of air and had to surface. Bliss, and I was almost in the center.

Silas would love this oasis. No fast-moving current here. I should tell him.

Ah no, I couldn't.

Damn, why had I said we need never even speak?

Right. To give him the chance to move on.

Someone's hands clasped my ankles from below, making me gasp. With a tug, I was towed under.

Oh, that someone moved fast, a blur of yellow swallowed within the dark beneath. Then another as well, no more than a wisp of red, and gone too.

Where was the culprit who'd sunk me? I swam, but found no one.

As I popped to the surface, a circle of older girls, all with sweetly innocent expressions, smiled at me.

"It wasn't me," Herianne said. I'd spoken to her on the walk out. She was eighteen, as I was.

Megein, beside her in a yellow swimsuit, grinned. "It was. I helped her."

Herianne splashed her with a wide arc of water that came out of nowhere. All she'd done was lift her hand and the water had flown and smacked Megein in the face.

I laughed. "You have the water skill."

Right, I'd get Herianne back. Slinking under the water, I grabbed her legs, only a slippery substance made it hard. I tried again, wrapping my arms right around. This time with more traction, I yanked and took her down, and darted away at the last moment.

She gave chase. Those with the water skill were faster, stronger and far sleeker in their movements within their element.

I was dunked more times than I could count as the older women joined us.

It was just what I needed.

Exhausted after so much play, I slogged to the water's edge

and crawled onto the sand and fell flat on my face. The younger ones giggled.

Elizara plopped down beside me. "I think I caught you five times," she teased.

With one cheek in the sand, I eyed her. "It was more like fifty-five. I see you have the water skill too." It hadn't taken me long to work out who did. I'd even seen some disappear below the water for several minutes at a time. Far more than humanly possible, something Maslin had never done.

"How many minutes can you survive down there? Maslin can't do that." If he could, I would have quizzed him so I could document it.

A glimmer in her eye confirmed my thoughts. "My affinity for the water is strong. My parents were mated, and because of that, I carry the full strength of the skill. It runs strongly in the Sol line. Having it is paramount in the desert."

"Where there's no water?"

"No. Because we have so little water. We use our skill to find it, collect it and hold onto it."

"Tell me about it. Maslin's parents aren't mated and he can't hold his breath like that." I elbowed up.

"You likely know water is made up of two parts hydrogen and one part oxygen to every molecule. I can remain submerged for several minutes because I draw the hydrogen away with my water skill, and form a protective bubble of it around the oxygen. It is done with a flick of my hand and a thought and I simply breathe the pocket of air in. Only those with the full strength can do so. There are twenty-three of us altogether, while Maslin and two others are at half strength and cannot breathe below water."

I nodded, taking in all her words. "Thank you for speaking to me of this."

"Of course. Bring your sister as soon as you've met her. Missing out isn't good and she should be here."

In the privacy of her tent this morning, we'd spoken at

length about Faith, of what I knew about her and Kate. It was a sad story, and tears had come to her eyes during the telling.

Elizara leaned in and brushed the sand from my cheek. "This is sticky." She flicked her fingers toward the pond and a wash of water flew at me. Like a missile, it splattered and drenched.

I spluttered, and then smiled.

"Sorry." She laughed. "I can fling water for some distance, more so than the ones who don't hold the full strength."

"If you ever wish to visit me at the station then come. We could use you."

"Absolutely. I have decided to travel to meet my nieces and my mate in a week as they make the return journey, but after that, yes, I'll be there. Let's head to bed." She rose and tugged me up.

We returned with the other women to camp. I would be on my own. No Silas.

Did he think of me this much?

Was he well?

At the tent flap, I hugged Elizara. "I can't imagine not knowing you. I wish I'd known Katerin too."

"So do I." She squeezed me tight. "Use whatever clothing you'd like from the pile I left. I'll see you in the morning. Sleep well."

I changed for bed into a short pink nightie with a teddy bear imprint on the pocket then spread a thin white sheet over top of the pelts and slid in.

An ache behind my eyes made me close them, and I opened my telepathic link with Silas. "*It's just me. I need the merge.*"

No answer, but we were connected.

Great. He must be mad, or hate me, or both. What a mess I'd made of things. With a sigh, I focused on the pinprick of golden thread in my mind. I channeled my mind-merge along it, weaving and letting it go as it disappeared from my mind to travel along the divide to his. After a few minutes, I was falling into his mind, rolling around in the soft spot which was all mine.

At least I'd always have this.

Mmm. I smoothed the pelt.

So good. I adored his mind.

Only my five minutes was up way too soon.

Probably should withdraw.

Ten minutes, and I let out a slow breath.

Fifteen and I choked up. Best to let go.

Taking a great gulp of air, I forced my withdrawal, pulling away until I'd fully released him and only the telepathic connection remained. *"Hey, Silas. Um, thanks."*

No answer.

I twiddled my fingers.

Should I tell him of my day? He hadn't broken the connection.

No.

"Elizara has the water skill." I couldn't help myself. *"I only found out today. There's this oasis. It's a magical spot. You would like it, or at least I think you would."*

I stilled for his response.

Nothing. Nada. Zilch.

My heart sank somewhere even deeper inside my chest.

I should stop and break the link. *"Elizara loaned me some clothes. She likes prints of teddy bears. There's even one on this nightie of hers. It's pink, by the way."* Right. I babbled but couldn't help it. *"She can hold her breath underwater for several minutes, and send water flying some distance with only the flick of her hand and a thought."*

I closed my eyes as a spasm of pain throbbed in my chest. He still didn't answer.

I missed him, so badly. This was sheer torture, not having him speak to me.

"Ooo-kay. Night then. Sleep well."

Best to end it, quick, which I did.

Hell, that was awful.

Rolling to my side, I wiped at my cheeks. The moon's glow illuminated the sides of the tent. Silas had carried me across the desert to this place. He had cared for me and made sure I'd gotten here. I had so much to thank him for.

I would never forget.

The compound went quiet as the hours passed.

By dawn, the heat of the rising sun turned the tent sides radiant yellow. Sleep. I needed the oblivion of it.

I yawned, finally succumbing as my eyelids slid shut.

* * * *

A heavy presence of desert heat covered my back.

Stretching and uncurling, I bumped into warm skin.

What the...

I jerked around and scrambled to my knees. "Silas?" This had to be an illusion. I rocked on my knees, and rubbed my eyes. It was definitely him, lying with his cheek on my pillow. On the floor lay his sword, as always close at hand. I touched the shadows under his eyes, so dark they appeared bruised. "What have you done to yourself?"

"I can't sleep without you." He snuck out a hand, encircled my wrist and yanked.

I lost my breath as I landed on him. "Me either."

"You shouldn't have spoken to me last night. It was the last straw."

"I couldn't help it." He was here. With me. That's all I'd wanted for the past day and two nights. I kissed his chin, his nose, his cheeks, nibbling all the way over his drop-dead gorgeous face. "I missed you. I thought you'd hate me."

He took my shoulders between his hands. "I've longed for our arguments. I am such a lost fool."

"An idiot for sure. I shall get the stamp made."

"I'm falling for you."

"Ooo-kay." My whole body shook.

"They'll be no more talk of separation." He kissed me. "We spend every night together, that's when you're on Earth and not in Dralion."

"What kind of spending the night are you talking about?"

"Nothing more than wanting you close." He rubbed his forehead against mine. "Merge, now. I've the worst craving for it, like an addiction."

I sent my mind soaring into his.

Oh yeah. Blisss.

Wriggling around, I sank deep into his mind, making myself completely at home. "Your head is so big, we can both fit in there."

He chuckled. "I'm sure it is. I brought you something." From the pocket of his tan pants, he removed a necklace and dangled the thin chain in front of me. A tiny white rose was masterfully painted on the silver charm.

"Oh, you didn't?"

"Last night I visited Silvie's favorite Earth shopping mall." He swept my hair over my shoulder and fastened the gift around my neck. "You said a white rose signifies the beginning of time, and that's what I want for us."

I played with the charm, so cool between my fingers. Tears welled in my eyes and Silas tipped up my chin.

"Hey, no crying. It's only a gift."

"You have a good memory."

"It's the big head. It holds a ton of information." His gaze softened. "Will you spend the day with me?"

"Yes."

"Good. Since I intend to have you sleep over from now on, I'm not raiding my sister's closet again. We're going shopping." His smile was smoldering.

"I could pack a bag."

"I'm buying you clothes. There'll be no overnight bag."

"Hope." The door of the tent flapped open and a rush of sunlight burst in as Elizara entered. She glanced from Silas to me, a slow grin forming. "Ah, you didn't turn up at breakfast, and I was worried. Obviously no need."

"Silas is here." I gripped the pendant, the most precious gift I'd ever received. "We're going shopping." I couldn't keep the giddiness from my words.

"Then I won't keep you." She kissed my cheek and set a hand on Silas's arm. "Look after my niece. That's an order."

"Yes. You have my word I will." He walked her to the door and held the flap for her as she left.

"Let's go." He returned and held me in his arms and flashed us away.

We arrived in his room. "Wow. Silas, I'm actually happy to be in Peacio. Weird. That's something I'd never thought I'd say."

"You can't wear that pink nightie to the shops, as cute as that teddy bear on the pocket is." He sighed. "I'll go sneak one last change of clothes from Silvie. I won't be long." He zapped away.

I skipped to his bathroom and searched his drawers for a toothbrush. After washing up, I gazed into his mirror. My face glowed. Being back with Silas was so right.

With the pendant in hand, I stroked it. A white rose. I loved it. The beginning of time.

"Silas, I'm preparing a special dinner tonight."

I jumped as a woman's voice came from the direction of his bedroom.

"Silas, you there?" She appeared in the opened bathroom doorway, her red-gold locks bouncing around her shoulders. Her gaze popped wide and she checked over her shoulder then stared back at me. "Faith, ah, this is my brother's room. What the heck are you doing in here?"

Crap.

"Ah, Silvie?" It must be her, Silas's sister. They had the same blue eyes and red-gold hair, only she was dressed in a short yellow denim skirt and red t-shirt.

"Yeah, of course. What's wrong with you?"

"I-I." You have a voice. Find it. Use it. You are now Faith. "Ah, I'm here because I'm hiding from Loveria."

Oops. No. Faith wouldn't hide from her mate.

Her eyebrow arched to a staggering height. "Whatever for? And why'd you just call him Loveria? Have you two had an argument or something?"

"Yes." I nodded frantically, going with that. "He's being a prick. An idiot. I can't stand him."

Okay, pull it back a bit.

"Uh-huh. So that's why you're in here? Why didn't you come to my room?" She stepped into the bathroom.

Sweat trickled down my spine. "I have no idea. That would have been the better choice. Gosh, it's hot in here." I fanned my face.

"Not really." She pressed her hand to my forehead, and then knocked her knuckles on it. "Yeah, it's empty in there. Your brain cells have gone on holiday."

"It's from the mind-merge. My mate's head is like a vacuum sucking all the good stuff away."

She laughed "Oh, that's good. You're fine, and to think for a moment I was worried. So, where's Silas?"

"Grabbing me some of your clothes." I picked up his hairbrush.

"What for?"

"Um…" I stilled mid-stroke.

"You have a closet full in Davio's room. I should know. I bought them." She perched against the countertop and eyed me.

"Sorry, your room was closer."

"For a teleporter?" She flicked her hand out. "Yeah, it doesn't matter. It's not like we haven't shared clothes a million times."

"We have?" How would that have happened? Silas had said Silvie and Faith were close, but they can't have known each other that long, certainly not to share clothes like a million times. She must have misspoken.

I fired up my link with Silas. *"How long have my sister and yours known each other?"*

"All their lives."

"Are you keeping a secret?" He better not be.

"No, but obviously I've omitted to tell you. Carlisio Loveria had forewarning after Faith's birth and sent my mother to Earth. He saw enough to interpret the child would have a soul-bound connection with someone close to him."

"So he presumed Davio?"

"He wasn't one-hundred percent certain, but yes. With Faith's father keeping his distance, Carlisio couldn't accurately identify if the man was of Dralion or Peacio. Since he didn't wish to risk Davio losing his future mate if she disappeared as her father had, he set precautions in place."

"What kind of precautions?"

"Along with my mother, he sent Silvie. Silvie was a baby at the time, but he thought two new mothers would bond better than any other he could send. That's how I came to be raised alongside Davio."

His explanation flowed swiftly and with unerring accuracy along our link. Every word he spoke was the truth. *"That's the first I've heard of this. Carlisio Loveria's forewarning must have been grave for him to take such firm action."*

"It was, but the task set to my mother was never a hardship for her, or for my sister. They spent half their time on Earth and the other half here. Silvie loves Faith, like a sister. Why did you ask about this? It's come out of the blue."

"Silvie's here. She thinks I'm Faith. And that's the way it needs to stay."

"My sister's with you? Hell. I'm on my way."

Footfalls sounded in the next room and Silas stormed around the corner. "Hey, Silvie. Ho—Faith needed some of your clothes. I hope you don't mind that I raided your drawers?"

"No problem."

"Great." He shoved the clothing into my hands. "You okay?"

"Couldn't be better." Silvie was cool, and I liked the idea of getting to know her better. She was Silas's sister after all. "Turn around, would you? Face the door."

"Why am I turning around?" he muttered as he did.

"I need to change."

"Shoot, you could have just told me to leave the room."

"It'll only take a second." I flapped the big-pocketed, beige cargo pants out and pulled them on. Next I slipped the black and white striped t-shirt over my head. Dark leather flats, and I was done. "Silvie, do you want to come shopping with us?"

"What kind of clothes are you after?" She straightened the bottom of my t-shirt.

"A couple of everything. I'm done, Silas."

With a slight turn of his head, he checked. "You'll know the best shops, Silvie. Come if you want."

I grabbed them both by the arm. "She's coming. Blinky-thing please, Mr. Convenient."

Taking hold of us too, he 'ported.

Through the darkness we traveled then arrived with the sun high above and pavement under our feet. At my back was a concrete block wall, three-stories high and painted sky blue. In front, a bright orange rubbish bin hid us completely from view.

Overhead a seagull screeched, and I opened my link with Silas. *"I haven't been here before."*

"This is the rear parking lot of the girls' favorite shopping mall. I bring Silvie here all the time. She and Faith will attend the same campus next year."

I played with the white rose pendant he'd given me. *"Oh, I see."*

"Hey, guys. Let's not stand around." Silvie side-shuffled out past the end of the bin.

I followed her movements to stand beside her. "What course is it you're doing next year?"

She arched a brow. "Ah, the same one we've always spoken about it, silly."

"Food technology." Silas edged in behind me. *"Te Puke is twenty minutes from here. That's where they both go to high school."*

"Sorry. I don't mean to be a dill. I'm just trying to get to know her, while remembering I already do. Not easy, you know." I leaned against him, merging my mind with his and sinking into my special place. Oh, I so needed that.

Whoops.

I jerked upright.

A strange look crossed Silvie's face. "You two are never this chummy, and as nice as it is to see you both getting along, it's making my stomach churn."

"Right." I darted a glance at Silas. *"Churn?"*

"Yeah, Faith and I don't see eye to eye. She argues with me too much."

"Don't you mean you argue with her too much?"

"Probably." He chuckled.

We continued to the entrance, and the glass doors opened automatically with a light swish.

"Oooh." Silvie lifted her nose and sniffed. "Who smells that?"

The scent of sugary bakery items from a nearby coffee stand and a hint of floor wax from the gleaming pale-speckled floors hit me. "Do you mean the donuts?"

"Of course I mean the donuts." Silvie shoved an elbow into my side. "What is with you today, girl?"

"Ah, I'm not feeling myself."

"Obviously." She strode off.

Silas tugged my hair. "It'll be okay. Come on."

He followed his sister as two little girls whizzed past me, one slightly older than the other. They wore matching pink silk ribbons in their brown hair. The eldest led the way, bounding onto an escalator. A woman called out as she gave chase and I jumped out of her way, the two white shopping bags in her arms almost clobbering me. Others on the escalator moved aside as she ran to catch them up.

Shopping malls. They were a minefield.

Not to mention busy. Families everywhere, and couples strolled hand-in-hand.

"Where would you like to go first?" Silvie asked as I came in beside her.

"I thought you said donuts?" The display of pink, yellow and blue-iced round donuts from behind the glass counter's front cabinet had my mouth watering. "I missed breakfast, and is that hot chocolate?" I licked my lips.

"It is. Do you want extra marshmallows?"

"Double. Or triple. I don't mind just a lit-tle hot chocolate with my marshmallows."

"Gotcha." Her hair swished forward as she leaned over the counter to place the order.

Silas eased in closer to me, his fingers warm against my elbow as he cupped it. He bent his head, his lips almost on mine, when he stopped with a growl. "Damn, that's frustrating."

Was it ever.

"Here we go."

I snapped to attention as Silvie turned and passed me a donut and a cup of hot chocolate in a foam cup. "Thanks. Love it."

She passed Silas a donut and drink, and then grabbed her own.

We walked. Gee, would it really hurt if Silvie knew exactly who I was? Would she keep my secret? Surely Dad would speak to Faith and Kate soon.

"Hey, look at these." At the front window of a jewelry shop, Silas paused. "These earrings have a tiny glass pyramid with orange sand inside. You know what I'm thinking, H—I mean, Faith?"

"Oh yeah, they'd be perfect for Elizara, as a thank you."

"Exactly." Patting his pocket, Silas headed inside.

"Who's Elizara?"

"Um... I met her a couple of days ago. She's been extremely helpful."

"You mean in Dralion? You met her there?"

Shoving the donut into my mouth, I mumbled a no.

"Where and how was she helpful then?"

"Ah—" I jammed the rest of the donut into my mouth.

"Something is up with you today." Silvie crossed her arms and tapped her fingers along them.

"Uh-huh, I need clothes." I linked my arm through hers and whisked her to the next shop, leaving Silas to buy the earrings.

Keeping her busy without time to question me was a mission. I buzzed around several stores, trying on jeans, shirts and blouses of every style and color. We bought shoes, jackets, sweatshirts and summer dresses for the warm nights to come.

Silas's arms overflowed with packages. "I'll zap these bags home and we'll stop for lunch across the way. You two good with that?"

"Yes." I rubbed my belly. "Shopping's exhausting. I definitely need food."

"We'll see you there." Silvie nodded to him. "Come on, you." She led me toward the cafe.

We sat opposite each over at a corner table in the rear. I moved the center posy of flowers to one side. As her brother's mate, surely she'd keep my secret because he did. It still niggled at me she didn't know.

"There's something I want to tell you, but you have to keep it to yourself." I spread a napkin over my lap, crinkling the edges.

"Hello, eighteen years and I didn't whisper a word of Peacio to you. I think I've proven my worth." She angled her head. "I can't believe you even asked that. Spill."

"Okay, but I can't tell you until Silas gets here. He's part of the secret."

"What?"

"May I take your order?"

A waitress with a pen and pad in hand smiled at us, and Silvie grumbled a loud, "No."

"Sure you can. Is there a chicken salad?" I smiled at the waitress, glad for the intervention.

"Yes, there is." She jotted the order down and glanced at Silvie. "And you, miss?"

"The same." Silvie thumped her feet under the table.

"Ladies." Silas swept in and pulled out a chair. *My sister looks frustrated. What have you done to her?*

"I'm going to tell her about us."

"Sir, what would you like?"

"A steak and egg burger, thanks. Iced water." He snatched my hand under the table. *"Heck. I can't stand not touching you. Make it quick."*

Silvie's gaze narrowed to tiny slits as the waitress left. "If I'm correct, I believe you two are holding hands...under the table. Don't get me wrong, Silas, but Davio will kill you. After eighteen years of learning all your pranks, I'm used to you and I'd quite like to keep you around."

I took the deepest breath, ready to tell all. "Silvie, Davio won't kill him because I'm not Faith. My name is Hope Wincrest. Faith's my sister and we share the same mother, well, the same father too, but I lived with him, not her."

Shoving her cutlery to the side, she stared. "A-are you serious?"

"Very. I wasn't raised with Faith, although obviously she's my twin. Instead I was taken by my father to Dralion, right after my birth."

"Twin? My best friend has a twin?" Her breathing became loud as she fought to drag in air. "Please tell me this is a joke."

"It's not. I live half my life in Dralion, and the other half on Wincrest Station in the outback."

"Australia and Dralion?" Scratching her head, she turned her gaze on Silas. "Is this for real?"

From underneath the table, Silas lifted my hand clear. "Hope is my soul-bound mate. She can't approach Faith until Kate's become more settled. Alexo Wincrest's asked it of her."

"Oh hell." Silvie's eyes went saucer wide as she gripped the table's edge. "This is mad. You two are soul-bound? We'll have another Wincrest on Peacian soil?"

"Yes." I merged my mind with Silas's, needing the comforting space. "We have issues since I'm not one of your people, but we're dealing with it."

"How did this happen?"

"You believe me? Us?"

"Yes." She snapped her fingers at Silas. "My brother doesn't lie. Tell me everything."

"Here we are. Your meals and drinks." The waitress set our plates before us and Silvie scowled at her.

She moved away quickly and Silas said, "I think you've well and truly scared her off. And I was drawn to the station because of our bond. We've had quite the journey, even headed to No-Man's Land where we met Elizara. She's Katerin Sol's sister."

"Wow. Don't stop." She picked up her fork and stabbed a wedge of chicken from her salad, her gave riveted on Silas.

"Hope has the skill of mind-merge."

She choked on her food and Silas pushed one of the glasses of water toward her. She coughed, and drank half the glass. "Whoa. The skill that kills."

"Yes, but unlike Faith and Davio, Hope and I have created a telepathic link. Elizara has the same skill and taught Hope how to merge through the link. We have a way to reach each other, negating the three-day effect."

Silas answered all of Silvie's questions as we ate. She sometimes shook her head, other times, sighed as if in understanding.

Eventually, she simply stared. "This will kill Faith if she finds out I've withheld this information. I can understand why you've asked me to, but I know Kate well, and even though she's been through so much, she's still a strong woman. She could handle this."

"No speaking of it, Silvie." Silas's demand was firm. "I abide by Hope's wishes and so will you."

"Please," I implored. "She doesn't know about me, and right now, she can't. Alexo's request comes first. He has forewarning. He wouldn't have asked this of me without good reason."

"Hope is my mate," Silas reiterated.

"I get that part." She swung her hand toward me, knocking her glass. It tipped to the side and she made a grab for it. Fumbling, she missed and it toppled.

I reached to catch it, but the water didn't spill. It stayed in the glass.

No way.

I'd just kept the liquid inside. I hadn't wanted it to flow over the table's smooth surface and into my lap. With my mind, I'd held the water at bay.

The glass rolled into my plate with a clunk and Silas picked it up. He peered inside then turned it toward me. "Would you care to explain why the glass is still half full?"

"I must have the Sol's water skill."

Silvie was half out of her chair, snatching the glass to double-check. "Holy, moly. You didn't just do that?"

I directed my thoughts to the water within the glass and with a twirl of my fingers, sent the water flying upward. It skimmed Silvie's nose and hit the ceiling with a tinkle then sprayed out. Beautiful crystalline drops showered all over us.

On my feet, I twirled around. "I have another skill."

"Silvie, get the check. I'll get this one out of here and come back for you." Silas snagged my hand and tugged me from the cafe with lightning speed.

"Oh my goodness. Did you see that?"

"Keep moving."

We raced out of the mall and stopped behind the closest parked car, a solid black SUV. Silas checked all was clear then 'ported us.

As we arrived in his bedroom, I jumped up and down. "The water skill. This is the best one to have."

"Incredible." He twirled me around, his excitement now as great as mine. "You'll need training."

"I can go to Elizara for that."

"I'll take you whenever you want. I want to see everything you can do."

"This is amazing." I plopped onto his bed, which bounced packages of clothing to the floor. "I need water. Lots of water."

Leaning over me, he planted a kiss on my lips and I wrapped my arms around his neck, kissing him with so much energy I was ready to explode.

"Hope." Deep breaths as he drew away, his hands sliding down my sides and over my hips.

I pulled him back, until every hot inch of him sent heat into my skin. "I'm not nearly done with you."

"I thought you wanted water?"

"Oh yes. I'll take you and water." I rolled off the bed and

heaved him by the hand with me. Once in his bathroom, I plugged his deep bathtub and set the water to run. It trickled through my fingers, warm, wet and gloriously wonderful. Needing to be surrounded by water, I kicked off my shoes and in I went, down onto my belly where I sloshed around.

Silas bent over the tub's edge, scratching his head. "I should return for Silvie."

"I want you in here with me."

"One never ignores Silvie."

"You shouldn't ignore your girlfriend either. Come and play with me."

The heated look he sent had my toes curling. Then he stepped in and rolled in beside me.

The water rose and splashed over the rim. I peered over the edge and with a flick of my hand, directed the spilt water into a bubble. It lifted and hovered an inch or two from the white-gray tiles.

"That's amazing." Silas planted delicious kisses all over my face, and more water gushed over the edge.

"Hold on. Let me get that too." With a single thought, I guided it into a bubble and lifted it so it fused with the first.

His blue eyes sparkled. "Okay, let's dump this water out. I've gotta see that again."

He had a deal as his lips met mine.

Chapter 8

"Hope, catch." Out in the station yard, Goldie raised a pail of water and tossed it right at me.

I started to duck, but stopped and lifted my hands. The flying water halted, rolled into a giant bubble that gurgled until it smoothed out.

"That is the coolest skill." Goldie beamed.

From the moment Silas had brought me home after having spent yesterday with him, I'd practiced hard.

"I seriously cannot get enough of seeing you do that. Okay, float it back to the pail again."

Maslin whistled from where he perched on the top railing of the corral. "No. Bring it closer to you, Hope. Being born of the mated bond, you hold the full strength. I don't, but I have an idea I'd like you to try. Something I can't do." He jumped down from the railing, and the dust rose and settled over the tips of his boots.

Above the sun's rays blazed, the outback heat as relentless as ever, and I fixed my tan Stetson higher on my head and rubbed my hands together. "Sure. I love ideas."

"You'll have to insert your hands into the water." He strode to the bubble, which I still floated, and tapped his chin as he walked around it. "I can't levitate water like this. I can drive its natural flow further across the land, but this is beyond my reach.

What kind of quantity do you believe you can float?"

"I don't know. I did a bath-full yesterday." Only because Silas had near emptied it. I smiled at how we'd accomplished that.

Maslin clicked his tongue. "A bath-full is nothing. Those with the full strength can lift and move a small pond-full. I don't see why you should be any different."

"I'd love to do that." I jiggled about. "Oh yeah, like right now. I don't know nearly enough about this skill."

"We'll visit the river to collect water, and then head to the front field's watering hole. We'll see what you can move." He glanced at Goldie. "Coming?"

"Absolutely." She dropped the metal pail and it bounced with a twang on the rock-hard ground. "I want to see everything Hope can do."

Focusing on my bubble of levitating water, I pushed my fists into it. The water melted around my hands with a slight gurgling sound. Nice. So cool and refreshing.

Goldie edged around the bubble as she eyed my position. "Now, this really is water on the go."

Maslin chuckled as he set his hands on my waist, taking care not to jostle my arms. "The water is connected to Hope. You follow in our 'porting airstream in case this doesn't quite work out." A teleporter could do that, provided they caught the scent within a second of the other's leaving. It was a way to ensure they came out at the same spot, but without traveling together.

The dark consumed us as he 'ported, the water swishing down to my elbows, but with a thought, I kept it from sliding further. Seconds later, we returned in the sunlight, the great winding outback river before us.

Goldie arrived in our wake. "Excellent. You transported it. Now, aim for the stars."

I lowered the water I had to the river then turned my hands

palms-up and focused on taking so much more.

A wave rippled outward from the center, and with a sweeping motion of my hands and a thought to scoop all I could, a huge mass rose, bubbling around the edges. Water poured in on itself until I controlled and drew it into a circle.

Up. It had to go up. My focused directive made the new bubble rise.

Wow. Goldie gasped but I didn't dare turn.

A rolling sphere of precious liquid, murky and holding sandy particles, continued to rise. As I plucked it free, waves rolled out to each side of the river and washed onto the bank. The river quietly settled.

"I'm loving it." Maslin had the widest grin on his face. "Lift it above us. You're going to have to insert your hands into it as you did before. We need the connection for 'porting."

Whoa. That was one monster amount of water. No, I could do this.

I lifted my hands high, and energy poured through me as my decision was set on its course. The massive bubble caused a shadow as it ascended over us and bobbed into place.

Lowering it a fraction, I drove my fists into the surface.

Goldie dipped her head. "Don't you dare drop that. That's much bigger than the last one."

"I won't." My heartbeat sped into high gear.

"I'm ready when you are." Maslin set his hands on my waist.

"Go." Sweat beaded along my brow and more trickled between my shoulder blades as we traveled through the dark.

Then we were there. Above me the balloon of water churned, an energy of its own forming and swirling within from the jump through space. It wobbled and liquid sloshed and spat to the ground. It hissed and steam plumed from where cool water hit hot, dry soil. "Um, guys. I'm not sure I can hold this."

"Set it down in the watering hole. You've reached your

skill's limit!" Maslin yelled as the bubbling mass stewed.

I sent the water from me in a flash and covered my head with my hands. It boomed as it hit.

Goldie squealed and grabbed my hands. "You did it."

A rush of water streamed to the outside of the watering hole. The surge of water cascaded over the bank and flowed over thirsty ground to our feet.

Wiping my damp sleeve over my face, I grinned. "I really did it."

"Hell, yes." Maslin strode to the water's edge and shoved his hand into it. "It's a touch warmer than usual, but it'll cool."

"I can see it, but I can't believe it."

"What you did is amazing. I'll test it properly." He kicked off his boots and walked in to hip depth then dove. He was going for a swim?

I laughed as his head broke the surface and he spat a fountain of water from his mouth. "What are you doing?"

"Celebrating."

Goldie looked skyward as birds appeared and flew down. They skimmed the surface, flapping their wings with a gaggle. "You filled it. So quick. This changes everything."

Maslin let out a hearty shout as he fell back, arms splayed wide as he went under again.

Where there was water, there was life.

Another bellowing shout came from Maslin as he took to swimming from one end to the other.

"I don't think he's coming out anytime soon." Goldie slapped my arm.

We relied on water for the necessity of life, and now it was here, where it hadn't been mere minutes ago. I couldn't stand still. I grabbed my boot. "I'm going to join him."

"*There won't be any time.*" Dad's voice rang clear in my mind.

I dropped my foot to the ground. "*Hey, you were watching.*"

He rarely missed the big stuff, and this was pretty big.

"*I'm so proud of you.*" Deep satisfaction laced his tone. "*It's an incredible skill to have.*"

"*Are you sure I don't have time for a swim?*" Maslin swam with fast strokes, and I wanted in.

"*Yes. I was with Donaldo when my forewarning activated. I shared the news of your water skill with him. He's asked for your return, for you to meet him in his quarters. Have Goldie bring you. I'll keep your mother busy while you're here. I can't risk a chance meeting.*"

"*Gotcha.*" I closed the link and jumped about. I was going home, for the first time in weeks. "Donaldo wants to see what I can do. His quarters, though."

"Of course he would. Now block your nose. I know how much you hate the stink of the dome room." Goldie grasped my hand.

She always warned me. The dungeon-like room was located deep within the lower bowels of the palace.

"Maslin," she called to him. "Donaldo's asked to see Hope. We'll catch you later."

"Later." He sent a returning wave.

Goldie flashed us away, and I braced for the smell and pinched my nose tighter as we arrived in the dome room. No doors here, just four gloomy walls of gray-black bricks with slabs of floor-stones in a dull gray-green. I skidded on the slimy floor, as always covered in moist layers of sticky mildewed moss. It was a wretched place, but then that was necessary, because our enemy would never guess this would be the image needed to successfully 'port through to reach us.

Taking care with my step, I headed to the central well. This well led to the energy source Guy's grandfather, Gilles Moyer, had first linked his enchantment to forty years ago. This was the spot where he had brought the energy field to life.

My chest tightened as I thought of Guy's father and our

other captured warriors. They never left my mind for long.

Goldie tugged me away. "Donaldo will be waiting."

I held onto her tight as she 'ported us, focusing only on what was ahead. We reappeared in the foyer leading to Donaldo's study. Here the ceiling was twelve feet high, with ornate plaster work surrounding a magnificent chandelier dripping in crystal. A dozen high-backed chairs covered in black silk lined the walls. I'd scrambled over those chairs many times as a child. I was home.

A maid stepped forward and bobbed her head. "Miladies, you have perfect timing. Donaldo awaits." She turned and opened one of the two oak paneled doors.

"Goldwyn. Hope." Donaldo's booming voice traveled to us, and we hurried. "I haven't seen my daughter or granddaughter in too long."

"Father." Goldie sped up as Donaldo stood.

He tossed the papers he held onto his solid desk then came around and embraced her in a firm forearm hold. Gold insignia rings on his thumbs glinted in the sunshine beaming through the large square windows to the side. Through the panes of glass was the most glorious sight. Black granite cliffs, an impenetrable structure never more obvious than from this high vantage point on the fourth floor, stood like a sentinel. Beyond was the deep blue of The Great Orbiting Ocean. Throughout my childhood, I'd been fascinated by the natural wonder, and to this day still was.

"Hope." My grandfather embraced me.

"Granddad, you look good." He wore an impeccably pressed blue-collared shirt with silver chains looped from his shoulder to his top pocket. His long legs were encased in tough black leather pants.

Swiping a hand over his full, dark beard, he eyed me. "As do you. Tell me of this rare Sol ability you have with water. I understand what Maslin can do, but Alexo tells me yours is at full strength. Showing me would be even better."

It was Donaldo's way to get straight to business. He ran a nation, and did it with precision.

I glanced at the long glass vase atop his side cabinet holding one white lily. Lifting my hand, I focused my mind on it. "I can manipulate water as Dad said." Swirling the water within, the vase moved with a gentle rattle, rocking on the polished wooden surface.

With more strength behind my thoughts, I increased the water's momentum until the vase jiggled and tipped.

As it fell, I swept the water upward but still within the vase. I used the liquid to lift the glass from within and hold it upright. It required pressure to keep it there, but with a single thought it was done.

Goldie clapped as I levitated the water within the upside-down vase. "The law of physics no longer comes into play around you."

"Incredible. I mean it." Donaldo grinned as he stepped around the floating vessel. His violet eyes glinted. "And what of Alexo saying you moved a massive quantity of water from the river and dumped it into one of the watering holes, filling it to capacity?"

"I did. I wish you could have seen it."

"Then show me now." He caught Goldie and me by the arm. "We have an ocean of water right on hand. Let's go."

Donaldo 'ported us to within thirty feet of the ledge. No. The vase of water I'd left behind would have fallen to smash on his study room floor. "Ah—"

"No." He took my shoulders and gave me a nudge toward the ledge.

I should have guessed he'd do this.

I paused a few steps from the edge, lowered myself to the ground and crawled toward it. Such a steep drop, of two-hundred feet to the base. Jeez, I never got this close, not when my fascination was well sated from further away.

"If there's any danger, I'll 'port and catch you. Other than that, you can do as you wish," Donaldo called out.

"Great. Thanks for that!" I yelled back.

Oh boy, this was crazy.

There was a fortress behind me, yet I sat on the edge of a cliff.

Come on. You can do this. You're a Wincrest.

Focus.

With my heart racing, I curled my hands around the ragged granite that would spell my doom if I toppled over it. Whoa. My vision swam and I dragged in a deep gulp of air. This was a whole lot scary. Silas would certainly freak if he saw me right now. Luckily though, he didn't know what I was about to do, and it was just as well I hadn't had enough time to contemplate it either.

"*Hope.*"

Uh-oh, stupid heart alignment. "*I'm fine.*"

"*It doesn't feel it. Where are you? I'll come.*" His tone was urgent, but then again so was the pounding of my heart.

"*I'm in Dralion. You can't.*"

"*What the hell are you doing there? My heart's about to jackknife out of my chest.*"

I held tighter to the granite. The waves far below slapped hard and sprayed high in an impressive display of nature versus life. I loved the water, but not like this.

Once I'd scampered away from the edge on my bottom, my heartbeat slowed a fraction. "*Is that better?*"

His voice was a deep growl, which rumbled around in my head. "*Not nearly enough.*"

Right. Not for me either.

"*Silas, you're not helping me focus. I'll get back to you. Real soon.*" I closed our link and blocked any reconnection.

Returning my attention to the waves meant I returned to the

ledge. Make this fast. I raised my hand and swept it in a wide arc, drawing as much of the swelling seawater from below as I could. It roared and churned, fighting capture, but I rolled it and created a funnel then lifted it with all my mental might.

A geyser jetted, spraying a fountain of sea spray over us.

Ah, not quite what I had been after.

I tried again, this time maintaining more control over the funnel and capping it as the water levitated free of the sea.

Lifting it high was a magical moment. I grinned as the swirling waters, a quantity that could fill a large pool, rose over our heads.

I scurried to my feet and rejoined Donaldo and Goldie. Above, the pool of water floated.

"I'm never going to tire of seeing you do this," Goldie whispered. "It has to be thirty feet in height and half as wide."

Shucking off my boots, I eyed my grandfather. "I've set my hands into the water before and teleported with it. I don't see why I can't fully hop inside and swim. It should hold me, provided I keep kicking."

Donaldo gripped my shoulder. "You want to go for a swim? In that?"

"Elizara Sol has this skill. She can breathe underwater for several minutes and she told me how to do it. I want to try. It's just a pool of water."

"A floating one." He stared at it.

"Did you hear about Elizara?"

"Yes, Alexo kept me updated once he caught sight of you in the Sol compound."

I glanced at the palace, to the slender towers, which rose to double the height of the gray-black stone walls near Dad's wing. "Is he—"

A brisk wind swirled and Dad wavered into view. He drew me into a hug and dropped a kiss on the top of my head. "I saw you from the window. I hope you realize this display of yours out here is rather obvious. At the moment, I have Jilly keeping your mother busy and far away from this side of the palace. You need to make this quick."

"Will do." I gave him a wobbly smile.

"If you're going for a swim, get to it."

"You haven't had forewarning, right? I'm not about to drown?"

"No unexpected activation of forewarning. You're safe to go."

Donaldo cleared his throat. "I look forward to seeing what you can do."

I approached the water. My nervousness hadn't left and now it banged away with even more force.

No hesitation. A Wincrest didn't falter.

I stopped in front and pressed one fist into the water. It suctioned around my arm, all tingly and cold. While pushing another fist in, the same strange sensation swept over me. Come on. Get in. I jumped and was swallowed by the chilly seawater.

Yee-ha. Holding my breath, I kicked swiftly to the center.

Wow. Such freedom in my movement. This was no different than being in a pool, only it was ocean water with seaweed and flotsam floating around. Oh, funny, and a jellyfish.

Holding my position, I thought only of the water and the breath I would soon run out of. That couldn't happen, and with a flick of my fingers in front of my face, I separated the hydrogen and pushed it outward, away from the oxygen until it formed a protective bubble around the precious air I needed to breathe. With no time left, I pressed my nose into the air pocket and drew in a deep breath. Only the air bubble rose. Drat. I kicked swiftly upward with it, dragging in the oxygen I needed. Oh, that worked.

With enough air, I dived, returning to swim lower. Silas. I had to tell him. I unblocked our telepathic link and threw it open. *"Guess what?"*

"Tell me." A dark edge to his tone said I'd better speak fast.

"I can breathe underwater. That's what I'm doing right now."

"Come and show me and don't block me again." A darker sense of urgency.

"I'm with my family. I told you I was in Dralion."

"I want you back."

"Hey, you knew this would happen. I spend half my time here."

"What are you saying?" His voice was too loud, almost ringing in my ears. *"How long do you expect to be there?"*

"My father won't permit me to stay long. Hold on, I need to take a breath." I focused on forming another bubble of oxygen by pushing the hydrogen atoms away. With my nose in, I inhaled and swam upward with its natural rising. *"Yes."* I did a little spin in the water and dived down.

"What was that yes for?"

"The air I'm breathing. I can form pockets of air, only they rise naturally. It means I have to chase them, but it's pretty cool." I rubbed my arms and a shiny gel smeared over my fingertips. *"Oh. I should feel cold since this is ocean water, and I did at the start, but now it's..."*

"What? What?"

"Don't be anxious. It's all good. There's a clear coating on my skin. It's keeping me warm."

"Did Elizara get a coating on her skin?"

"Hmm, in the oasis with the other women, those with the water skill were faster, sleeker and slippery to the touch. They must have. This is their element." I grinned, recognizing it was now mine too.

I worked at creating another bubble of air. Rising with it, I drew a breath in then turned cartwheels, playing as the water slid over my insulated skin.

"Are you still underwater?"

"Uh-huh. How long's it been?"

"Too long. Get your feet on dry land."

"It's been a minute."

"More like five."

"Maybe two."

"Four," he grumbled.

I laughed. *"I think I may need an incentive to get out. I like this too much."*

"Come to me and I'll give you that and more."

"I don't think so. This is heaven."

"Heaven would be you getting out."

"Tell me what you're up to while I swim."

"Hyperventilating. I have a paper bag shoved under my nose."

He so did not. What a liar, and I would have argued, but Dad circled the perimeter of the watery shield, signaling me out.

"I gotta get out. Dad's calling."

"So, you'll go for your father?"

"He's bossier. You haven't mastered that yet." With a chuckle, I closed our link and kicked to the water's edge. I pressed a fist through and hit air.

Dad grabbed and drew me through.

With a suctioning gurgle, I was out. The surface behind me rippled, and then resettled as I maintained its shape with my mind.

"What's this on your skin?"

"This gel protects me from the cold. It must be part of my water skill to create it."

Donaldo approached and rubbed at his chin. "Simply amazing."

Goldie touched the slick stuff on my hair. "How do you get this off?"

"I don't know." Or perhaps I did and all I had to do was send it away with the same focus I used with water. My heartbeat skipped in excitement. Oh, that was it.

With a sweep of my hands, from my head to my toes, I directed the gel away. It slid to the ground and coated the soil at my feet.

The breeze lifted my hair, the dry strands fluttering across my face. The salt of the ocean was on my skin, but it was perfectly dry. Even my sleeveless outback shirt ruffled in the wind, and when I patted my jeans, not a drop of water remained. "I can't believe the control I have."

"It's wonderful, but do not forget the wall of water behind you." Donaldo wagged a finger at it. "As much as I hate to see that go, it better."

Raising a hand, I swept the water out in an arc. It cleared the cliff and crashed far below.

Dad ran his hands down my arms. "Incredible. You were underwater for several minutes."

Goldie skipped in a circle around me. "Mar-vel-ous."

"It is," he agreed. "But you two need to go."

"As do I. I have meetings. I will see you girls later." Donaldo inclined his head, and flashed away. No surprises there. He always had a mountain of work to do.

With a sigh, I glanced up at the windows of Dad's wing. My mother would be in a room somewhere within. "How much longer do I have to wait, Dad?"

"I've seen your purpose is great, as is your sister's."

I rolled my eyes. "Dad, that's not helpful. I asked when I'll meet my mother."

"The day you and Faith were born, you arrived tangled together, arms and legs holding onto each other when the doctor performed the caesarian and delivered you both. Faith is not the eldest. Neither are you. You were born together." He tapped my chin. "You will find each other again, and soon. It shall be as it was then. Your bonds will be renewed as if never lost, because your blood-bond with your twin is the strongest I've foreseen.

Afterward, I will surely speak to your mother of Katerin Sol and No-Man's Land. There are so many issues. We will take them one at a time." He darted a look toward the palace. "I have to go, now. I'm sorry I can't stay, and that neither can you. Look after her, Goldie." He shimmered out of sight.

Kicking the space he'd been in, I growled. "This wait is excruciating."

Goldie passed me my boots. "Yes, but you have a fantastic skill, and I wonder if more will come. You should have asked your father when your rising will begin. He may have seen it."

One's rising was the completion of our skills coming together. It was an occasion we honored and celebrated, because as our rising began, an overpowering assault wreaked havoc on all our senses. Adrenaline pumped through our bodies, causing an all-time high. Hormones swung, but most of all, strength-levels three-times greater than normal hit us. Only those closest to us could best aid us in draining the excess energy spiraling out. So, yes, I should have asked about it.

"Boots, and ask him another time." Goldie dragged up one of my legs by the cuff of my jeans. "The station doesn't run itself, and you have a lot to do."

"You mean I have to fill all the watering holes?" I tugged on my boots, hopping about.

Her eyes brightened, the violet all Wincrests shared shimmering to a sparkling amethyst hue. A dangerous hue, in her case. "C'mon, don't tell me you're not up for it."

"There has to be at least fifty watering holes, and half that number completely dried out."

"Think how happy you'll make Maslin." Goldie's laugh was a tinkle of sound. "Oh, he's going to be over the moon."

And without waiting for my answer, she took me with her through the dome room and on to the dusty red plains of home.

Yeah, Maslin was delirious. I worked at transferring river water with his teleportation aid until the night sky was a thick blanket of black.

It was the longest day, and later that night after having filled half of them, I collapsed on my bed, all of me covered in mud and dirt.

"Hope."

I lifted one eyelid. Oh, what a sight. I lifted the other.

Mmm, Silas looked as gorgeous as ever in a pair of butt-hugging black jeans and a white cotton t-shirt stretched tight over his broad chest. "You look sooo good. Come here."

"You need to get up."

"I would, but my legs are dead. And I'm dirty. Don't tell me you missed the state of my dress."

"You don't look like any princess I know."

I sighed and merged my mind with his, sinking into sweet oblivion. "Being a princess is completely overrated. Seriously, it is not at all like those fairy tales make it out to be. There is no crown, no glass slippers, and surely no prince."

"Up with you. I'll be your prince." He scooped me from the bed, his lips softly touching mine, and he 'ported us.

I glanced around his bedroom as we arrived. His bed looked completely inviting, only he headed in the wrong direction and away from it. "This princess wants the bed. Where are you taking me?"

"I'm starving and Silvie cooked. You're getting changed so we can have dinner."

"You made your sister cook?"

In his dressing room, he set me on my feet. "She's amazing. I told you she's been accepted into the university's food technology course. It's like a culinary school."

He tugged his mucky t-shirt over his head. I zeroed in on the splendor of his rippling muscles. Oh boy, Silas had muscles on top of muscles. "You train with the sword daily?"

"Usually."

Delicious. I licked my lips. I could certainly stare at him all day.

He removed a starched dress shirt in the palest shade of blue from the rack and pulled it on. Drat. I'd lost that sweet view.

"You should be showering. You stink."

"What?"

"You should—"

I slapped his arm. "I heard you. I wasn't asking you to repeat yourself. A little more tact wouldn't go amiss."

"Sorry." He nuzzled my cheek. "I can't stand you being away from me, but right now I can. Is that better?"

"Not much, but it'll do."

"Great. I'll master this bossier side of me yet." From the side where my clothes now hung, he selected a violet spaghetti strap dress of mid-length with a flared skirt and a pair of matching heels. He passed the clothing to me. "Silvie doesn't like her guests turning up late, and you're not moving. Bathroom's that way."

"Even when bossy, I should get a proper kiss."

His gaze moved over my face and his breathing accelerated. "If I kiss you now, I won't stop. I didn't like knowing how far away you've been from me today. And Zac and Viv are expected at dinner, so we must leave. Belle too. She's our empath, and she senses feelings, so be prepared for it. She's more curious than I imagine you'll enjoy."

I cocked one leg out. "Then sense this. I can't think of any place worse than being with a bunch of protectors. I'll probably choke on my food."

He turned me toward the door. "You'll do this for Silvie."

I grumbled the whole way to the bathroom and gladly shut the door on him. He was mastering bossy quicker than I liked.

Twenty minutes later, I was dressed and turning around in front of the mirror. The dress had thin crisscrossing straps over my shoulders and back. The bodice was fitted and the exact shade of violet as my eyes.

"Are you coming out?" Silas knocked on the door.

"Go away."

He came in and crossed to me. "I couldn't hear you."

"Sure you couldn't." Sheesh, what a liar.

"I bought something for you, today." He reached into his pocket and pulled whatever it was out. When he uncurled his fingers, a silver charm, the tiny rose pattern delicately painted in sunshine-yellow, glinted in his palm. "It's a yellow rose, for the gift of friendship. Will you accept it?"

"Oh my goodness, yes." Turning around, I swept my hair to the side. "Could you put it on with the other?" My hands shook. I loved it.

As he unfastened the link, his fingers brushed against my skin. He added the yellow rose. "There's something else I'd like to do tonight."

I fingered the white and yellow rose charms with a soft sigh, feeling completely lost for words. Well, except one. "No."

"You haven't heard my request."

"I don't need to. You're in a dangerous mood. You gave me this."

"You're a Wincrest. You live for danger." He dropped a kiss on the tip of my nose.

"It's still a no."

"We'll see." His cheeky grin returned, and I was lost. "Next time I'll know not to ask, just do."

"I'm hungry. Do we walk or do we—"

Everything darkened, and we arrived in the middle of a brightly lit dining room. Silver-edged emerald curtains adorned the windows and underneath was a seated area with covered pads of the same luscious fabric. Cutlery and glasses sparkled on a long dining table draped with a silver-threaded tablecloth. Beyond, double doors led to another room.

"Silvie's kitchen is through there, and the rec room is next to that. This wing was designed by Genevy for us younger ones some years ago, and only those closest to Davio have access to it. You're completely safe from coming into contact with those you don't know here."

"Thanks. I think."

The doors swung open and the two protectors who'd aided Silas in his search for me by the river came in. Zac wore a pair of gray dress pants with a paler shaded shirt, and Viv had dressed in a short black leather skirt and red blouse. She had killer red heels and a dagger holstered along her wrist.

I gripped Silas's forearm and found his dagger hidden underneath his long cuffed sleeves. They were always armed, but then so were our warriors. Something I was used to.

"Good evening." Viv nodded at me. "Silas told us this afternoon you have the water skill. Congratulations."

I eyed the two of them, because being in the same room as protectors, even though they were polite, made my skin crawl. Still, I would be civil. "It's a skill needed on the station, a valuable one."

The door opened, and a woman in a red dress, with the longest locks of brown hair crossed the room. She looked just like the lead actress from the musical movie I'd watched on Earth one night. Yeah, the one about an American high school.

Silas whispered in my ear, "This is Belle, our empath."

She popped a hand over her mouth with a soft exhalation. "Oh, you must be Hope. Silvie just warned me you'd be here. You look just like Faith."

"So I've heard." There were four protectors in this room, counting Silas. I'd never been around so many. Not good.

Silas smoothed a hand around my waist as I inched closer to him. *"Relax. No one here will harm you."*

Gripping his hand, I held on tight. *"You're outnumbered if they decide to attack. It's not hard to miss that."* To the depths of my heart, I didn't doubt his protection stood strong, regardless of who we were around.

Belle's lips lifted. "I sense your connection with Silas is strong. That's good, but I also feel your concern radiating through. There's no need. No one here would hurt Silas's mate."

Empaths were tricky to be around. They identified emotions with precision and were a pain in the butt. "You shouldn't pry."

"I wasn't prying." She advanced, and I held up my hands.

"No, you don't. You stay there." Empaths had a terrible habit of being overly friendly.

She engulfed me in a hug, the sweet scent of roses coming with her. Shoot, and this one was no different. "I can tell you have a big heart simply because you care for Silas, and there is honor and pride emitting strongly from you."

"I'm sure there is," I muttered, trying to push her away. Damn it. Why wouldn't she move? "Silas, a little help here."

He snickered, and then coughed. "Sorry. Belle, do you mind?"

A sigh came from her. "No one cares about the empath. We have feelings too, you know." Still, she retreated a few steps. Thank heavens. "You radiate the same emotional responses as Faith did after I first met her."

"I do?" I slanted my head. "How can you tell that in so short a time?"

"It's the strongest part of my skill."

"Here we go, everyone." Silvie breezed into the room carrying a large crockery pot with steam escaping from the sides of its glass lid. A long ladle balanced on top, and I rushed to help her, took the serving spoon and cleared a spot in the center of the table.

"Oooh, that smells delicious." I peered in.

"It's the starter. Spiced pumpkin soup. Great to see you." She gave me a hug.

Silas pulled out a chair. "Come sit here, Hope, at the quiet end of the table."

"There's a quiet end?" I was all for that, and scurried to him.

Everyone sat and Silvie passed a basket of crusty herbed bread to me. "Did you have a good day?"

"I did." Not that I'd talk about it in front of Zac, Viv or Belle. Dinner was one thing, but getting chummy another.

Silas squeezed my leg under the table. "You're here. That's all that matters."

I gave him a small smile as Silvie plated the soup and set a bowl before me. "Thank you. This looks amazing." I sipped a mouthful from my spoon. Oh, de-li-cious. She was good, and the herbed bread was melt-in-the-mouth divine.

"Hope. I hate to interrupt."

I froze at Dad's voice in my head, an undeniable urgency in his tone. *"Yes."*

"Your sister's coming. She heard Silvie had cooked and the last meal Silvie prepared for her didn't end well. She wants to make it up to her."

"How long?"

"Five seconds, but I've seen it's time for you to meet her."

I dropped my spoon and stared at the door. A tingly numbness pervaded my limbs. *"Now?"*

"Yes. Four seconds."

"I'm not ready." My heart thumped and Silas gripped my hand.

"What's wrong?"

"Three."

"Faith comes. It's time for me to meet her."

His chair scraped as he pushed it back.

"Two."

"Dad, I'm not sure I can do this."

"One."

"Flip, stop counting down, Dad. I'm not a two-year-old."

The door flew open and a young woman dashed in. "Silvie,

I would have been here already if Davio had told me sooner you'd cooked."

My gaze got stuck on her face as she spoke. She had pink cheeks from running and sparkling violet eyes. Her blond hair swept down her back. This was my sister. My twin. The one person I should never have been separated from in life.

Loveria panted as he hurried into the room. "You are too crafty for your own good, Faith. I said I had other plans for us."

I soaked in every detail of her, from her casual Earth clothing, a short white skirt with a ruffled candy-pink blouse, to the three silver hoops on one wrist and the small digital watch on the other. I couldn't wait another moment to meet her.

"Faith." I gripped the table with both hands as I said her name.

She swiveled around, her gaze boggling wide. "What?" She blinked rapidly and squinted. "Um..." She flicked her fingers in front of her face. "Guys, I'm having a little problem with my eyesight." She glanced around the room, looking from one to the other until she returned to me.

"No, you're not." Silvie grasped Faith's shoulder. "You have a twin. This is Hope."

Faith's legs wobbled and her eyes rolled until the whites showed. Loveria caught her as she fell.

Okay, not the best first meeting.

* * * *

Slowly Faith came to. Loveria fanned her face, holding her upright. "You fainted," he murmured in her ear.

"I never faint." She frowned. "Unless I see someone just like me and my best friend tells me I have twin. Then I do." She gripped his shoulders, her knuckles turning white as she turned my way. "Oh. You're still real."

"What Silvie said was true." I shoved my shaky hands behind my back. "I know this is...unexpected." Crazy was more like it. "But if you'll allow me to explain, I will."

She flattened her hand on her chest. "You won't see me stopping you...whoever you are."

"You and I are true sisters of the blood-bond, born eighteen years ago to the same mother."

Her gaze narrowed with precision. "Are you sure? I believe my mother would have mentioned there being two of us."

"Our mother isn't aware I live. I was born with a heart blockage and after our birth, I died. Alexo took me home to Dralion. His intention was to bury me on home soil, although because of the teleportation jump, my heart restarted. It was unexpected."

Her gaze now held more interest and less suspicion. "You're saying you grew up in Dralion? Oh my." Her breath caught and she fluttered her hands at her sides. "You're that Hope. Alexo once mentioned he had a sister named Goldie who was currently off-world caring for another family member named Hope. Australia, I think he said. Why did he not tell me exactly who you were?"

Dad had hinted at my existence? My heart lightened. "He had his reasons."

"Why didn't Alexo return with you, since you lived?"

"You believe me?"

"It's a little hard not to with you standing right before me. So, why didn't he return with you?"

"Dad was worried about what another jump would do, so he called in the healers and Donaldo was informed. Dad's actions at that point were impossible to reverse. Kate's safety had to come first."

"The mated bond thing. I have that maddening relationship with Davio. I can't bring any harm to him, which right now, sucks." She eyed him. "Why'd you attempt to prevent my return? You knew she was here, huh?" It was not a good sounding *huh*.

He took her hands in his, squeezing them. "Hope requested

through Silas the two of you not yet meet. I withheld only for that reason."

"What the heck does Silas have to do with this?" Her gaze swung to Silas's, slitting with deadly intent. "What have you done?"

"Hope is my mate," he stated and placed a hand on my shoulder. "I've done nothing but accept the bond."

Faith's gaze pinged to his hand. "You're mated...to my sister?" She took one-step forward, her hands twitching at her sides. "Get your hands off her. I don't know her, but I already know I don't like you touching her."

"We are soul-bound. Touch is expected."

"I don't care. Hands. Off. Her. Now."

"I only have the one hand on her, but if you'd prefer I can make it two."

She took another step forward, a very menacing one. "I want to hurt you, Silas. You've now given me the best reason to."

"I'd like to see you try."

Was he egging her on?

At an intense moment like this?

He tucked me in closer to his side and her face went bull-fighting red.

Oh, he was.

Silas had said they didn't get along, and now I believed.

I cleared my throat. "Silas, you have to behave."

"No, I don't."

My hair whooshed across my face as Faith rammed into him.

She pinned him to the floor, one knee pressed into his belly and her elbow against his windpipe. "She asked you not to touch her. I have the battle skills, don't forget. I like to fight."

"She said for me to behave."

"Same thing."

"Let me up."

"You've been hiding her. My own sister. From me."

"Wincrest requested it of her. She obliged him, and so did I."

"Since when did you start doing something a Wincrest said to do?" Dropping her elbow deeper, she scowled. "Damn it, and what's wrong with me? I feel incredibly connected to her."

Loveria wandered across and sat on the padded seat under the window. "It's the blood-bond. The ties between you and your sister will be as strong as those between us as mates, only I hold your soul." He eased his legs out and idly crossed them at the ankles. "This is refreshing to see, Silas. I think this is called retribution."

Silas gawked about the room. "Does no one want to help me out here?"

A chorus of "nos" came from Zac, Viv and Belle.

Teeth clenched, Faith snorted at him. "I want to kill you and that thought isn't going anywhere. It doesn't help she looks like me. It gave me the creepies when you touched her."

Silvie huffed. "Faith, you've gotta let Silas go. He'll behave. I'll make sure he does."

"I have a twin, Silvie."

"It's a shock. I know." She tugged her up. "Everyone, to the table. This little display is over."

"But a sister?" Faith's gaze jumped between Silvie and me. "I've always wanted a sister. This is unreal."

Silvie pulled out a chair and plunked her in it. "Now you have one. Ask her some questions. It'll take your mind off wanting to hurt Silas, and me, since I withheld too."

"You withheld?"

"Silas did first. He told me to."

"Thanks, sis. Dump me in it a little further, why don't you." Silas smoothed out the collar of his shirt then tucked his loose tails in and guided me to my seat. "You still really want a sister?

I forgot to mention, they're a pain in the butt."

"I do." More than ever, now that I'd met her.

Faith wrinkled up the tablecloth as she leaned forward opposite me. "Goodness. It's like I'm staring at my own reflection. Wow. Seeing you before me is a shock, but the greatest one I've had so far, and trust me, there's been a ton in the past few weeks."

I inched my feet out and touched my toes to hers. "I've only known of your existence for a short time." I itched to get closer still, my blood-bond with her the strongest ever. It called me to her as Dad had said.

She laid her hand on the table and wriggled her fingers. "More."

I gripped her hand. "I have the ability to mind-merge as you do. I'm merged with Silas right now, and since he and I met, we've discovered where Katerin Sol came from."

She rocked forward and clutched my hand. "Our grandmother?"

"Yes. We're not alone with our ability of mind-merge. Katerin's sister, Elizara, spent time with me. The Sols come from the desert of No-Man's Land. Ours is a rare skill, but there are four at the Sol compound who hold it. I also came into my water skill. It's another that runs through the Sol line."

Her gaze searched mine. "Mum knows nothing about No-Man's Land. She would have said."

"Dad intends to speak to her of it. He was waiting for you and I to meet, but there are so many other issues, like her own abandonment. He deals with one at a time and won't be rushed."

"He's definitely persistent where her safety is concerned." She nodded.

"Yes. They've been apart for eighteen years and I don't want to press him after he's waited so long for her return. What's a little more time?"

She squeezed her eyes shut and bowed her head. "I hate that

I understand."

Loveria tugged his chair closer to hers. "Your mother is a strong woman, Faith."

"Yeah, but she was abandoned as a child, and that's always been her one weakness. If she finds out she had a child she never met, no matter that"—her voice wobbled—"Hope died. In her opinion she'll be no different than her mother, a woman who gave up her child."

My hand shook as I held hers. "But these circumstances were out of her control."

"I know, but will she accept it? Alexo must have seen differently."

I dropped my chin to my chest. My heart ached for my mother. I wanted to meet her, not to cause her more agony by my presence. I longed to know her.

Silas eased an arm around my shoulders. "You've met your sister today. Think only of that."

Faith switched her gaze to Silas. "Excuse me. I'm still not okay with you touching her."

"She is my mate."

A determined look lit Faith's eyes. "As you keep saying, but it's going to take me a little time to get used to seeing you two together. My blood is fair singing at being this close to her. It's the whole blood-bond, but totally ramped up." She stood and came around the table then pulled me to my feet. "And I'll need to deal with it my way." "*Can you swim?*"

Her voice in my head caught me by surprise. "*How'd you know I was a telepath?*"

"*You're a Wincrest, and the one thing I've learnt is our line is highly skilled. You said you had the water skill, so I take it you swim?*"

"*Yes, of course.*"

"*Great, because we're about to take a dip in the river to mask our airstream. I've learnt how to escape Davio when needed. You up for some sisterly bonding without the overabundance of protectors in this room?"*

"*Hell, yes.*" I grinned. "*I just can't 'port.*"

"*I've got you covered. Okay, let's have some fun and ditch this Peacian joint.*"

I was all for that. "*What are you waiting for, sis?*"

She beamed. "*Yes, you are, sister-mine.*" She flashed us from the room.

Chapter 9

Faith teleported us to a river shrouded by nightfall. We sprinted into its depths, Silas and Loveria having followed hot on our heels.

"Dive," she yelled with the tightest grip on my hand. "Davio hates me leaving, in every possible way."

"I'll give us some leeway." I swept my hand behind me and sent a wave of water into Silas and Loveria. It slapped into their chests and pushed them back.

"Wow. Love your water skill. I think we're good to go." She tugged me under and 'ported us.

We arrived on our bellies on damp sand, the surf crashing in. Sticky grains stuck to my palms as I propped myself on my elbows. White froth rolled in and tickled my feet. "Where are we?"

"Papamoa beach. I live close by, in Te Puke."

"Oh, I've not been here before." The moonlight touched the ocean, glittering along its surface.

"This is one of my favorite spots."

On the landside, lights glowed a few hundred feet away in the windows of a restaurant, illuminating diners as they ate. Streetlamps positioned along the driveway of a beachside parking lot showed a square of grass and several deserted picnic tables.

"This place is beautiful." I scooped a handful of sand and opened my fingers, letting the fine white grains slip through. Dralion's beaches were predominantly black and the sand always so hot. "Thank you for bringing me. I can't believe I've finally met you...my sister."

She pulled me into her arms. "It's always been just Mum and me. Now I have a father, a grandfather and all of a sudden, you."

"Wait until you meet Goldie. She's only a year older than us. Did you ever wonder if there were others?"

"Mum never spoke of Dad over the years, and I never asked. On top of that, I had no grandparents or cousins or other family. I've always longed for a sister, which is why Silvie and I have always been close, but no, I never wondered about others. I could never have guessed what's happened in a million years."

"Dad stayed away to protect her."

"I know, and I can't fault him for his decision. But, if he turns up now, he's gonna be in a heck of a lot of trouble." She looked skyward and glared. "You hear that, Dad? Trouble, and a lot of it. So, if you don't mind, get cracking on telling Mum I have a sister, or else."

"You know he does what he wants. Or should I say, what he believes is best."

"Oh, this is in his best interests. He better believe that."

I grinned, stretching my hands to my knees then played my fingers in the surf, which rolled in. "Tell me all about you?" I wanted to know it all, and this was the perfect spot. "Silas said you're studying at high school."

"Exams are in a few months, although I've struggled to focus these past weeks with all that's gone on. What about you? What's in Australia?"

Well, that wasn't enough. Still, she was clearly as eager to hear about me as I was to hear about her. "I'm in the outback, at a place called Wincrest Station. Oh, you have forethought. Take the image from my mind. It's of the stables." I flicked it up.

"Oh yeah, I love this part about my skill." Her brow creased as she concentrated. "I see horses and a corral."

"There're two-hundred breeding mares. We rear stock for Dralion, grazing thirty-five thousand head of cattle. I spend half my time there, as does Goldie. She and I were raised together." The incoming tide splashed over my legs all the way to my waist.

"It's chilly now." Faith jumped out of the water and rubbed her arms.

Joining her, I swept my hands down her body, sending the water away.

"Did you just—gee, that's incredible." She patted her hands over her blouse and skirt. "The fabric's dry."

"It's part of my skill." I dried myself next.

"Wow." She reached out and straightened my hair. "I love your skill. How cool."

I laughed and fixed her hair.

"Hope. You there?"

I darted a look toward the sand dunes. Silas stood at the top of the bank, a hand to his brow as he peered through the dark.

"There they are." Loveria slapped his shoulder as he jerked his head toward us.

"Don't you dare move, Hope," Silas demanded.

With super speed Silas blinked in front of me, so fast the rush of wind rocked me on my feet. "Hey, long time no see."

Faith planted her hands on her hips. "For goodness sake. What is it with these Peacian men?" She let out the loudest sigh. "Me. Woman. Must. Have."

I knocked my shoulder against hers with a giggle. "Surely you were warned about the males within the bond."

"Not nearly enough." She screwed up her face.

Loveria flashed in and caught her against him. "Let's you and me talk. Privately." He tugged her five strides away.

I went to reach for her, but Silas held me at bay. "No, remember Faith will have mind-merged with him and once they're touching skin-to-skin, they're fine. You though, I don't need getting angry." Silas stroked my back. "You didn't have to run. I would have understood if you'd wanted time with her."

Merging, I sank into my spot because it was hard not to when he stood this close. "I don't need your permission to do every little thing."

With a grin, he bent his head and pressed his lips to mine. "I know, but it'd be nice if you did."

I clutched his shirtfront, a very wet one. "My wave of water didn't stop you for long."

"The only reason we searched here, is because it's one of Faith's favorite haunts."

"Let me dry you." Sweeping my hands down his body, I pushed the liquid away.

"Whoa, that's clever."

"It's part of my skill." I smoothed my palm over his cheek. "Won't your sister be mad at you for leaving after she prepared such a lovely meal?"

"You left first."

"Don't put this back on me." Ah, but he did have a point.

"She'll understand, but just in case..." His gaze lifted over my head. "Davio, do you and Faith want to return and pack a basket with some of Silvie's food? I'm not game catching sight of her right now. Tell her I'm sorry, but we'll eat here."

"Sure. You build a fire to keep us warm."

Faith rubbed her hands together. "I love that idea." She looked at me. "We'll be back real soon. Don't go anywhere."

"I won't." Although, I didn't care one bit for her leaving, no matter how long.

Only the two of them shimmered and flashed away, and I stared at where she'd been.

"Hey, what's that on your feet?"

The surf tickled my toes on the tide-line. I lifted my foot, and a shimmery gel coated me from my knees downward. "This is the gel I mentioned when I was in Dralion. It keeps me warm." I stepped out of the water and with one flick of my fingers, the essence slid to the sand.

"Which means you must have been cold." He led me higher onto the sand, gathering pieces of driftwood. "We'll need this for the fire. So, what do you think of Faith?"

"I already miss her." "*Faith.*" I called along our link.

"*I'm here. Do you like marshmallows?*"

"*Yes. I love them.*" I relaxed my shoulders.

"*Have you ever tried marshmallows melted over an open fire and squished between two chocolate cookies? Not everyone has.*"

"*I like chocolate. I like cookies. Marshmallows are a given.*" My mouth watered. "*Please hurry.*"

A giggle resounded in my head. "*We won't be long. Silvie has her own kitchen in the castle and we're just dishing up plates. I'll nab some of my favorite things from her cupboards.*"

As much as I wanted to be alone with Silas, I longed to see her, to know her. "*Tell Silvie I'm sorry.*"

"*Will do.*"

"Are you speaking to Faith?" Silas drew me toward the sandy bank where it was sheltered from the breeze.

"Yes. She won't be long."

He set his armload of firewood on the ground then knelt and scooped a hole in the sand. I settled beside him, removing the husky bark from the largest pieces then dropped them into his pit.

"You two are going to become inseparable. I can see it now." He took a piece of flint from his pocket and struck his dagger to it. Sparks flew and caught on the husks. "Not something I particularly like."

"We have eighteen years to catch up on."

"I know, but when you're gone, I miss you." His admission was soft as he blew the fire carefully to life and laid sticks and wood overtop.

"That's why you followed?" I kissed his cheek.

"Yeah." The fire crackled, glowing bright as the stars twinkled above.

"Show me how much you missed me."

"Always." He grinned and ducked his head to mine.

"Ah-hem."

We turned to see Loveria standing across the other side of the fire holding onto Faith.

She shot a venomous look at Silas. "I didn't want to see that, thank you."

"Then you shouldn't have looked. Talk about nosy."

Oh boy, they were back to bickering. "Ah, people. We can be adults, right?"

"It's okay, Hope. I'll keep her distracted as I can." Loveria tugged Faith in beside him as he sat further away. He was coming in to bat for me? Interesting.

"Thanks, Davio." Silas saluted him.

"No problem." He flipped the lid of the basket he'd brought, removed two covered plates and set one on Faith's lap. "Refrain from throwing that at Silas, love."

She gritted her teeth. "I wouldn't waste Silvie's fabulous food in such a way. Sheesh, I just don't like seeing him touch her, is all."

Silas took the remaining two plates from the basket and passed me a meal and fork. Mm-hmm. Grilled fish in some kind of white sauce flavored the air, and lightly roasted parsnips and buttered cubes of potato sat at the side. My taste buds tripped over themselves in delight.

"Your sister can surely cook." I speared a piece of the fish and dropped it in my mouth. I moaned in delight as it melted over my tongue. "I'm going to have to apologize in person when

I see her.”

“Oh, that is sooo good.” Faith licked her fingers. A smear of white sauce remained at the corner of her lips.

Silas stroked my arm, tickling my skin. “So the way to your devotion is through your stomach?”

“Uh-huh. What about you?”

He scooped up a wedge of roasted parsnip. “I think you have my devotion nailed.”

Faith made a gagging sound. “Where is my knife, Davio?”

Loveria scratched behind his ear. “I only got you a fork. It was a calculated move.”

“Scaredy-cat.”

“Or a very wise cat.”

I smiled as Faith continued to send Silas dirty looks, not so worried now. For some reason her relationship with him was actually amusing me. It was as if they were feuding siblings, neither able to get enough barbs in.

As we ate, the wood sizzled and burned in the fire, orange and yellow flames flickering bright. A small drifting of woodsy smoke rose to permeate the air. Loveria kept Faith close at his side, maintaining their skin-to-skin contact as she needed to ensure their blood didn’t war, yet Loveria still sat five strides from me, keeping his distance which was what I needed.

He was being compassionate and kind, and as long as he continued to care for my sister, I could get along with him. He was making an effort, and so would I.

“What are you thinking?” Silas touched his palm to my cheek then rubbed his fingers gently back and forth until I turned to face him. “You were away somewhere.”

“I-I’m beginning to accept what is.”

“And...”

“That my blood wars with Loveria’s, but I’ll deal with it.” I glanced again at Peacio’s prince. His gaze on my sister was faithful. Constant and committed. It made my stomach churn a little, but I'd get over it.

Faith and I were both mated to Peacians, something I couldn't deny. And for us to have a future, we'd have to consider ways to bring peace between our two nations. How that would happen, I had no idea, but I'd give it a go.

"We'll all deal with it. Together." Silas pulled a packet of marshmallows from the basket along with a metal skewer. Onto the tip, he threaded marshmallows and set it to toast over the fire. The moment they were gooey, he slid them between two chocolate cookies and squished them together. "Want a bite?"

"Yes." I snuck it from his hands, only it was quickly plucked from mine. "Hey." I swiveled around and gaped at Faith.

"Thank you." With a crafty tilt to her eyebrow, she gobbled it down. "Oh yee-ah."

"You little thief."

"Yep, but a content one." She rolled onto her back and kicked up her feet, doing a happy-dance with them.

"Here." Silas passed me another newly made one, and before someone else could steal it, I squeezed the marshmallow until it oozed out with chocolate then took a big bite. I fell back. "Oh boy."

"Can I have another, Silas?" Faith dropped her hand across my chest to reach for one.

"Since you brought the goods, yes."

Giggling, she snatched what he passed her and clunked her cookie against mine. "To some-mores."

"Some-mores?"

"Here we call these some-mores. Don't you want *some more*?"

I laughed. "I get it, and yes I do."

Silas passed me another, and I ate two at one time. I patted my belly when I was done. "I love your beach."

"Me too."

Loveria tossed more driftwood onto the fire. He stoked it and it burned higher. Looking satisfied, he then came around and sat on the other side of Faith. He took her hand and rolled her into his side. The two of them quietly spoke.

Silas threaded his fingers through mine, and tugged me to face him. "You doing okay?"

"More than okay." I leaned into his ear. "Meeting her feels unreal. I can't lose her. Not now I finally know her."

"It's real."

"No, I mean I don't want to wake in the morning and find out this has all been a dream. Or for someone to take her away from me."

"I get it." He pressed his lips to my forehead. "She spends a lot of nights at the castle. Davio's rooms are two floors above ours."

"Ours?" I smiled. "You're calling your room *ours*?"

"Your place is with me." Another kiss, this one on the tip of my nose.

"Half the time."

"I would take more if you gave it."

"You can't have it."

"Please." His lips brushed mine.

"Silas."

He stole in and nibbled at my neck. "You taste delicious."

"What am I going to do with you?" I cupped his face and returned his gaze to mine.

"Whatever you wish. Right now, I'm having the most sinful thoughts."

Goosebumps raced across my flesh. "Maybe you need some time out."

His gaze heated, exponentially. "I don't doubt it. Say goodnight to your sister. It's late and I know how you like to be up at the crack of dawn."

"I don't want to say goodnight to her." I let out a slow

breath. "Ask anything else, but that."

"No, it's bedtime." He pinched my butt.

"Ouch. Talk about bossy."

"Have I mastered it yet?" He pulled me to my feet as he rose.

"Not by a long way."

"Ha. Now who's lying?"

I faced Faith, who'd stood as we had. "Apparently, I've got a curfew."

"It's okay. I've gotta be up early in the morning too. We'll catch up then." She hugged me.

"This has been the most amazing day."

"For me too. Sweet dreams, sis."

"'Night everyone." Silas flashed us to his dressing room with no further warning.

I sagged against his dresser. "Where do I find some pajamas?"

"I folded your things into the top three drawers right behind you."

"Okay, out of here so I can change."

"You got it. I'll meet you in bed." He walked from the room and closed the door quietly behind him.

In the drawers, I found what I was after and pulled out a pair of sleep shorts in cherry red and a white tank top then changed.

When I came out, Silas was propped up in bed. I merged my mind with his as I tossed the covers to one side. Whoa. I searched for a breath as I stared at this low slung pajama bottoms.

It was expected, but still. He'd never once slept like this. He'd always worn clothes.

"You sleep here." He tugged me in.

"So much has happened so fast between us."

Flicking off the light and plunging the room into darkness,

he said, "We're together. It doesn't matter how that happened."

I wriggled to face him in the dark. "What are your plans for tomorrow?" The barest sliver of moonlight from a gap in the curtains illuminated his strong jaw and high cheekbones.

"Work, but I have training first thing in the morning. I've let it ride lately."

"Where are you working afterward?"

"Sunider. It's one of the villages on our desert border with No-Man's Land. Davio's put teams of protectors there since our trip of discovery to the Sol compound. We've neglected that area, and if we hadn't, we may have learned of Elizara's tribe sooner."

"Later in the week I'm going to the Sol compound to begin documentation."

He stroked my head, playing his fingers through my hair. "I'll come when you do."

"I have to finish filling the watering holes first. I've only completed half, and no doubt, they've begun to dry again. Maslin will want all of them done."

"I do not like him."

"You don't have to."

"Sol sits in the wings waiting for you. He's being patient in his desires. I see it."

I skipped one finger down the center of his chest. Such deliciously hot skin.

"Hope, are you paying attention?"

"Nope." I stroked down his sides and he shivered.

"Sol's always in your vicinity. I don't care for it."

"Do you truly want to talk about Maslin right now?" I rubbed my cheek against his.

"Yes. I want you to keep a certain distance from him."

"Not possible. You do realize we're in bed, right? Why isn't your mouth on mine?"

He tipped up my chin. "I need your agreement."

"Sure, kissing's a great idea. I totally agree."

"Not kissing. Sol. We're talking about two different things."

"Kiss me, and then we won't be."

His forearm muscles bunched as he wrapped his arms around me. "You are my mate."

"Uh-huh, and a mate who wishes to be kissed."

"You are merged and I'm near addicted to it."

"I do it because I need it, and you like it." I spread my mind deeper into his.

"I'd like it more if you kept your distance from Sol."

"We are alone, and you keep talking about another man. Tut-tut." I pushed him onto his back. "I want your kisses before I go to sleep. I have much to teach you about meeting my needs." I dropped my mouth to his, and got bossy, until he no longer considered speaking an option. Wonderful. A silent Silas was a perfect Silas.

Chapter 10

"Are you awake, Hope?"

Faith's voice swam inside my head. I pushed myself up to my elbows and squinted through the dark toward the heavy drape of Silas's curtains. A trickle of light peeked through. *"I am. Just."* I turned back the covers and peered at my mate as he remained asleep.

"I had to hear your voice. I'm finishing my morning run, and then I'm coming to collect you."

"You are?"

"Yep, I've got a study day, which means I'm skipping school so you can show me the outback. I want to meet Goldie."

Taking care not to disturb Silas, I slid my feet to the floor and curled my toes into the plush carpet. *"I'll dress. Give me a couple of minutes."* After sneaking a pair of low-rise blue jeans and a berry-red V-neck shirt from the dressing room, I then tiptoed to the bathroom and shut the door.

I dressed and brushed my hair. What a mess. I detangled the nightly knots and pulled my hair into a ponytail.

After slipping back to Silas, I knelt on the floor beside him. His cheek was pressed to his pillow and he breathed ever so quietly. I gazed at his closed eyelids, at the long sweep of golden eyelashes touched with a hint of red. The stubble on his jaw was the same light color, but looked incredibly sharp. I smiled at the memory of shaving him. So much had happened since that time. I'd found Elizara Sol and my water skill had come in. Now I had my sister, and I would never let her go. I kissed his cheek then nibbled to the corner of his mouth. My soul was bound to his, an unbreakable tie no one could pull apart.

"Hope, Davio's asleep. Do you want to sneak out? I've found that's best. You ready?"

"Silas is usually my ride home." My gaze wandered over his face. Every moment I had with him was precious.

"Now you have me too. Whenever you call, I'll come. Within an instant. I know where his rooms are and I'll wait outside. Nice and quiet now."

"On my way." I let out a slow breath as I eased back and stood. If I dallied, it would slow my day. And taking me home wasn't Silas's favorite thing to do. He generally grumbled and would no doubt raise the issue of Maslin again.

Having snuck to the door, I turned the knob, and then slid through the small gap. Faith was there wearing navy three-quarter Nike pants and a blue sports top with white stripes down the sides. Like me, her hair was drawn into a ponytail.

She held a finger to her lips. "Should I use the image of the stables you've already given me?"

"Yes, Goldie's usually there at daybreak. That'd be perfect." My mind-merge slipped from Silas's as we tiptoed further away. I rubbed my head.

Faith's brow shot upward. "Forewarning. He's about to wake." She 'ported us.

As we flashed in at the station, the sunshine near blinded me. Another scorcher of a day awaited.

"Whoa, it's hot." Faith darted a look about. "Where's the grass?"

"We don't have much here, but the lower fields along the river where we graze the cattle are green. Let me give you the image." I pulled it up.

"Oh." Her violet eyes brightened. "That's so much better." Turning to face the homestead on the hill, she lifted a hand to her brow. "Nice digs. Which room is yours?"

I gave her the visual, and then one of the room next to mine. "If you want to stay, this one is yours. It leads onto the same balcony as mine." It was almost a mirror image.

"Fabulous. I love the New Zealand rimu by the way. It'll feel like home away from home. Except that I'm collecting a few of those. I have a room in Dralion, one near school, and now there's Davio's. Sometimes I don't know where I'm sleeping."

"Well, if you don't know what you're wearing either then just raid my wardrobe or Goldie's. We're the same size."

"Thanks." She nudged my shoulder with hers. "If you're here, then I'll stay. I want to know my sister. We have eighteen years to catch up on."

I couldn't hold back from giving her a hug. She smelt like fresh air and violets, and she squeezed me in return.

"Hell, where are you, Hope? I wake up and you're gone."

"Good morning, Mr. Sleepyhead. I'm with Faith. We're bonding, so stay away."

"I'd rather you bond with me."

"I know you would. Go to work."

"You'll return tonight, right?"

"Yes."

A loud mental sigh. *"If you don't, you're in trouble."*

I closed the link and smiled. He was so predictable.

I took Faith's hand and pulled her toward the stables, my favorite place in the world. "Do you like horses?"

One grating cough came from Faith. "I've never ridden a horse in my life."

"What? You're missing out on so much."

"I'm not a horsey person, but Mum is. Don't forget I can zip-zap here and there, which means I'm going with teleportation over a sore butt in the saddle any day."

"Hope, is that you?" Goldie's voice traveled from the interior of the stables. "Maslin's looking for you."

I skipped through the wide open doors. Goldie was halfway up the stack of hay bales on one side. It was a small supply, just for the stalls, but quite high. She reached for the top bale, grabbed it by the ties and tossed it. It rolled and bounced to the ground, kicking up a plume of dust as it came to a stop in the center of the room.

"Goldie." I coughed and wet my lips as a surge of thirst hit me. "I brought Faith with me. My sister."

"You brought—" She pivoted, clapping a hand to her mouth, her gaze riveted on Faith. "Oh my. You brought—" She dropped to her butt, and then bumped from one baled platform to the next and landed with a jolt and "oomph" on the last level. On her feet, she engulfed Faith in her arms. "Welcome to the family."

The blood-bond would surge between them, and the familial Wincrest ties would bind strongly.

Faith held onto Goldie, her shoulders shaking. "I don't know what to say. I have an aunt."

Goldie hugged her hard then pulled back. "If you're feeling overwhelmed, so am I."

"Who's—" Maslin halted in the doorway, his gaze darting from Faith to me. "Wow." He removed his Stetson and thumped it against his legs. "Well, I never…so alike."

"Maslin, come meet my sister." I waved him forward then rubbed at my throat. I was parched.

He extended his hand to Faith and she shook it. "Nice to meet the mysterious Faith Wincrest."

"Mysterious no more." She smiled. "Nice meeting you."

Maslin glanced at me. "You've been waiting for this. How are you feeling?"

"Incredible. Like my heart wants to soar from my chest." I pressed my closed hand to it, my gaze returning to Faith's.

"Maslin knows all about us and the protectors. He's also distantly related to you and me through the Sol family line."

"You mean through Elizara?"

"Yes." I wet my lips, my thirst having increased. "They're all part of the same tribe."

Maslin nodded his head toward Faith. "Elizara will want to meet you. She won't wish to wait."

She lifted onto her toes and jiggled about. "Neither do I. Could we go now?"

"Whenever you'd like." He looked to Goldie. "Does now suit you?"

"Absolutely." Her cheeks puffed out as she bubbled with excitement.

Faith snagged my hands and twirled me around. Goldie laughed and joined us. Maslin linked in and grinned. "Ladies, Elizara's it is," he said.

I held my breath. I couldn't be any happier. My sister and Goldie had met, and now we were going to see Elizara.

Travelling through the dark took no time at all, and then we were there and my feet sank into the orange desert sands of No-Man's Land. Next to us, the bright yellow of Elizara's canvas awning rippled in the breeze.

Faith rubbed her chest, looking about in all directions. "My heart's beating so fast."

"Me too."

Maslin lifted the flap and called out to Elizara. "I've brought visitors. Both your nieces."

A squeal sounded from inside. There'd be no more waiting. In the past twenty-four hours, my life had taken on new meaning. This was all too much. My mouth dried completely out.

"My nieces." Elizara erupted from the tent in a blur of white, almost knocking us all to the ground. "Look at you." She cupped my face, and then Faith's. "Both of you. Welcome." A beaming smile for Goldie and Maslin. "We have so much to speak about. Come inside."

Maslin lifted the flap higher as Elizara yanked Faith in and Goldie laughed as she followed. I stood, grinning as sheer pleasure coursed through me.

"You need to go in, Hope." Maslin still held the flap.

"I feel too happy." I tapped my dry throat. "I've never imagined such bliss." I coughed and thumped my chest and wheezed. Oh, so thirsty.

"When was the last time you drank?"

"Yesterday afternoon, no, morning. I've got to drink. It feels like all the moisture is draining right out of the air."

"Those with the water skill can't go without it for any long length of time. It's worse for us than any other. You must drink constantly throughout the day."

My sight dimmed to one singular pinprick of light, and I swayed.

"I've got you." His arms came around me.

"*Hope?*" Silas's muffled voice resounded in my head. "*I can feel your accelerated heartbeat. What's going on? Where are you?*"

So much heat.

It blazed through me, like fire, singing my throat.

"Water," I croaked to Maslin as my entire world spun. Then nothing. Darkness enveloped me.

* * * *

"I didn't have forewarning. She has to be all right." Faith's voice echoed inside my head.

"Those with the water skill must drink water continuously." Liquid dribbled into my mouth and down my throat. "Nice and slow, Hope."

I dragged my eyelids open. Maslin held a cup to my lips and my head to his shoulder.

Elizara stroked my arm. "Maslin will take you to the oasis.

You'll need skin-to-skin replenishment for full recharging."

I gulped the water, desperate to get more.

"You had me so worried." Goldie squeezed my hand.

Faith had the other. "You have to drink. All the time. Elizara and Maslin said so."

"I'll take her now. We won't be long." Maslin set the cup down.

"Go quickly," Elizara urged.

Dark replaced the brightness of her tent as he 'ported us. At the edge of the oasis, he removed my boots then carried me in until the blessed water rose over my hips and to my chest. I swam free and dunked to my shoulders.

I shuddered with need, pushing my hands through the water and spreading my fingers out. The water swirled like liquid silk, a lavish sensation I wanted to curl into and be absorbed by. I kicked away, diving and tumbling below the surface, desperate for more.

As I came up, I slicked my hair back and treaded water. "This is perfect."

"Water is your lifeline." Maslin swam beside me.

"*Where are you? I've searched your bedroom and you're not there.*"

Silas's voice pounded down our link.

"*I'm swimming. I'm fine.*"

He sighed, almighty loud. "*What aren't you telling me? I couldn't get through to you and you weren't blocking. It's like you blacked out.*"

"*I did. Apparently, I can't go without drinking water.*"

"*You lost consciousness because you didn't drink?*" His tone was incredulous.

Swirling his hands through the water as he treaded, Maslin said, "Carver?"

"Uh-huh." "*I'm fine now, Silas, and you shouldn't worry. I have to return to Faith and Goldie.*"

"No more blacking out or I'll chain you to my bed so you can never sneak away again."

"I'd like to see you try. Later." I laughed.

Maslin eyed me. "He cares for you, but that doesn't mean your soul-bound match is a good one. I'm here if you need me. I have sworn my allegiance to the Wincrest family, and to the people of Dralion, and I swear it personally to you. Whatever you need, I will give."

His words were a deep promise, one that touched my heart.

I blinked, barely holding back tears. "You're my friend."

"That's a good start." He dove with a grin, his feet coming up into the air before he disappeared below the water's surface.

Palm tree fronds rustled in the breeze. Maslin tugged on my leg, and yanked me under.

Chapter 11

Sitting on the end of Faith's bed in Dralion late that afternoon, I was not surprised to see she'd been given the bedroom next to mine on the third floor of Dad's wing. Faith had snuck me in after we'd left the Sol compound. She'd 'ported us both after promising me she'd see any problems with her forethought, and that our mother was elsewhere and wouldn't spot us. It was just us. Goldie and Maslin had returned to the station.

"How does this look? We're twins. We should at least dress alike occasionally since we missed out as kids." She wandered to the freestanding full-length oval mirror and turned side to side in front of it. Her blond hair swung around her shoulders. Even the long length of our hair was the same, and now with her dressed as I was in a pair of white shorts and tank top, no one would likely tell us apart.

"I have a feeling your motives for dressing the same run deeper than that." Pressing my hands to her violet silk bedspread, I pushed myself up, and joined her. "What's ticking through that mind of yours, my tricky sister?"

"A plan of intrigue. You took me to meet Goldie and Elizara. Now it's my turn to bring you to Mum. That's my plan, and I'm sticking to it. Sorry for the subterfuge." She sidled closer. "Now, spill on what's going on with you and Maslin?

He's most attentive. I was surprised."

"He's a warrior and family. We're linked through our Sol line."

She slowly stroked her jaw. "I felt a touch of the blood-bond with him too. What about Silas?"

"Silas and I are soul-bound. I never want to be separated from him."

"I understand. I can't survive without Davio, mind-merge skill or not."

I blew out a breath. "As much I want Silas, I still understand the danger which lurks with him being a protector. At this moment, those warriors who know of our relationship protect me by keeping my secret, as they will with you. But that doesn't change the fact our countries are at war."

She squeezed her eyes shut, and then opened them. "Why can't our lives be easy? We need to think of our future. We have to find a way to bring peace between our nations."

"I've thought the same, but we have one major obstacle ahead of us. Donaldo. He'll never tolerate us being mated with Peacians, let alone protectors. Dad only does because he reveres the bond and wouldn't take from us what Donaldo took from him." Rubbing my arms, I stared out the window. "We have each other, and we'll work on the rest, but it will take time."

"I'll keep a watch with my forethought. Perhaps I'll see something in our future which may help." She dabbed the corners of her eyes. "Which reminds me, I used my forethought when Elizara showed me the album and the portraits of Katerin and Nathwer. I tried to get a fix on them."

"And..."

"Nothing. I know we don't physically age, but is there a possibility they could've altered their appearance in some way?"

"If they disguised themselves, maybe, but I can't imagine why they'd think to do that. Katerin was banished and the sentence had already been handed down."

"So, if there's no reason for a disguise then it doesn't look good. I doubt they live."

"I'd hoped…" I dragged in a deep breath.

"Hey." Faith touched my quivering chin. "I keep making you sad. I never look this down and Mum will notice."

"I can't meet her."

"Oh yes, you can." She slung an arm over my shoulder.

"Is there any way I can change your mind?"

"Huh, hardly. You'll come to learn that fairly soon."

I groaned. "What's your plan?"

"You're going to spend some time with Mum, and I'll be there."

"Girls."

We swung around as Dad strode into the room. Dressed in a midnight silk shirt and black pants, the colors enhanced the equally dark look on his face. "This isn't going to happen. You're not meeting your mother, Hope."

"Why?" Faith edged in front of me. "I know you delayed my meeting with Hope because you saw I'd tell Mum about her. Well, too bad. Mum has to know."

"Do I need to repeat myself?" His gaze flicked between the two of us and his frown deepened. "Hell." He stared, then his chest heaved and he dragged us both to him. "You two are finally together. I've been watching with my forethought, but being—look at you."

Faith wrinkled her nose. "Aw, c'mon, Dad. We're eighteen." She speared me a look. "Hope, please, we should be able to work out some kind of guilty parental angle with this. What you got?"

"I don't know. I've always done what he's said."

He huffed, continuing to squish us. "I can hear you both."

Faith nodded at me. "We could ignore him and just go with my plan. That would work."

"I'm still listening," he growled.

"I will if you will," I added, going for it.

"No one's will but mine will be obeyed." He released us and paced the room. "I don't know what to do. Every time I run a scenario, my forewarning blares with the same problem. Kate finds out she had a child she's never met, and no matter that you died, Hope, she sees her actions as no different than her own mother's. It destroys her to know she gave her own child away and never acknowledged you. Not even to Faith. She didn't grieve. She blocked you from her mind, which includes your birth, your death. It all."

"I didn't die."

"It doesn't matter. After she finds she struck you from her heart, it tears her apart. I can't see that happen."

"I want to meet my mother. Even under the ruse of acting as Faith. What about that scenario?"

He halted his pacing and tapped one foot on the polished wooden flooring. "I've never thought to work that angle."

"We should." Faith closed her eyes. "Found her. She's outside with Jilly. She looks like she's about to go riding."

Dad crossed to the glass doors overlooking the balcony and peered toward the stables. "Kate and I were about to head out when I had forewarning about you two. She enjoys riding."

Faith gripped my arm. "Good. So does Hope. She's going to join Mum and you...as me." Without warning, everything darkened and Faith and I arrived inside a clean stall, the scent of the hay strong in the air and the ladies' voices close by. Faith tugged me to my knees behind the half-height door.

Dad flashed in beside us and hunkered down. "I'll pull you out, Hope, if anything goes wrong." His whispered warning was clear, as was the grave look on his face. "I will not allow your mother to have a breakdown."

"Of course you won't." Faith peeked over the top of the swing door. "How about you guys just go saddle a thingy and stop over-analyzing everything."

"A thingy? You mean a horse?"

She gave me a snide look. "Don't be a smarty pants. A thingy, a horse. Who cares."

"First"—Dad urged her down—"I cannot believe I'm hiding out like this. Second, you stay here. Hope and I will go."

He took my hand and flashed us outside. "Wait here." He strode away and asked the lad who held the reins of the two horses to ready another. "Kate, our daughter is coming along with us."

Oh my goodness. My heart fluttered within my chest. My mother was maybe ten feet away, a horse the only obstacle between us.

"Don't be silly. Faith's not ridden before. She doesn't care for horses."

"She's gotten over it. Rather quickly."

I looked upward, my heartbeat racing as streaky white clouds hazed the sky. I never wanted to forget this moment.

"Hope, I swear this heart alignment is making me crazy. What are doing, now?"

"I'm in Dralion."

One loud snort. *"I'm buying handcuffs before this day is out."*

"I'm about to meet my mother, but as Faith. A twin-swap thing."

"Right." Several seconds of silence passed. *"I want to see you the moment you're free. I'm still in Sunider, but I can return in an instant."*

"I'm so nervous."

"You can do this."

His solemn words reassured me, and I closed our link and rolled my shoulders.

"Hey." Faith's voice in my head. *"Pay attention. She's coming."*

"Faith? Where are you?" Kate rounded the horse,

smoothing over the animal's sleek rump with a hand.

I stared, and my heart thumped like thunder.

My mother.

Blond streaks shone through her long chestnut-brown hair. Her eyes were the prettiest shade of brown, her skin smooth, just like that of our people.

"Faith." She snapped her fingers in front of me. "Honey, what's wrong?"

Her lips moved. Oh boy, my mother spoke to me. For the first time.

I wobbled and she propped a hand under my elbow. "Are you all right?"

"I'm nervous."

"I'll be here to help you." She turned and took the reins from the stable hand as he arrived with my ride. "Hop up, and you'll be fine. I'll go slow for you."

I propped my foot in the shiny silver stirrup and swung up. I could do this.

Dad set an arm around her waist. "Faith will be fine. She's a fast learner." His smile was tight. "But not too fast."

Faith moaned. *"You hear that? Not too fast."*

"Let's go," Dad called out as he mounted.

I snapped the mare's reins and followed the gravel drive to the main gates.

"Slow down. And slouch. Some fumbling with those long leather things would be good."

"They're called reins, Faith."

I nudged the horse's flanks and trotted in alongside Mum. Dad was two lengths ahead and he veered slightly to the left, taking the forest path.

Pine trees grew tall and strong either side as we entered the thick tree line. Above the sun was masked by the canopy, but the ocean and its rhythmic crashing reached me on the breeze.

"Look at you." My mother chuckled, looking quite amused.

"Like a duck to water."

"Like you wouldn't believe." I licked my lips, finding them dry. Gosh, I had to remember water was now a necessity, something I had to drink every few hours. "This duck needs a drink."

I lifted the leather flap on the saddlebag and withdrew a water flask from the supplies which were always well stocked for rides. I took a long swallow.

"How did school go today?"

"School? Oh, it was a study day." "*Dad, did you tell Mum about Elizara? You said you would.*"

"*I did. She's aware we sent a team of warriors to the Sol compound for information. I told her what was discovered, only not by whom. Remember, she is spellbound to Dralion and cannot leave to visit them.*"

"And..." my mother continued.

"I visited No-Man's Land. I met Elizara Sol."

"You did? What's she like?"

"The best. I met Dad's sister too. Goldie took me to the compound."

"She's in the outback, right? Alexo mentioned her to us a while ago." Reaching across the small gap between our horses, she squeezed my arm. "Tell me about her and Elizara. Everything."

I smiled, because I wanted to speak of this so desperately. "Elizara has the water skill. It's amazing to see what she can do."

"Alexo briefed me on it. He said one of his family members was going to document what she'd discovered. The skill flows through the Sol family line and could turn up within any future children we have."

"That's right." I glanced ahead to where he rode. "Did he mention more information has come to hand on mind-merge?"

"No, and I only want to hear it if it's good news. I'm so sick of the bad stuff. Like death. Ugh."

"It's all good. I've discovered if both within the mated bond have a telepathic link, the one with mind-merge can use it to draw the merge along. It removes the whole three-day death sentence."

"What?" Her horse shifted at her high tone and she patted his neck. "Sorry, but you're a telepathic. Can you merge along this link?"

I wanted to say yes for myself and Silas, but Faith couldn't with Loveria. "Um, no. I don't have a link with him. Warring blood and all."

"*Tell her Davio and I won't stop trying.*" Faith's words rung clear.

"I won't stop trying, Mum." My spirits lifted as I called her Mum for the first time. "Mum. Mum. Mum." I just had to repeat it.

"Y-e-s?" She scrunched her brow up. "Something wrong?"

"Nothing. You just have the best name in the world."

She laughed. "Thanks, honey. I can't wait until I have more little lunatics like you."

"*Ew.*" Faith griped. "*I didn't want to hear that.*"

"How many lunatics do you want, Mum?"

"*No. Don't go there.*"

"Because I'd like a sister for sure."

"*You're in dangerous territory, sis.*"

"Actually scrub that. I'd like a brother instead."

"*Shut up.*"

"*You shut up.*"

"You look a little flushed, Faith."

"I'm fine. Amazing, actually."

Releasing a soft breath, she lifted her face to the sky. "Me too." Sunlight sprinkled through the thinning canopy. We were close to where the trail meandered toward the black granite cliffs. "I can't put my finger on why, but for some reason I feel...complete."

"You do?"

She touched a hand to her chest. "There's always been an emptiness in my heart I've never been able to explain, but right now, it's strangely gone. It's like I have everything I've ever wanted."

I drew in a slow breath. "I feel the same way."

"I have an idea. How about we do some girly stuff after this? It's been ages since we have."

It was the best idea I'd ever heard. And my yes couldn't come fast enough.

* * * *

The next evening, I stood thirty feet from Dralion's magnificent cliff face. The setting sun dipped on the horizon, the last rays of the day touching the ocean's rippling blue surface. Another beautiful day had passed with my mother, my second one.

Faith had watched me with her forethought from close by. I'd told Mum more of Goldie and the outback and Elizara Sol. We'd painted our nails and gone for another ride. Now though, she dressed for dinner, a family meal. So simple, yet I couldn't wait for it.

"Faith has just turned up. Where are you?"

Silas's low growl rumbled around in my head. Faith had not left in the two days we'd been here, but with her head pounding these past few hours, I'd insisted she leave and mind-merge with Loveria.

"I told you I wasn't coming."

"I'll send her back to get you in five."

I rubbed my head, at the ache that had settled between my eyes the same time Faith's had. *"I'll merge now, from here."* Finding the beaded end of the telepathic link, I sent my mind along its golden threaded path, merged and sank into Silas's mind as quickly as I could.

Rocking onto my heels, I squeezed my arms. It was bliss,

and yet of a torturous kind. I wanted to go to him, but couldn't. I wasn't leaving here, not when I wanted to be around my mother for as long as I could.

Footfalls sounded from behind, and I turned. Mum crossed to me in a dark chocolate-brown dress with thin straps over her shoulders. The lower flared folds rippled with milkier tones and skimmed her ankles.

"I saw you from the window." She wrapped an arm around my shoulders, staring out to sea as I did. "I'll never get used to this sight. I often come down and stand here as you are."

Leaning into her, my heart melted. "I wanted to tell you how wonderful these last couple of days have been, Mum."

She arched an eyebrow. "Something is different about you. You're more introspective. Has something happened you need to speak of?"

Yes, because I'd so had enough of Mum not knowing the real me. I'd told her all about Goldie and Elizara, but never me.

How I wished...

Now, why not take the plunge and tell her who I was? Perhaps the right time would never come, in Dad's eyes.

I breathed deep. "Mum, I want you in my life. I want you to know me, the daughter who died." I lifted the lower edge of my cream blouse and exposed my childhood scar. "I've been told Faith had surgery at birth, but so did I."

Her forehead wrinkled. "Honey, what are you talking about? I only have one..." She dragged in a shaky breath. "You have to be Faith."

I grasped her trembling hands. "My name is Hope. I'm Faith's twin."

"No. No. Don't do this."

"You sense something different about me. I know it."

"There isn't another." Her gaze pleaded with me to stop.

"Why is there no other?" The knowledge had to be there. Buried deep, but surely still there.

With a slow shake of her head, she moaned low in her throat. "I would never abandon a child of mine. The other baby never survived. Have you *seen* something, because I can explain. I remember some words the doctor said."

"I am the child who didn't survive. You don't have to explain anything to me." I kept my tone as gentle as possible.

"How—" Thumping her chest, she struggled for breath then her knees buckled.

I grabbed her as she fell and lowered her carefully to the ground, not letting her go.

Dad appeared and knelt beside us. "She fainted. I'll take her."

"No." I clutched her tighter. "She remembered something."

"Are you sure?"

"Yes." I withdrew from Silas's mind, having held onto the connection through it all. "*Tell Faith to return. Immediately.*"

"*She's right here in the rec room with Davio and me. What's happened?*"

I stroked Mum's forehead. "*My mother knows the truth about me.*"

"*Hell.*" He was gone for a moment, back the next. "*Faith said she didn't have any forewarning. She said to hold tight.*" His words registered and I frowned at Dad. "Did you have forewarning of what I would do?"

"No. I was watching you two from the window above and saw her faint."

"Oh my goodness. No forewarning? What does that mean?"

He held up his hands. "I don't know, honey. Perhaps this was the right time."

Mum stirred then blinked. Her dazed gaze cleared and traveled over me. So wary. "Who are you?"

"Hope. I grew up here, in Dralion." Below, the surf crashed into the rocky cliff-face and a light mist sprayed over us. I flicked out my hand, directing the finest droplets to me. They shimmered and revolved in the air, forming one perfect drop, which I lowered into my hand.

She peeked at my palm, her eyebrows pulling down. "How did you do that?"

"Unlike Faith, I have a different skill set. I can manipulate water. Hold out your hand." She did, and I tipped the drop into hers.

"Oh my. It's real." She wrapped her fingers around it and looked into my eyes. "Faith can't manipulate water."

"You believe me? That I'm not Faith?" I had to make sure, to hear her say yes. I couldn't breathe.

She nodded, slowly but surely. "I do recall the doctor saying the other child's body couldn't be found. Those words have always haunted me, no matter how deep I tried to bury them."

Dad gripped her hand. "Hope died at birth, Kate. She couldn't be found because I brought her home to bury her here, but the act of teleportation kick-started her heart. She was a sick child, but our healers cured her."

Faith wavered into sight and dashed to us then dropped to the damp ground and hugged Mum. "I'm gone for half an hour and look what happens. You meet my sister and I missed it."

"I'm so sorry. When did you two—"

"The day before you did. It was Hope on the horse. We swapped places."

"Oh." Her eyes alighted on me then misted. "That's when I felt complete, like a part of me was back." She reached out and caught me to her, her tears falling. "The time of your birth is a blur because of the meds I was on. Then Alexo was gone and no one could find him. I was depressed for so long, and the pain in my soul was almost too much to bear. I remember a detective who came. He said something like what the doctor had, about a child's body being missing. I just couldn't listen. I at least had Faith, and I never let her go. She's what kept me sane in those days."

Dad edged closer, tightening our bound circle as he wrapped his arms around us all. "We are a family now. That's all that matters."

Faith rubbed her cheek against mine, wet from her tears, or were they mine? I wasn't sure. We all cried.

Chapter 12

"This area surprised me when I first saw it." Mum sat at the side of the indoor palace pool in black cotton pants rolled to her knees, swishing her feet through the clear water. Her gaze remained solidly on mine, where I treaded in the deep. She'd barely let me out of her sight in the days since the cliff.

"Donaldo likes the conveniences of Earth." The pool was three lanes wide and seventy-five feet long, a luxury he'd had installed on the ground floor some years ago. "With my water skill, I'm rather grateful now."

Faith splashed in from finishing a lap and heaved herself in beside Mum at the edge of the pool. Water sluiced down her red one-piece swimsuit as she grabbed in air. "I'm exhausted."

"You look like a drowned rat." Mum grinned at her then returned her gaze to me. "But you, honey, look as fresh as a daisy, no matter that you've been in the water for hours on end. I wonder if you're close to your rising. You have so much energy. It's almost boundless."

Faith propped her hands behind her as she leaned back. "I loved having three-times the energy. What a hit that was." She eyed me. "And Mum's right. We can't get you out of the water."

I kicked away on my back, scooping water at my sides. "I'm not coming out now either."

Standing, she snatched a fluffy white towel from the

wooden slatted bench and wrapped it around her waist. "Where'd Dad go?"

"To a debriefing with the leading eight. Killian collected him and said to say hi to you."

She sagged over. "Please tell me you're lying. I wish he'd wear a shirt. Have you seen the fire-breathing dragon tattoos he has all over his chest and arms? And what's with that metal mallet he's always holding? It looks like something right out of a Thor movie. And the blood. Ew. I swear all I can smell on him is blood."

"I think he likes you." Mum laughed as Faith pinched her nose and did a dramatic roll of her eyes.

"What's wrong with Killian?" I asked her. "He's quite the catch. He commands one of his own fighting teams."

"Hello. Taken." Still rolling her eyes.

I chuckled. "Right. Maybe we should hook Goldie up on a date with—"

"Oh, that reminds me." Mum jumped to her feet. "When do I get to meet Goldie?"

Faith rubbed her temple and squished up her nose. She appeared in pain. "Ask Dad. He can have her here in a jiffy, if you want."

"Are you all right?" Mum tipped up her chin and looked in her eyes. "You need to mind-merge, don't you?"

"How'd ya guess?" Faith glanced at me. "What about you? You merged with nuisance?"

"I am. He wouldn't stop complaining in my head, so I merged instead." A spurt of energy thrummed through my veins. "Hold on. Gotta swim for a bit."

Kicking out, I powered through the water. I missed Silas. So badly.

Releasing the merge, I freed our link. *"Hey."*

"About damn time." His voice bounded through. *"I've been wanting to speak to you for hours."*

"I'm swimming."

"Hope, I need to see you. It's been days."

"I've been getting to know my mum."

"You know I understand, but it's late. That means bedtime. My bed."

I was parched and swam to the side of the pool to grab my water flask. I guzzled half the bottle down.

"You're not answering me."

"Just drinking. I've missed you too, but I can't be everywhere." I dunked my head under the water and came up again. *"Oooh. My hair is dripping down my back and it feels so good."*

"Do I need to buy a water bed to entice you home?"

I laughed, and then promptly stopped. *"Oh my. Is that even possible? I'm definitely coming if it is."*

"I should be able to pick one up from somewhere on Earth. How are your energy levels?"

Last time I'd checked in with him, I'd told him they were increasing. *"Everyone says they've noticed the upward spike."*

"I want to see you before your rising, and it sounds as if you're close." He knew I would stay here for it. That was already decided. One needed family, those closest to them to aid in expending the excess energy until the closing moment when the accumulation of skills peaked and one completely collapsed. That draining was intense and took hours to recover from. One was limbless.

"Come see me now." His tone held longing. *"I'll take you swimming."*

"I'm already swimming."

"Not with me, you're not."

"You are incredibly observant."

"I swear, Faith's snarky attitude is rubbing off on you." The loudest sigh came from him. *"I'm exhausted, and I can't sleep without you."*

My mother picked up my empty water flask. "I'll fill this up. If you have to go to your mate as Faith does, I understand."

"Out of there." Faith tossed me a towel. "I've just checked with my forethought, and Davio and Silas appear a pitiful mess. Let's give them a break."

"But I need to swim."

"No problem. I'll take you to Papamoa beach. The boys can come." She hugged Mum. "Tell Dad we'll see him tomorrow."

I eased out of the pool and wrapped the towel around my waist. Peeking back at the water, I dipped my toe in it.

"No, you don't." Faith grabbed me and between one second and the next, we were gone, flashing through the dome room.

We arrived in the warmth of Loveria's rec room, and ten feet away, Silas and he lay crashed out on two of the white leather couches. Both wore their training leathers and light colored shirts soaked through with sweat. Their swords hung from their limp hands, the pointy tips brushing the thick carpet.

"Did you two kill each other?" Faith stepped toward them.

"You're back." Loveria launched to his feet and swung Faith in a circle. "Hey, Silas, you have a visitor."

"I do?" Silas's sword clattered to the ground as he rolled off the couch and stared at me. Then he was no longer there. He 'ported the ten feet then wrapped his arms around me like bands of steel. "Are you real?"

Cupping his face in my hands, I grinned. "Kiss me and find out."

Pushing me against the wall at my back, he did, or devoured was more like it.

I couldn't think straight, and in that instant I didn't care. I wanted him and only him.

Oh sweet heaven. More.

"We need privacy." I clutched his shirtfront, my world spinning. "Bedroom. Now."

"Whoa." Faith was there, shoving us apart. "I heard that.

Don't forget your rising is close. That means hormone levels are raging just as strength levels do." She glared at Silas, and then at me. "You two can't be allowed this up close and personal. I remember that from my own rising."

I tried to push her away. "Let go of me. I want him." The need was strong now he was within my sight.

She tilted her head toward Loveria and he was there. He grabbed Silas from behind and yanked him away.

Silas jerked one arm free. "Davio, she's been gone for days."

"I have to keep you two separated. If you give into Hope physically now, it'll be all the more difficult for her when her rising takes firm hold. You can see she's close. Distance. You've got to have distance."

I hissed, curling my fingers into my palms and wanting to snag Silas back, but Faith was solidly in front.

"Look at me." She gripped my shoulders. "I know what you're feeling. The physical pull toward one's mate is excruciating if there's been some time apart, and trust me, you've just had that."

"Right now, I don't care. What kind of sister are you?"

"One who loves you."

I froze. "You do?"

"I've always wanted a sister. And family. Now, I have all I've ever dreamed of." She wrenched me into her arms. "I'll even put up with Silas...for you."

Loveria coughed. "Now, that's some love."

"Faith, I didn't know you were missing from my life until you came into it. I love you too."

"Good, then believe me when I say I need to get you out of here. Papamoa beach, okay?"

"Yes."

She glanced at Loveria. "Get changed and we'll meet you at my favorite spot." Everything darkened as she 'ported us.

Moonlight glazed over the ocean's slick, dark surface and my feet sank into the softest white sand. The air was still, the ocean peaceful, like the calm before the storm. The skies above were clear, an inky-black spread with a million twinkling stars.

I walked forward. Oh boy. Water. Lots of water.

"They're here. Hey, wait up."

Faith's words came from afar, and then the pounding of footsteps, but the ocean called to me. Silky smooth, the water rose to my knees, then my waist.

Deeper. I had to go deeper.

"She's not listening, Silas. Hurry."

Faith stood in front of me, her hands on my chest as she skidded backward.

What was she doing there? I pushed her away.

Glorious water swirled over my shoulders, skimmed my chin. Ahh, perfect.

"Wait up."

Someone lifted me off my feet, and I blinked. Oooh, Silas wrapped his arms around me.

Oh yeah, he had no shirt on.

I licked my lips and stared at his muscled chest. "You took too long."

"It was bare seconds. I had to change for a swim."

Seawater glistened on his skin, the most gorgeous sight. I tickled my fingers across his flesh, only my vision wavered.

Water all around... I needed him. No, I needed it.

"Hope?" He clicked his fingers in front of my face. "Her eyes are glazed, like she's in a trance." Silas spoke to someone over my shoulder, only the gentle slapping of the water against my back seduced me. Like an invisible hand which caressed, water swept around my legs, tugging at me as if to come, to play.

"I want to go, Silas." I focused on my skin, on the essence I needed to coat it to prepare for the cold.

The gel gathered and I slid free of him.

I was away.

Power thrummed through my limbs, a strength three-times greater than ever before as I kicked and moved beneath the water's surface. Like a seal, I glided out into the depths.

Air.

I slowed and held my position, thinking only of what I needed, and with a flick of my fingers in front of my face, separated the hydrogen and pushed it outward, away from the oxygen. I pressed my nose into the protected bubble of air and breathed, moving with it as it rose. Purrr-fect.

"Where are you? Are you breathing underwater?"

Silas's demanding questions echoed inside my head.

"Damn it. You're freaking me out. The water's pitch black and I can't see you."

I moved through the dark, a few feet below the surface as I continued out to sea. Deeper. Ever deeper.

"Answer me."

I stopped, but only to draw in more air. I couldn't have him halt me.

Away again. Further still.

"I need to hear your voice." His abrupt tone sizzled along my senses as a slick-skinned dolphin drew beside me.

With a smile, I smoothed its silvery-blue flesh with a hand.

"Hope, it's Faith. Silas is going crazy here, and ordinarily that wouldn't upset me, except his worry is over you. I can't see you with my forethought."

Hmm. No, she wouldn't. I was under the surface, in the dark. *"I'm fine."*

"No, you need those closest to you. Your rising has begun."

"I know. I like it, and I'm not telling you where I am unless you promise not to take me from the water. I gotta stay."

"Of course you do. Give me some direction. We're organizing a boat. There's a Surf Club and Davio's borrowing one of the inflatables. Well, stealing it really, but let's not get

into technicalities. We'll head out and motor beside you in the water."

The dolphin circled me as I came to the surface and treaded water. *"I'm west of the Surf Club. I'll be the one swimming with the dolphin."*

Slick nose butting my arm, the dolphin pressed me to play. I laughed and curled my hand around his fin.

Oh, this was wonderful. The ocean was alive, and the water was mine.

"We'll bring the boat to you. Stay still."

"Not a chance."

Holding onto the dolphin, I clicked my tongue. "Take me for a ride."

With a flick of his tail, he obeyed, skimming the glassy surface and making a high-pitched squeal. I giggled as water flew into my face. Such a rush. It was a moment I wished would never end. Only the inflatable was close, its engine roaring as it sped toward me. Seated at the rear, Loveria worked the motor control, and Silas and Faith were at the front searching ahead.

The dolphin dived and I let go and waved out to them.

Loveria slowed the craft and brought it in beside me. "Heck, you can swim fast."

"It's my rising."

"Rising or not, you shouldn't have run," Silas growled as he leaned over the side.

"Officially I swam. I can't believe you stole a boat, and what's with the wetsuits?" They all wore the Surf Club's black and red gear with the lifesaving logo emblazoned across the front.

"We didn't have a choice. You're in the deep and we don't produce the gel."

"Unbelievably deep." Faith scrambled across Silas to reach me.

I grinned at her. "I can't believe my rising is finally here."

"It is, and we're here for you. I can come in. Do you want me to get Dad first? Or Goldie?"

This was a time to celebrate, to have my closest near. Except, with Silas on the scene, not to mention Loveria, having Dad or Goldie in the inflatable begged trouble. "No, you better not get either. I'll have to do this without them."

Her gaze flickered with understanding. "What about Elizara? Or Maslin? They have the water skill and I know they'd come."

"Oh, that'll work. Yes, get them." The ocean rocked me in its watery arms and I longed to slip below the surface. "I'll be back in a—"

"No. You're not going anywhere." Silas grabbed my arm, only I was a little too slick.

I bobbed away with a smile. "The boss man isn't going to get his way on this."

"We can't have the warrior here."

"You can't, but she can." Faith pinched his cheek. "Just deal with it. It's only for one night." She crawled to Loveria and kissed him. "I'll return in a few minutes, and I'd appreciate you not moving the boat, or I'll end up in the drink when I return."

She flashed away and I came in closer to Silas. "How did you expel your excess energy from your rising?"

"In the arena, with the sword. I think I'll come in."

"My hormones are raging and I'd be all over you in a second. You have to keep your distance for now, plus I'm not cold, even out this deep. Maslin and Elizara can swim with me."

"I want you to keep a distance from Sol."

"He's a warrior and my friend. We work together."

"You chose him when I released you."

I huffed, wanting to kiss him and smack him all at once. "Barely, and so long ago, my mate, it doesn't count."

"Hope." My name was a growl from between his lips, and as Faith reappeared with Maslin, his fists clenched.

She raised her shoulders in a shrug. "Sorry, I can't spot Elizara. She must have snuck into the gray area. As soon as I see her, I'll get her."

"I'm here, Hope." Maslin shucked off his jeans and stripped down to a pair of shorts. "I can produce the gel, but you'll need to help me breathe underwater if we go too deep. I can't form the bubbles."

Silas glared at Maslin. "Touch her, and I'll remove your head from your shoulders."

"You don't frighten me, Carver. She's my princess. I'll protect her as I see fit, even from her own mate."

"No fighting, you two." This I didn't need.

Maslin dove in, came in underneath and grabbed my legs. The water slid over my head as I went down.

Ten feet under, and Maslin came face to face with me, his gaze locked on mine in the murky depths. "*Do you hear me?*"

"*Yes.*" The telepathic link of trust was strong.

"*Create a bubble of air for me, larger than what you make for yourself.*"

I did, and he leaned in then chased it up a foot as he drew in a breath.

Returning to me, he grinned. "*You are my perfect woman.*"

"*You are going to get yourself into trouble with that kind of talk. I'm mated.*"

He shrugged, his copper hair floating about his face. "*Do I look like I care?*" No, he didn't. He grasped my hand, and even with our slippery gel, kicked us upward.

We hit the surface and I swam for the boat. Silas was swearing, rather full on.

I grabbed hold of the looped side rope then dispersed the gel from my hands for a better grip. "My redhead has a temper. Come here."

His gaze speared into Maslin just a few feet behind me. "I'm trying to see the bigger picture, but right now, there isn't one."

"Uh-huh. Right, so I have to go for a swim, but I'll stay in a straight line from this point, keeping parallel to the beach."

He maintained his glower at Maslin.

"Silas, I truly need you"—his gaze jolted to mine—"to remain sane."

"Usually I am. That's currently impossible."

I drew in closer. "Kiss me. We'll both feel better."

Faith clambered in between us. "Okay. Here I am. I think we've covered this whole kissing thing already. Silas is out of bounds for you during your rising. And a lot longer, if I had my way."

"Having you around is frustrating." I frowned.

Silas crossed his arms with a slap. "You don't know the half of it."

Faith held out a bottle of water toward me. "You want a drink?"

"Oooh, but I still love you, sis. Yes." I unscrewed the lid and gulped. A surge of energy raced through me. "Whoa. That's got a power-punch to it. I have to dash." I touched my necklace and held up the gift Silas had given me. "You'll always be with me."

"Not the way I intended to."

Best to go. So I did.

I swam to Maslin, who lifted his chin while he treaded water. "Don't forget you'll be running at triple the strength for your rising. I'll try and keep up, but double-back to me if you need."

My blood fired. "Will do." I dove then swam underwater where I had to work harder. I surfaced every sixty feet so the others knew where I was. But nothing could have prepared me for what happened. The sudden clarity between mind and body and the massive wave of energy which rode me.

It was the most magical experience, even with the roar of

the boat's motor close.

"*This is the perfect night for a swim.*" Maslin spoke directly to me, and as the hours passed, I did as he instructed, making sure he was never too far away.

So many hours, I lost count.

At times, we dove deep, finding schools of fish. I created air pockets as we needed them. Other times, we swam along the surface, the moonlight rippling over its midnight beauty.

"Do you need some water, Hope?" Silas called out.

"I'd love some."

He signaled to Loveria at the rear of the inflatable to guide the boat closer to me then leaned over the side with a bottle. "It's been six hours."

"That long already?" I guzzled down the precious liquid and tossed him the empty.

Faith nudged in beside Silas. "How are you feeling?"

"Fantastic." I did a tumble-turn in the water, knocking into Maslin, who plucked me upright.

His eyes were bright, his enjoyment as great as mine. "This is our playground, but you must be getting near the end. Stay close."

"Yeah, but not too close," Silas grumbled as he jerked on the long sleeves of his wetsuit. "I'm coming in for a bit. I've had enough of sitting like a duck."

I held up a hand. "It's all right. I know at the end I'll lose all strength. I'll take care." I faced Maslin. "Ready for another swim?"

He leaned in and kissed the tip of my nose. "Always."

I gasped. Oh no, he hadn't just done that. Not in front of Silas.

With one almighty splash, a wave of water hit me in the face. When I opened my eyes, Maslin was gone and Silas was nowhere on the boat.

"Silas took him straight down!" Faith screamed and

pointed, almost toppling her and Loveria out of the boat. "Go and get him. Silas is acting all kinds of crazy right now."

Chills raced down my spine, and my legs went rubbery. "Gotcha." I tried to dive, but numbness invaded my limbs.

Ah, that wasn't good.

My lower body became a dead weight and dragged.

I went down, like an anchor thrown from the boat.

Yeah, more than not good.

The shadowy depths of the water swirled over me. No, I wasn't ready for my rising to finish. Focus. You're going down. Create some air. You're going to have to grab it on the move.

Damn. My arms were floppy.

I tried twice to flick my fingers in front of my face and barely managed it. On the third attempt, I finally succeeded and poked my nose into a bubble as I sank past it.

I was descending fast. So deep.

My head swam. Silas.

Throwing open our connection, I called to him. "*You have to come get me. My rising is done and I'm sinking.*"

"*What? No! Where?*"

"*I'm already well below the surface and falling fast. Can you free-dive forty or fifty feet? I think that's about where I am.*"

"*I'll do whatever's necessary. I can 'port in spurts.*"

And I needed oxygen. I created another bubble, getting the distance close as I sank past and managed a half breath before it floated away beyond my reach.

"*I'm coming in a direct line down.*"

Forming another bubble, I snatched what I could.

"*Make it fast. I'll be the one sinking.*"

"*Not for long.*" His tone held a deadly bite. "*Where are you?*" Something brushed against my back but it wasn't him.

"*I'm deep. I can't slow my descent.*" I struggled, fighting to move, but my limbs were useless. Focus. I had to make another bubble. I did, getting a pitiful amount of air.

"I'm coming, love."

My lungs burned. *"Silas?"*

"Stay with me." His words echoed in my head.

"I'm not making enough—" I coughed, expelling the precious air I'd drawn in.

My vision swam, and I caught a flash of black and red, and then nothing.

Chapter 13

My head exploded with pain. My chest throbbed as if someone sat on it.

I was tossed around as voices echoed all around.

"Carver's not getting her back."

Was that Maslin?

A scream shattered the air and my heart lurched within my chest.

"Get off Silas, Maslin." The boat rocked underneath me, or at least I'm sure it was the boat. "There's so much blood, Davio. Is Silas breathing?"

Faith was yelling, and why would Silas not be breathing? And what blood?

"Silas is unconscious, and the wound is deep." Loveria for sure. "I'll take him to the healers. Look after your sister."

"Carver came after me first." Maslin again, puffing with sharp breaths. "I had to defend myself."

I tried to move. Silas needed me, only I couldn't.

The voices drifted.

The dark embraced me.

* * * *

"Goldie, her lungs had to be near to bursting, but she's healing. Davio said so is Silas. I can't believe he and Maslin fought with their daggers on the boat."

I tried to push my eyelids up as my sister's voice washed over me.

"They'll both be fine, Faith. Your forewarning would've activated otherwise, and let's not forget Maslin had to defend himself. He is a warrior first and foremost."

Striving for the surface, I moaned deep in my throat.

"That's it. Open your eyes, sis."

I blinked as the overhead light blazed. Faith and Goldie were perched beside me on the bed. The station. "Why am I not with Silas?" Not that I was happy with him right now. He'd fought, and at a time when I'd needed him most.

Goldie enveloped me in her arms, the scent of horse and hay coming with her. "I can't have a protector here and this is where Faith brought you. You had me so worried. Boy, I don't know whether to hug or growl at you."

"You're doing both already."

Faith wiped her cheeks. "It's my turn to hug and growl." She wrapped me up tight. "You did it. You've gotten through your rising. Silas is still healing though, and I'm under strict orders from Dad to wait here until you wake. He wants to—"

With a swirl of air, he shimmered into the room, and I pushed myself upright. "Hey—"

"Don't *hey* me. Your mother is not happy with what I had to report." He smothered me next. "She'll be all over you when you come home. That was the warning I had to pass on."

"I can't wait," I said, my voice muffled by his silk shirt.

He glanced at Faith. "Goldie and I have always kept a close eye on her. Although with your forethought, you're now called to help. As you can see, it's a never-ending job."

"I'll help, but there has to be hazardous pay involved. She's a lot of hard work."

"Ha, I'm not that bad."

Faith swung to look at me. "Oh c'mon, yes you are."

"No, I'm not."

"Don't argue with me."

"Then take me to Silas so I can argue with him. He'd appreciate it, and I've got a lot of arguing to do. He's truly okay, right?"

"Yes. I would have told you otherwise." Still dressed in her wetsuit, she pulled me with her off the bed. "Let's get changed. I'll gladly take you to him."

Dad cocked a brow. "I'll head home and reassure your mother. I'll see you both as soon as possible. In Dralion." He shimmered and disappeared.

Goldie grabbed me by the shoulders. "Hold on. Maslin wanted to see you too." She tapped her head. "I just 'pathed him you were up."

A knock sounded, and we all turned. Faith crossed to the door and opened it.

Maslin hurried in. "Are you healed?"

"Yes." Maslin was my friend and always would be. Our lives were intertwined because of our love of this station. He had always stood at my side, never having left when I needed him. "What happened out there? Between you and Silas."

"It was a tense moment when he brought you to the surface. Once we knew you lived, I told him he wasn't getting you back. I reacted from my gut, and well, I'm sorry, he attacked and I defended. I realize he's your mate, and in hindsight, neither of us were likely thinking straight. It won't happen again. Your safety will always come first."

I took his hands in mine. "What am I going to do with you?"

He gave me one of his assured grins. "We're blood-bound. I'll always be by your side. Tell Carver I apologize for my part in what went down, but more than that, I accept his place in your life. He saved you. That I can never forget."

Goldie rubbed my arm. "Carver dived deep to get you. I can forgive him his lapse in judgment for what happened afterward since Maslin wasn't harmed."

Maslin popped a kiss on my cheek. "I'm truly sorry for my part in it. Make sure you take plenty of time to rest and recover. We have a ton of watering holes to top up once you have. Stay safe."

"You too. I'll see you later."

"Absolutely." He flashed away.

"That goes for me as well since I imagine you'll want to be elsewhere. Get lots of rest like Maslin said." Goldie 'ported as he had.

Faith smiled. "I really like Maslin. In fact I'm even a bit jealous he got to—"

I clapped a hand over her mouth. "Don't even think of saying it."

She pried my fingers away. "He got to cut Silas. Lucky dude."

"Sheesh, you weren't supposed to say it." I headed to my dressing room.

"Who knows?" She sighed wistfully as she followed. "Maybe one day I'll get my chance. I can but dream."

"What we actually need to do, and not just one day but soon, is work out a plan on how to bring peace between Peacio and Dralion."

"I'm with you there, sister of mine." She pulled me into her arms. "Sorry, just needed another hug."

I squeezed her back. "I love having a sister. Thanks for being there during my rising."

"Of course. I wouldn't have been anywhere else, and I'm with you on working out a plan." She eyed the rack and snagged two pairs of black jeans then tossed me one of them. "We'll go and see Silas, before he wakes up and comes over here. I need to see you put him in his place."

"Oh, I'll be having words with him." My chest tightened as frustration and worry equally collided. "Is he truly all right?"

"I'll check again, but I would have had forewarning if not." She closed her eyes. "Yeah, he's still out to it. Silvie's with him though, as well as Davio."

I nabbed two violet stretch t-shirts and handed one to her.

"Silvie's flicking him in the leg now, telling him to hurry and wake up. She's getting impatient. His chest wound is healing, though. I can see the pink line and it's getting fainter. You ready to go?"

"Yep." I straightened the hem. "Don't dally. I've gotta show him who's boss."

"Good. Hold tight."

Everything darkened and my heartbeat raced as we arrived in Silas's room. His thick beige curtains were drawn against the dark and the bedside light was on. He lay still, his wetsuit rolled to his waist, the slash across his chest healing, as Faith had said.

"There you two are." Silvie motioned me closer. "Come talk to him. Do something. He'll respond to your voice for sure."

I crossed and took her spot as she moved away. "Hey, wake up. Enough of this lying around." I merged my mind with his, sinking into my soul-blending spot.

He didn't answer, or even move.

"I'm awake. Why aren't you?" I picked up his hand and glanced at Faith.

"Keep trying. He's just napping, the lazy sod."

I cupped his stubbly jaw and leaned in. "If now isn't a good time for you, I could come back later. I'll have worked up a little more steam by then."

He moaned and his fingers tightened around mine. "You were down so deep."

"There were extenuating circumstances. What were you thinking?"

"I wasn't. I was an idiot for going after Sol when I should have been watching you." He lifted his eyelids, then blinked. A tear escaped from the corners of his eyes as he focused on me. "I thought I was too late. You were so limp in the water."

"Nah-ah, I've been known to return from the dead, and I certainly would have come back to haunt you."

"Not funny. Let's forget the handcuffs. I'm going to lock you up in the cells so no harm can ever come to you." He tried to sit, but groaned and slumped into his pillows.

"You could try." I nipped his nose. "Although in your current state, I doubt you'll be successful."

"If there's a will, there's a way."

"Then you'll need a lot of will, because my way is the way. Officially, I'm now the boss."

"You're fully healed?" His gaze traveled over me, inspecting all he saw.

"I'm fine, but in the future, no fighting with Maslin. He said it won't happen again from his side, and I want your promise on that too."

"Your safety is all that matters. I give you my promise, and I'll apologize to him when I see him."

"That's one very agreeable mood you're in right now."

"I shouldn't have fought with Maslin. My jealousy almost got you killed, and it'll never happen again. Whatever you ask, I'll do."

"Now, that sounds better."

Loveria coughed. "Ah, if you two are about to make up, then we're out of here." He wrapped an arm around Faith's waist.

She sighed. "I'm not sure we should leave them alone. You heard. An agreeable mood."

"Ha," Silvie snorted. "Well, I'm not agreeable. I want to go and talk to this Maslin Sol and hear his promise to not fight with my own ears." She snagged Faith's hand. "Take me to see him, please. Now."

"Nope." Faith shook her head. "I know you too well. You'll hurt him yourself."

"So? He's a warrior. He can handle a little pain."

"It's still a no."

"That's so unfair." She trudged to the door. "I'm not going to forget this. I'm not making you rocky-road again."

"Oooh, hold on. Now for rocky-road, I might take you." Faith skipped after her. "I mean it. Make me a huge slab and we have a deal. I'll find a way to protect Maslin from you."

Loveria chuckled and gave Silas a thumbs-up as he followed the girls. "Take the rest of the day off. You've still got some serious groveling to do." With a silly grin, he shut the door as he left.

"Come here." Silas tugged on my hand and pulled me against him. "Do you forgive me?"

"Maybe. Serious groveling, remember?" I rested my head on his shoulder and cuddled in. I was so tired. "What a day. I'm glad it's over."

Here with him was where I longed to be. Nowhere else. He was my home, just as Dralion and the wide-open plains of the outback were.

"Faith and I are going to work on a plan to bring about peace."

"That's a tough one, but I'll do what I can to help." He stroked the nape of my neck. "As long as we're together, that's what counts."

I edged up and looked him in the eyes. "Thank you for saving me." Undeniably he had.

"You've saved me too, in more ways than one." He reached to his bedside drawer and removed a small black velvet pouch from within. Sitting up a little, he tipped out a silver charm, one of a red rose. "I gave you a white rose for the beginning of time, a yellow for the gift of friendship, and this red rose." He kissed me, deeply, until we finally had to pull apart for air. "I want you to know there is a love which consumes my heart, and it's only for you."

"Oh. Wow."

"You have my heart, now and forever, Hope." His breath whispered across my neck as he added the red rose to join the white and yellow charms.

Love, it stole all good sense and was an agony unto itself. Still, my heart burst with the emotion. "I love you too, Silas. You're my mate, and I'll never let you go."

"You don't have a choice, and I'll make sure I never allow you to slip from my grasp again. You are the only woman I want. Always." He took my face between his hands. "And I have our entire lives to prove it. Are you ready for our journey to begin?"

I looked deep into his eyes, because I could never get enough of him. "For the first order of business. Kiss me. Then I'll tell you."

He did, and with absolute devotion, I lost my "yes" against his lips.

Read on to Catch a Bonus Novella.

Princesses of Myth

Hunter, (Novella – Book 2.5)

HUNTER

Lieska's Story, Book 2.5 (Novella)

HUNTER

~ BONUS NOVELLA ~

Princesses of Myth, Book 2.5

JOANNE WADSWORTH

Chapter 1

A light breeze swirled, scratching nettles against my face where I crouched within the bushes near the enemy's battle-training arena. I swatted the brush aside, wishing it were just as easy to eliminate the protectors I could never get rid of.

"Lieska, I can't believe you did this." Hope, my princess and friend, shoved a pesky branch out of her way. "Why'd you teleport us right into the enemy's camp?"

"My warrior hunter instincts are on alert, and this is where they led me."

"A little warning would've been nice."

"Shh, keep your voice down. If we're found here, it'd look suspicious."

"Ya think?"

"Hey, you're the one always up for an adventure."

"This isn't a flippin' adventure." She blew out a long breath. "Maybe if we acted like normal people, we'd be less likely to catch a second glance."

"Or you could consider this a training exercise. Your new skills could use the practice."

"And hiding out in a bush is called practice?"

"It's called scouting, and it'll be a handy addition to your warrior arsenal."

"Yeah, but Silas is one of the enemy. I don't need to be

scouting here." Hope peered through the bushes, her long blond hair snagging in the scrub. "He trains in this arena every morning. If he saw me without protection this close to his hangout, I'd be in big trouble."

"I am your protection. Huh, I can't believe you're mated to the enemy, and your twin is soul-bound to their prince. What is this world coming to? Next thing you know, they'll be no protectors on Magio left for me to fight."

"Actually, the few protectors Faith and I've met haven't been all that bad." Hope squeezed my arm. "Sorry. Don't hate me for saying that."

"Your opinion is skewed. Silas ensures you don't meet any of the protectors outside his inner circle. Prince Davio does the same with Faith."

"Yeah, which means they'll be hundreds of protectors in there I don't know, and shouldn't know." Her gaze narrowed, and the deep violet denoting her strong Wincrest line, targeted on me. "That is danger times hundreds in case you weren't counting."

"You'll never be in any danger with me. And you can telepath Silas in a heartbeat if you have to."

"Did you not hear me say big trouble?" She sighed and rubbed her neck. "You've gotta tell me. What's really bugging you? I've never seen you this anxious."

"I don't know." Those with the hunter skill had to hunt their prey, whether we knew who they were or not. The urge ate at us until we did. "All I can say is my hunter instincts are blaring at me like never before. Although this time it's different. I want to hunt, but not hurt."

"Well, that's a bonus." She knocked her shoulder against mine. "It would've helped if you'd said that in the beginning. How long has this blaring thing been going on?"

"Five days, but my senses are narrowing in on one. That's why I decided to bring you."

"So I'm like your wing-woman?"

"Yep, I need you to keep me sane."

"Ha. Give me the easy job why don't you." She tweaked my chin. "Seriously, what happens next? You intend to hunt then what?"

I rolled the cuffs of my loose black shirt to the elbow, exposing the sheathed daggers at each wrist, weapons I was never without. The pointy tips sparkled under a sliver of sunlight trickling through. Hunt and fight. The desire always fired my blood, but today it was hunt and… Hmm, yeah hunt and something else. "I'm not sure. Be prepared for anything."

"Anything isn't good. You can hunt, but not hurt. Wing-woman's orders." Hope plunked her tan Stetson on her head. "Unless we can ditch this joint? Wing-woman really wants to do that."

"You wanna get back to the roundup?"

"I'd rather roundup cattle than have Silas find out I was here."

"Nope, the outback can wait." Wincrest Station in the Australian outback was King Donaldo Wincrest's off-world holding, and where I spent my time when not in Dralion. Goldie and Hope Wincrest ran the place.

"You are one stubborn hunter, Lieska. I wish I could 'port. It'd make my life a lot—"

Chains cranked, and the solid paneled iron gates at the entrance rolled open. This was what I'd been waiting for. Finally I'd be able to see inside the three-story high open-aired arena. It was a beauty with its ancient circular architecture.

"Wow. Do you see that?" Hope whispered.

I shoved the brush farther aside, and we both poked our noses in. The protectors' arena was close in size to our fighting force's in Dralion. Their blocked seats were layered back and up and able to hold thousands of spectators. Groups of protectors trained on the central sandy floor with swords and spears and axes, with likely more beyond. Some of the men wore red tunics with leather-flapped skirts, and they lunged and parried, as accurate with their brutally sharp weapons as any warrior would be. The women trained in their battle leathers. So close. This was the chance I'd been waiting for. It had definitely been right to bring Hope. Hopefully she'd be able to help me keep a level head.

"Let's go." I gripped Hope's hand and 'ported us. Everything darkened as I made the short jump through space.

Hope wobbled as we arrived near the wall. "Lieska, what the heck are you doing?"

"You saw the gate open. It's an invitation I can't turn down." I plucked the sides of my hip-hugging black leather pants. "Look at us. I'm dressed no differently to any of the protector women, and you're completely unassuming in jeans and a t-shirt. Except for this. The Stetson has to go. It screams Earth." I nabbed it and tossed it behind a flax bush growing beside the wall. "Now no one's going to suspect we're from Dralion unless we announce it. We'll be normal people, not catching a second glance."

"Geez, I hate how my own words come back to bite me." She shook her head. "Just make sure you don't announce our arrival your way. No throwing any daggers at the protectors, because that would be announcing it, in case you weren't aware."

"I'm aware, and I'll try and keep them sheathed, maybe." I couldn't stop from rubbing my hands together. Finally I'd have a chance to sort this problem. The hunt was on. I strode in and the breeze lifted my long brown locks and swept strands across my face. Two men battled close by and one of the men's blade's struck flesh and bone. Blood spurted in a wide arc. My blood thrummed to join the fight. Oh yeah. I wish I'd been the one to inflict that wound. The injured man grasped his arm, holding the edges closed. His blood ceased running and his skin began to knit together. A fast-healer. Damn. What a shame.

"Ew." Hope puffed as she caught up. "Are your senses still on fire?"

"Burning bright. So stay close in case I need to 'port us out of here quick." I followed the safety rail around the perimeter. My senses flared. There. A man in black jeans stretched as if readying himself for training. The denim molded his butt. Mm-mmm.

He selected a two-handed sword from the rack and twirled it in a precise figure eight. Slowly he built up speed, and moved through a series of fluid training moves. He held the battle skills, and only those who had such an affinity for their weapon did.

"Is that him? The one you're after?" Hope hauled me to a stop.

"Yes, and it appears he needs a battling partner. Wait here."

"I'll wait provided you agree not to kill anyone."

"We'll see, just don't draw any attention to yourself."

"Huh, I can't believe you're telling me not to draw attention to myself. Hello. Give yourself your own pep talk." With a harrumph, she snuck under the railing. She plopped onto the wooden bench and grasped the edge under her knees, squishing her knuckles.

"I would take my own advice, except I don't think I'm up for listening. That's why I have you." She was one of my best friends, even though she'd accepted a protector as her mate. I could deal. Stroking the hilt of my ever-present side sword, I walked toward the one my senses had flared on. "Hey," I called out. "You look lonely." Good, keep it casual.

He jerked around, his gaze landing on me.

Whoa. I missed a step. His eyes were to die for. Stunning gold flickered through the darkest shade of brown. The pinpointed gaze of a hunter. My eyes. He had my eyes and my skill.

"Who are you?" He stood an impressive hand over me, and

I was close to six feet. Not intimidating, but tall enough I notched up my chin.

"Lieska Alura."

"Another hunter. Your eyes give you away."

"As do yours."

His nostrils flared as he circled me. "I wasn't aware we had a new recruit with the skill."

Hmm, interesting. Being a new recruit would explain why I was here, except my skills were too advanced. Best to keep as close to the truth as I could. "You don't. I came into my adult skills a year ago on my eighteenth and I've been training ever since."

"Not a recruit then. Why'd you walk in?" He shot a look at the gate as a horse and cart rumbled in, loaded with supplies.

"Sorry, it seems the hunter in me couldn't be denied."

"Civilians aren't permitted within this arena." His gaze moved toward Hope who watched us with eagle eyes. "She's a civilian too, although I've seen her at Loveria Castle with Silas Carver. What's her name? How do you know her?"

Was this protector within Silas's inner circle? I opened my telepathic link with Hope. *"Do you know this man?"*

"No, I would have said if I did. I've seen him around a couple of times, but not formally met him. You're taking care, right?"

"Care is my middle name."

"Don't give me that. It's more like lunatic."

"Thank you."

"That wasn't a compliment."

"Yeah, but lunatic goes nicely with insane." I waved, and then grinned as she scowled. She was so easy to rile.

"Excuse me." The man cleared his throat. "You appear rather relaxed for one who just defied Prince Davio Loveria's rules. No one enters this arena unless sanctioned by him, or Silas Carver, his cousin and second."

"Then let's not tell either of them." I nodded toward Hope. "Hope's my friend, and also a friend of Silas's, if that's of any help." He'd seen them together, but I wouldn't go into any further detail. "I simply wanted to see what all the fuss was about, you know, being a protector and all. I'm itching to hone my battle skills, and I'm picking this is the best place for it. You could help me out with that, right?" Although he had a good point about my relaxed state. My hunter skill had calmed and so had I since crossing to him. Strange. Such a thing rarely happened to me, not unless I was amongst my closest.

"Davio and Silas have taken a team out to Sundrimer. I could let this slide, but only if you both remain within my sight. Are you serious about wanting to join the protectors? We could use more hunters."

"As long as I'm allowed to whip some butt today, I might consider joining." I probably shouldn't be trying to antagonize him on his own turf, but I was a warrior. That's what we did. Riling protectors made our day. "What's your name?"

"Cole Cyrano." The wind rushed into him, plastering his shimmery silver shirt to his wide chest. Broad and heavily muscled. So hot.

Hold on. I was relaxed and now ogling the enemy? What was going on?

"Ah, nice to meet you, Cole." I slid my sword free, tapped it against his. "Feel free to show me what you can do. And don't go easy on me 'cause I'm a girl."

"If you say so." He whipped around and his sword slashed down. I moved with lightning speed and met his attack. Our blades crashed dead center, steel ringing loud against steel.

"Oooh, I like a man who can fight." I leaned past our crossed blades and tousled his golden-brown hair. The silky strands brushed his shoulders, glimmering in the sunlight. Whoa. What was I doing touching him? Get it together. He's a protector.

He grasped my hand, his gaze flickering with frustration. Nose to nose, he eyed me. "You feel it too, don't you?"

My heartbeat thumped at his closeness. "Yeah, but I have no idea what it is. What's happening?" Inside me an urge to be even nearer burned, and I was quite close enough.

"The bond." He threaded our fingers together. "You're my mated one. I've only ever felt the male's drive within the bond toward Earth, and at other times beyond Dralion's protective dome. I've suspected this past year my mate was a warrior since it's only Dralion's elite who have the freedom to travel. It's why I stayed away from you. Did I get my bearings wrong? Are you a Peacian?"

Oh my goodness. The truth blazed in his eyes. That's what this was. I'd never in my life felt an attraction to any man and my skill had brought me here. From the moment I'd seen him my emotions had settled. We were mated, the soul-bond pulsing to life between us.

Crap. Crap. Crap.

"Cole, I think we have a problem, a very big problem." I was mated to a protector. Only half our people were soul-bound. The bond was what I desired, but not with my enemy.

"Hell, I'm right. You're a warrior from Dralion. We need to talk. Now. In private." Grip tight on my hand, he stalked toward a gap in the rail and tugged me along the first row of seats.

"I can't leave Hope behind."

"She can wait here. You said she's a friend of Silas's, which means she's safe enough."

I threw open my link with Hope. *Change of plans. I'll be back shortly. Go nowhere without me.*

"What's wrong? Should I be worried?"

"His name is Cole Cyrano. My stupid hunter senses led me straight to my mate. I'll be back before you know it though. I've gotta dump the big guy."

"You know the whole dumping thing, Lieska?" She snorted

down our link. "*Yeah, not that easy. Don't worry about me. I'll just hang here. If Silas finds out, I'm mincemeat, so whatever you do, make the dumping snappy.*"

"Are you speaking to her now?" Cole continued to tow me along behind him.

"Yes, and I didn't say I wasn't a Peacian." I had to try and talk my way out of this if I could.

He stared into my eyes, the gold in his sparking intensely. "We're soul-bound, and I can sense when you lie. I can't hurt you, Lieska. It's impossible because of the bond. Hell. If these protectors knew who you were though, they'd slice and dice you. Let's keep moving so they don't." He turned left and strode between two rows that dipped into a darkened corridor. "This is the way to the barracks. I have my own quarters, and that's as private as we're going to get."

The tunnel came out before a short flight of upward stairs. At the top we passed through double doors and into a bright passageway. Doorways were recessed into paneled walls of pure white. Light streamed in from windows positioned between every other doorway on alternate sides. I slowed before the first window since the passageway remained clear. Wow. Flowers bloomed in a myriad of colors amongst thick green foliage. Talk about cheerful, nothing like our barracks in Dralion, which were dark and gloomy. "Nice place."

"Yes, and one you're only going to visit once." He opened a door. "This is my place. Come inside."

"Are you sure that's wise? Us, alone in your room?"

"Inside now, and before someone comes and asks me who you are. I don't care to lie and protect a warrior's butt, even if it is yours."

"Puh-lease, I wouldn't ask it of you." I strode past him and into his quarters, allowing my hunter senses to roam. A massive bed was pressed against one wall, a brown comforter with flecks of gold, spread over top. Four plump white pillows rested against a dark wood headboard, the letters *CCC* skillfully engraved along it. "Hmm, I take it those are your initials?"

"Yes, take a seat."

"No thanks. What does the middle *C* stand for?" I strolled toward his corner desk. In delicate scrollwork on the back of the dark wood chair were the same matching initials. I trailed my finger over the etching. His wooden pen was engraved too, as was the polished stand it sat in. "Either you have a fascination with your name, or you have a furniture maker in your family."

"Maybe. Is this room too distracting for your hunter senses?" He leaned against the wall as he eyed me.

"Nope. Oh, I know. Maybe the *C* stands for Cabinet. Cole Cabinet Cyrano."

"What?"

"It's a wild guess going off the whole furniture maker thing. C'mon, you've gotta give me something, otherwise I'll think the worst. What about Choo-choo?" I'd drag his full name out of him somehow.

He chuckled. "Where'd you come up with that middle name?"

"I'm inventive. What about Chimpanzee?"

"Are you calling me an ape?"

"I wouldn't do such a thing." I picked up his black leather jacket slung over the padded chair seat. The inside tag again read *CCC*. I shoved my hands into the sleeves and tugged it on. His jacket swamped me, but cocooned within, I drew in his spicy scent.

"Why don't you sit and I'll tell you."

"Is it Confident?"

"Sit."

"I really don't have time to get too comfortable." Although he did have a rather cozy looking padded couch of beige with floor length curtains of the same velvety fabric tucked behind it. I crossed to his glass door, pressed a hand to its warm surface.

Sunlight bathed his private garden. "I like the golden roses. Flowers barely survive where I live."

"And where is that?" His hunter skills had him as intrigued as me by the drilling sound of his voice, and it wasn't good to leave a hunter with unanswered questions. I'd tell him what I could then get this day over with. There wasn't a chance we could work out any form of relationship. Hope and Faith had, but they hid a ton of secrets to make it work.

"In Dralion my parents have a cottage in a village near the snow-capped mountains. Snow equals no roses. Then there's the warriors' barracks. Not one garden to speak of there. On Earth, I live on a station in the blazing heat of the outback."

"Ahh, that explains why I was drawn to Earth." He moved in behind me, his chest brushing my back. Usually such a move would have my defenses on alert. Instead I eased back and allowed his presence to surround me. He was my mate, the one man meant to be mine. Destiny though had backfired with this bond. "Lieska? You know what we need to do, right?" His voice was a soft murmur in my ear.

"I sure do." I tugged his jacket tighter around me. "Time to break up, not that we've actually gone out, but you know, it's not likely to work."

"Protectors and warriors don't mix." He stroked my arms.

"I take it that's why you never came for me. You'd already decided to let our bond pass?"

"There's a war, and we'd never suit."

"I know."

"I'm not happy you're here, but at least it'll give us the chance to end things the right way." Yep, releasing each other would mean we could move on, even though we still held the other half of each other's soul. Distance and time though would aid in the separation.

I turned in his arms and faced him. "Speak the words I need to hear, Cole. Release me, and I'll release you."

His gaze intensified. "I like your strength."

"Yes, and you're—oh, perhaps the *C* in your name stands for Challenging?" Geez, I really had to know. He had to give me something before the hunter in me got really serious.

"That's not it either." He cupped my cheeks. "It's Chase. I've always gone after what I wanted and never deviated from the set course."

"Cole Chase Cyrano." My pulse sped up. I liked his warm hands on my face and the intense look in his eye, all for me. "That's why we hunt. Thank you for telling—"

"*Lieska? You gotta minute?*" Hope's frantic voice rang clear in my mind.

"*What's up?*"

"*I hate to interrupt whatever's going down, but it seems I've attracted some attention.*"

"*I'll be there soon. We're almost done.*"

"*Maybe I should have said a lot of attention.*"

"*Hold still then. I'm on my way.*" I covered Cole's hands and squeezed. "Sorry, but there's an emergency. Hope's in need of a pick-up. An urgent one."

I flashed us to the safety rail since I had the image. Oh boy, and a lot of attention was right. Four beefy protectors, their swords drawn, towered over Hope.

Shoot. What had she done now?

Dralion's princess certainly knew how to find trouble.

Chapter 2

"Put your weapons away!" Cole bellowed as he heaved in front of me and faced the others. "This is Hope, a friend of Silas's. I can vouch for her."

Wow. My mate was a rather imposing force. Nice. I liked.

One of the towering menaces spun around. "Cole, she still shouldn't be here. She's a civilian."

"I was keeping an eye on her."

"Not a close enough eye."

"It's okay. I'll leave." Hope eased past the brute in black leathers and whipped in beside me. "We're leaving, right?"

I glanced at Cole. He clapped the man on the back then urged him and the others away and into the throng of battling protectors. Well, this was it. We didn't suit, and now I'd made him lie to protect Hope and me. I couldn't ask anymore of him. A twinge of pain settled around my heart. Dismissing our bond wasn't going to be easy, but we had no choice.

I drew his leather jacket collar over my nose and breathed deep. If I had his scent close, I'd manage the separation with more ease, or at least the hunter in me would. "We'll leave, Hope, after one more small task. This won't take long."

I flashed us to Cole's quarters. If I was taking something of his to aid me, then I'd leave him something of mine in return. I wriggled my hands back through my shirtsleeves, jiggled about and managed to remove my black lace camisole. I tugged it over my head then shoved my arms back into my shirt.

Hope gaped at me. "What are you doing?"

"We're trackers. Having a piece of clothing that holds our scent will calm the craving to hunt. Taking in the scent is like a fix." And I couldn't go without my shirt or pants, so the slip was it.

"Are you sure? I've seen dogs go berserk when given a scrap of material to sniff. It makes them want to hunt even more."

"Did you just call me a dog?" I flicked her arm. "I'll get you for that later."

"Sorry." She chuckled. "I make the worst wing-woman."

"You just need more practice, and we were pretty much done. I'll leave Cole a note to make sure I've got my bases covered." I folded my camisole and laid it on his bed. At his desk, I scrawled him a message.

Dear Cole,
I have your jacket and I'm keeping it. In return, I'm leaving you something of mine. It was nice meeting you and all. Have a fabulous life, and go and chase the one you really want.
Yours no more,
Lieska.

Good. Brief and blunt. I tucked it on top of my slip.

"Lieska? Where are you?"

Cole. His voice echoed in my head. No fair. He couldn't go creating a telepathic link of trust with me. That really wasn't on.

"Lieska, answer me."

Should I? No. It was best not to.

"I need to know you've gotten away all right. Have you left?"

Holy moly. I better do that now before he thought I might

have returned here. I seized Hope's arm and brought the image of Wincrest Station into my mind. I 'ported us, and we arrived, the red outback dust swirling and settling over our booted feet.

Hope grabbed the corral railing. "Whoa. That was fast. Why the rush?"

"I sensed a problem, and now I've averted it." I hugged her. "Thanks for coming with me today. It helped having you on hand."

"No problem." She squeezed me back. "And if you need to talk, I'm here. I know how tough it is to be mated."

"We broke up."

Smiling, she patted my back. "Sure you did. Okay, I better go and get some actual work done. I'll catch you later." She walked toward the feed sheds, whistling chirpily as if she knew something I didn't.

"*Lieska, I'm in my room.*" Cole, back in my head, and sounding very aggrieved. "*You left me your camisole? Hell. Couldn't you have made it something less personal to stay my need to hunt?*"

"*It was all I had on me.*" Drat. I probably shouldn't have answered him.

"*Where are you?*"

"*It's okay. I got away without a problem.*" I strode into the long run of white weatherboard stables and nabbed my Stetson off the hook in the central holding room. Argh, Hope's hat. I'd have to retrieve it for her later. Or buy her a new one. I'm sure she'd understand about getting a new one. "*I'm in the outback. How'd you explain our disappearance to your comrades?*"

"*I didn't. The less said the better. That jacket was one of my favorites by the way.*"

"*I'll take very good care of it.*" I stroked the soft black leather. "*Promise.*"

"*I have an old sweater you might like more. I've worn it a million times.*"

"Lieska." Maslin jogged toward me. "Goldie asked me to look for you. That bushfire on the other side of the hills has spread. It's still some hours from here, but winds are now fanning the flames our way. We're going to need all hands on deck for roundup. Have you seen Hope?"

"A minute ago. She was headed toward the feed sheds." Damn. One could count on the land being ripe for bushfires in November, but we were only midway through October. Summer temperatures didn't even spike until after New Year's. "What does Goldie want me to do?"

"You're to ride out toward the closest watering hole. If there're strays, herd them down to the river."

"Will do."

"You still there, Lieska?"

"I am. Sorry." I grabbed my gear, raced out to the corral and saddled a bay mare. *"Cole, if you really need the jacket back, I can swap it for the sweater. Hand it to Silas and I'll ask Hope to get it from him."*

"You sound anxious all of a sudden. What's wrong?"

"Bushfires, but some distance away. Sometimes they arrive on our doorstep, and other times, well, they tend to get even closer."

"Damn. Do you need a hand?"

"No." Heck no. *"I'll be fine."* Any time we spent together would only strengthen our bond. I checked my saddlebags. Water flask and snacks. Good. I folded Cole's jacket and tucked it into one of the pouches. It was hot out, and only getting hotter. I mounted and galloped, giving my mare her head. Adrenaline pumped, blood flowed through my veins and invigorated me. This was life, riding free across the greatest plains on Earth.

"I'm serious about my offer, Lieska. If you're in any danger and need a hand I'll come. 'Port back and collect me."

"There's no danger, or at least not yet. I'll be sure to holler though if there is." Not. I didn't need a protector on warrior soil.

That would cause more problems than the bushfires, more unnecessary heat too.

I surveyed the northern horizon where Rocky Ledge ascended. The Ledge, a massive red rock sitting on the plains, ran as far as the eye could see. The cloudless sky above was a vivid blue and clear of any smoke. To the west, a different story hailed. The hills, rising far into the distance, displayed a swath of brown-green bush, one with the bushfire's telltale smog clinging to it. To the east where the mighty river lay beyond the plains, thankfully it all appeared clear.

"Where in the outback are you? Give me a location. I need to check for myself." Great. Perhaps I should've stuck around so we could speak the words of release and end our bond properly. Although my mate was a hunter, so his male need to come a-running had likely doubled.

"Cole, can you do me a favor?" I dug my knees in and urged the horse to a faster speed, keeping an eye out for any strays between the homestead and watering hole.

"You know the bond. If there's anything you truly need, then ask."

"I need you to close this connection and never open it again."

"Except that."

"You said anything."

"Yeah, but within reason."

"That's not unreasonable. We broke up. I distinctly remember leaving you a note."

"You can't speak of bushfires and not expect me to react. Tell me where you are. Don't make me hunt you down."

Ha. He'd actually like that. The thrill of the chase was what hunters thrived on. *"You'd never catch my scent this deep in the outback. Wincrest Station alone is spread over eight-thousand square miles."* Okay, why was I provoking him?

"Give me some coordinates."

"Nope, that's too easy."

"Which state?"

"The one apparently on fire."

"Lieska." He growled my name, a dark rumble down our link.

Oooh, hot tingles raced across my skin. Maybe I'd give him something. He'd never find me out here under the scorching sun anyway. *"Okay. Soon I'll be coming up on a cluster of bush trees bordering the closest water source to the homestead. Come find me. I promise a reward if you do."*

"What kind of reward?" Silky smooth words. *"You want me to chase you. I can sense it."*

"Think about what you really want, my mate. That's all I'm asking. It's not me, and it's too dangerous for us to pursue this bond."

"Danger is my middle name."

"Nah-uh, it's Chimpanzee."

"It's Chase." He chuckled. *"And for a very good reason. Hold onto your reins. I'm coming for you."*

My long hair whipped around my face as I rode low and fast. I bundled the locks of brown under my Stetson then petted the horse's neck. He'd never find me. Or at least he better not.

Gripping the reins, I allowed my love of the outback to comfort me. Tumbleweeds blew across the land, some catching in low brush before the gust freed them and they rolled on. The ride lengthened, and I changed my angle toward the east.

A half hour later, the watering hole came into view. Cattle munched on a small patch of grass growing along its shallow bank. I rode in and jumped down beside the half-dry creek bed. At the edge, the sun had baked deep cracks into it.

My horse snickered, pushing his muzzle into my back. "Are you thirsty, girl?"

I tied the reins to a low branch, removed my water flask from my saddlebags and poured some into one cupped palm. The horse whinnied then lapped at the clear drinking water. When she was content, I took a few sips then tucked the flask away. Even harsh and dry, this was the most beautiful place.

I eyed the red rocks rimming the basin. Hold on. What was that? A wisp of black fluttered between two boulders, completely out of place.

Hands clamped around my waist from behind. I jumped and thumped back into one very hard chest. A man's spicy scent enveloped me.

"Turn around, Lieska. I want my reward."

Chapter 3

My heartbeat thundered as I whipped around. Oh boy. Cole. It was really him. My mate stood before me when I should never have seen him again. "How'd you find me? That should have been near impossible, and never this quick."

"You dared me. And I've always gone after what I wanted and never deviated from the set course."

"Your set course is not me and we both know it." Although two hunters together would be a striking force. Nope, don't think it. You're not together, and it'll never work.

"Then don't dare me again."

"All right. I promise I won't." I motioned toward the non-danger surrounding me. "See, you came for no reason. No fire here."

He surveyed the smoky hills in the west.

"Hey." I clasped his face and brought his gaze back to mine. The slight rasp of stubble tickled my fingertips. "It's best you don't look over there."

"Once the danger's gone, we'll get back to our separation. Consider this a hitch in our plans. That's all." He leaned in, bent his head close to my neck.

"What are you doing?" I sank my hands into his soft golden-brown hair. And what was I doing?

He breathed deep, nose against my flesh. "So I wasn't

imagining it. Your skin holds the scent of chocolate. Your camisole held a touch of the aroma, but I couldn't figure out why."

"I use cocoa butter as a lotion instead of—" Okay, he didn't need to hear I preferred that over sweetly scented perfumes.

"Don't stop. Tell me why." His brown gold-flecked eyes sparkled.

Great. Apparently he did, and the hunter in him wouldn't rest until he knew. The same happened to me, time and time again. "In Dralion chocolate is nonexistent. We don't have the land to cultivate the cacao beans."

"And only warriors can leave your land through the dome."

"Exactly. This past year I discovered chocolate on Earth. It's everywhere, and with my heightened senses, I've become a bit of a chocolate addict."

"Have you tried chocolate ice cream drizzled with chocolate syrup, and finished off with a sprinkle of chocolate—"

"Hey." I shoved a finger against his lips. "Try not to mention chocolate when I'm out on a job. I've been known to flash straight to my favorite store and buy up large."

He smiled. "Even your hair shimmers with varying shades of milk and dark chocolate."

What was he talking about? "Ah, I don't think so. It's brown. Just brown."

"It's silky and long." He tipped off my Stetson and ran his fingers through it. "I like this shade."

"Cole, we're getting rather…close."

"Close is daring." He pulled back and looked into my eyes. "I've gotta kiss you. Just this once."

"That's a terrible—" His mouth dropped over mine and he kissed me, with a hunter's prowess. I clutched his wickedly broad shoulders, flattened myself against him and kissed him back. "We shouldn't do this," I mumbled against his lips. But oh, so good.

"One kiss can't hurt, right?" He deepened our kiss, and I was lost as my need for more took over.

I kissed him, and my heartbeat raced. More. He was my mate, and it wasn't a bond to be broken. Except, damn it, we pretty much had. What was I thinking letting this go on? Hands on his chest, I pushed him back, only an inch, but one valuable inch. "Okay, wait up."

He growled. "You shouldn't taste so good."

"Neither should you." Unable to help myself, I traced his full lips with a finger. "I liked the kiss."

"I'd like another." He sucked my finger into his mouth. Wow. Hot, and I was about to expire as it was. "What was your intended reward, my mate?"

"I think you've already had enough of one. Why don't you tell me how you found me. I need to make sure that doesn't happen again."

"I tracked Silas down in Sundrimer. We shared some information about yours and Hope's visit. He told me about his mated bond with Hope, and Hope's twin sister being mated to my prince. What a mess. I can't believe the deadly secret they're keeping."

"So he pulled you into his inner circle?"

"He did. I gave him my promise to keep their secret."

"If Donaldo Wincrest knew of his granddaughters' relationships, he'd forbid them. Only a few of Hope and Faith's most trusted are aware."

"So Silas said. I won't spill the beans."

The wind played with his hair, brushing it back and forth over his shoulders. I itched to touch it again. Focus. "Ah, Silas led you here then?"

"Yes. He knew exactly where the closest water source to the homestead was." He stroked my back. "I also asked him to take me to places you frequent. We buzzed by the stables, the river, and a couple of the more prominent watering holes."

Silas was a pest, and if I could kill him, I would. Sadly, that was no longer an option. "He shouldn't have done that. Warriors come and go, Cole. You have to take care."

"You walked freely into the protectors' arena. I've done no different."

"Yeah, but I don't ever intend to visit there again."

"And neither will I drop by the outback. I simply needed to ensure I had the images for 'porting. As a precautionary measure. That's all."

"What about your decision to 'path me? That has to stop too."

"Once we're done here, I won't get in touch."

"Promise me."

"Sure. Now let's get moving on this job you've got to do." He released me and jumped along the rocks. Carefully, he untied my camisole from the stick, folded the silk and slid in into his front shirt pocket. Grinning, he patted his chest. "Thanks for this. It appears I don't mind it at all."

"Don't thank me yet. I intend to swap that for a pair of old woolen socks, and as soon as I can." I grabbed my fallen Stetson and jammed it on. Mates. So frustrating. How did Hope and Faith cope with theirs? Hmm, maybe I needed to stand my ground a little more.

"You ready to go?" he asked.

"Yes."

He led the way back to the watering hole. After checking the straps on the saddle, he mounted then extended a hand. "Since there's one horse, we'll ride together."

"I should make you go saddle your own horse, except I don't want you near the stables." I slipped my hand into his. He lifted me up and settled me in front of him. I nabbed the reins. "But I'm in charge. I know where this horse needs to be led."

"So do I. Away from those smoky hills. Let's get the cattle moving." Arms around my waist, he held on.

"We're heading to the river. That's what Goldie's asked. It's the safest place for them on the station."

"Who's Goldie?"

"Goldwyn Wincrest is Donaldo's daughter. She's nineteen, the same age as me. Her and Hope are close since they grew up together. She keeps the girls' secret too. She certainly won't be happy to hear I'm mated to a protector, but I'll explain that it's over." I tugged on the reins, guided the mare around the cattle.

"You ride well." He leaned against my back, nuzzled my neck. "And this cocoa butter of yours smells good. I like it. Too much."

"I'll be sure to lather it all over those old socks."

He chuckled then tightened his arms around my waist.

"Hey." I smacked his hands. "A little less of that. I have weapons and I will use them."

"Of course you will." He blew a soft breath along my neck. "I enjoy a little excitement with my danger. Don't you?"

"No." I nudged the horse's flanks and kept a weaving pattern going as I skirted the cattle, urging them forward. "It might pay for you to stop talking, Mr. I-love-danger."

He chuckled. "It appears I also like teasing you."

"Well, you're doing a slap-up job." The sun dipped along the western horizon behind us, sending a flare of red into the clouds of swelling smoke. Bushfires were so destructive, taking everything in their path. I had to get this cattle as far out to the east as I could.

"Will we get to the river by nightfall? This terrain is pretty rough."

"There's a half moon tonight. It'll be enough to guide our way if we don't." The cattle bawled as I continued to press them on. "You sound anxious. If you need to leave, I won't complain. Don't you have duties to attend to?"

"Usually, but after training today the rest of my day was free. I had intended to visit my parents. Dad's got a special project on and needed a hand with it."

"What kind of—" Nope, don't let him draw you into any personal conversation. Bad, bad move.

"You were right about there being a furniture maker in the family. Dad's building Mum a glorious new desk. Wedding anniversary coming up. She's gonna love it."

"Will it be initialed?" No. No. No. Don't ask any questions.

"He monograms everything. It's his thing. Look at me."

I glanced over my shoulder. I really shouldn't have done that. The gold flecks in his brown eyes shimmered powerfully, weaving me under their spell.

"We'll get through this, Lieska." He cupped my cheek.

"I'd rather we not get through anything at all. There must be something I can say to convince you to leave."

"There's danger, so no."

The horse snickered, and I faced front. That's it. Keep your attention where it should be, and ignore the hot hunk at your back.

Only I couldn't. I leaned back against him, surrounded myself in his solid warmth. His spicy scent enveloped me, comforted me. The hunter in me settled. I was with my mate, and since he wasn't going anywhere anytime soon, I might as well enjoy this stolen moment.

I wouldn't have him for long.

Argh, but if only he'd stop breathing on my neck. Each time his warm breath glided over the pulse in my throat, it sped up.

I rode on, pressing the cattle forward.

Slowly the sun dropped behind the hills and the sky darkened. Twinkling within the darkest blanket of midnight blue, the stars added a touch of light to the moon's glow.

"Are we almost there?" Soft, silky words. Each one tingled my toes.

"There's a small rise up ahead. Beyond that the river flows." I couldn't get there fast enough. I crested the slope, and spread out before us, fields of lush green grass rippled like quicksilver. The mighty river snaked through it all. "These lower fields are thick because of the controlled river releases. Maslin, one of our warriors, has the water skill and drives the water as far as he can inland."

"There appears to be a lot of cattle here already."

A large herd grazed, but nowhere near close to our number of stock. "Usually we have thirty-five thousand head, although with the current drought, we're slightly shy of that. Dralion is such an inhospitable land. The cattle and horses we rear on this station provide for those back home. We have to save every animal we can from the threat of the fires."

"I'll help you. I promise." He searched the horizon. "I don't see anyone else on horseback."

Neither did I. A bonus for now. "The cattle won't want to move much from here. We'll make camp though and keep an eye out in case any get restless. Fires have a terrible habit of spreading when the winds get up. If any warriors turn up though, keep your head down."

"I won't cause any problems." He smoothed down my arms, around my hands then took the reins from me. "There's no ash in the air here. I can't scent a thing."

"Lieska!" A horse and rider rode in from behind. Hope. Her blond hair breezed over her shoulders. What a sight for sore eyes.

"Hey, I can't tell you how happy I am to see you." I waved to her.

"Silas is right behind me. We brought some cattle in too." Breathing fast, she pointed along the darkened rise. "Ah, there's the gear Goldie told me she'd dropped off. Bedrolls and such. She 'pathed me and said the four of us can monitor this end of the river belt. Have you spoken to Goldie?"

"No." And I really should have.

"I'll let her know we've all arrived. Won't be a sec."

I searched for Silas among the cattle moving past us from the herd they'd brought in. Our own had joined the other cattle on the plains.

Another horse and rider's silhouette appeared, bringing in the stragglers. Silas. He rode tall and strong as he came abreast of us, the moonlight glinting off his short red-gold hair. Dressed in leather pants and a dark shirt, a sword gleaming at his side, he could pass for one of our warriors.

He cocked a brow as he eyed Cole. "I see you found your mate."

"I did, but my released mate. Thanks for the bringing me in."

"No problem. So you've spoken the words of release then?"

"Ah, not formally." Cole shuffled in the saddle, creaking the leather. "We'll get onto that, ah, sometime."

Heck, that was something we needed to do. The note I'd left him didn't appear to be good enough. A formal release was best. We should do that now we had time. Yeah, why hadn't we done that already?

Hope cleared her throat. "Okay, Goldie's rounding up around the farthest outreaches with some of the other warriors. She said to say hi to you all."

"Ha. Sure she did." Silas snorted then patted his horse's neck. "So she knows about Cole here being mated to Lieska?"

"Um." Hope twiddled with her reins. "I mentioned it, and then had to cut her off when she started screaming in my head." She flicked my arm. "You should have told her. Goldie would've understood."

"Hello. You're the one who said screaming. You're lucky she understands the position you and Faith are in."

"I'm fortunate Dad does too." She cut a look toward Silas. "Don't say it."

"I didn't say a word." He sighed, long and loud. "At least he's not as bad as your grandfather, not that I care to meet either of them."

"I said don't say it." She slid off her saddle and jumped to the ground with a light thud.

King Donaldo would certainly cause problems if he ever heard of his granddaughters' bonds. All hell would break loose for starters, then, well I didn't even care to contemplate what would come next.

Cole rubbed my arms. "Why do you feel so tense?"

I covered his hands with mine. "Donaldo rules with precision and determination. For him there is no gray, just black and white. Our people and yours can't mix."

"We don't. Your dome over Dralion ensures it." He dismounted, reached for me and swung me down beside him. With his hands still on my hips, he brushed a kiss over the top of my head.

I looked into his soulful eyes. "Except we're not in Dralion right now, and his own granddaughters have mixed."

"That was their choice, and now I know what's happened, I'm glad no one's taken that choice from them."

"You are?"

"My parents are soul-bound and…" He dragged in a deep breath then shook his head. "Never mind. That's not for us."

"No, tell me about your parents. You don't keep information from a hunter."

"Sorry, but this time it's best I do." He leaned in and rubbed his nose to mine, a smile on his lips. "Relax."

He couldn't be serious? He wanted me to relax when any number of warriors could turn up. I motioned toward Silas. "Perhaps you've forgotten where you are. Silas would lose that pretty head of his if his true identity were discovered by a warrior not in the know. I don't need you losing yours too."

"Aw, thanks, Lieska." Silas chuckled. "You think my head is pretty? Did you hear that Hope?"

"She meant your head is big. She got her words mixed up."

Hope passed Silas her horse's reins and popped a kiss on his lips. "Why don't you go and tend the horses and I'll sort out the bedrolls. Take Cole with you."

"Sure thing."

"Hold on. Let me grab my gear first." I snagged Cole's jacket from my saddlebags and tugged it on. The days were hot, but the nights could be cool. I'd need this later.

Cole zipped the jacket to my chin. "You seem rather attached to this."

"It smells good." Like spice and all things nice. On my tiptoes, I kissed him. I just couldn't help myself. "I'm looking forward to getting the sweater though. I promise."

"You are the worst liar." Grumbling, he guided our horse away. Silas followed with his and Hope's mounts.

"Come on." Hope led the way toward the gear. "I hate it how they can sense every lie we speak, but still, I think you've got Cole sorted."

"Hardly. Sorted would be him, ah, leaving." Although did I really want him to leave? It would be for the best when he'd only get hurt by staying with me. I flapped out the bedrolls while Hope foraged through the food and set snacks and a bottle of water on each.

"You don't sound so sure. If you ask me, he looks both frustrated and smitten. I don't think he's leaving anytime soon." Hope sat on her makeshift bed. She kicked off her boots and eased her jean-clad legs out "Which means, totally sorted."

"Being mated to the enemy is asking for trouble." I removed my sword belt and Stetson then set them beside my bed. "It's best I not go there."

"Or you can accept it might be for the best. Just try not to overthink it, and give yourself time. You wanna make the right decision."

Except we didn't have time on our side. He'd be gone the moment the fires were under control. Great. I was going to make myself crazy with all the what-ifs if I didn't let this rest. I picked up one of the snacks, a plastic wrapped chocolate cookie. There was nothing quite like chocolate to bump my mood. A morale-booster if ever I needed one.

"You're supposed to eat the sandwich first." Hope picked up hers then her cookie and looked from one to the other as if weighing her choices.

"I would, but there's chocolate. Go for the cookie." I flopped onto my back, munched and stared at the array of stars. Nature at its most beautiful, even with the threat of fires so close.

Silas jogged toward us, unstrapped his sword and plunked down next to Hope. "Move over, love."

"You've got your own bedroll." She nudged his shoulder. "Over there."

"I don't think so." He tipped up her chin and kissed her. "Mmm, chocolate. Hope, why are you eating the cookie first?"

"Because Lieska is, and she's a bad influence."

Cole strode in, tucked his sword near his bedroll then settled in beside me. "What's this about chocolate cookies? I'm certainly aware my mate's a bad influence."

"I'm not nearly as bad as you, and you're on my bed." I should enforce more space. I shoved his shoulder, his immoveable shoulder. "Are you going to move?"

"Maybe later. You look like you need a little company." He heaved his bedding closer. "What's on your mind?"

"Nothing."

"Come on. Did you miss the soul-bond lesson on thou cannot lie? Because you suck at speaking the truth."

"Okay, everything's wrong then. Is that better?" Sheesh. Were his thoughts as tangled as mine?

"Right, where shall we start then?" With his snacks and water in hand, he relaxed on his side and smiled at me. "I'm listening. Tell me what you need."

"I need you to zap home, so I can stop overthinking

everything. You've got the image for this place now. You could drop back and pester me at any time. Think of the excitement and danger with that."

"Wrong answer. And I prefer to pester you now, which I'm getting rather good at." He unwrapped his sandwich and bit into it. "You want a sandwich?"

"No. But feel free to give me your chocolate cookie." I shot a look at Hope, hoping to give her a signal that I could use some help, but she and Silas were quietly talking, their heads bent together. She truly needed some serious wing-woman lessons.

"Here you go." He handed his cookie over.

"You're really giving me this?" Damn. How adorable was that?

"It's all yours, for some information. I want to know more about you. How much time do you spend here?" He passed me my water flask. "I mean as compared to Dralion."

"About half." I took a couple of sips and set it aside. "Why?"

"I'm curious. Where do you usually—"

"No. Don't ask."

"—sleep?"

I almost bopped the cookie over his head, but it would be a terrible waste. I couldn't do that to the cookie. "You don't want to know, Cole. You really don't."

"Don't dare me. Leaving me guessing will only backfire on you." He rolled me in under his shoulder. "Spill. Curb my curiosity."

"You don't fight fair, but you're also lucky I understand." I rested my cheek on his chest and snuggled. "I have a room on the homestead's second floor. A perfectly safe room. In Dralion, I have my own quarters in the barracks. And when I manage to pop in to see my parents, I catch a few winks in the sleep-out next to their cottage. That's provided there's a spare bunk. It kind of gets overrun by my three younger brothers, so I just go with the flow. All I've ever really needed is a pillow and a warm blanket. I even love sleeping out on the range when we're mustering."

He caressed the back of my neck, his fingers warm as he grazed them back and forth against my skin. I almost purred. "See, that wasn't so bad."

No, not bad at all. I liked being with him. "I'm glad you're here, Cole."

"So am I," he whispered. "So am I."

His statement rang with truth, as mine had.

Trouble, big trouble.

The breeze picked up, and I breathed deep, testing it with my heightened senses. Thankfully it was still perfectly clear of even the smallest taint of smoke.

"*Lieska, it's Goldie.*" She fired up our link.

"*Hey, Goldie, we've still got clear air at the river.*" Goodness, what was she going to say about Cole?

"*Good. I want you to remain alert though. You know the drill.*" I sure did. Bushfires could rage for days or weeks, and smoke could drift some distance from the heart of the blaze. New fires often spread through the ash in the air. "*Lieska, and about being alert. Hope told me about Cole. Give me the run down.*"

"*Um...well...ah...*"

"*Spit it out. Are you two together? Or is there still a chance I can harm him and you won't get angry?*"

"*He's helping out. He'll be gone once the fires are out, and no, you can't hurt him.*" I'd never let her touch him. He was my mate, and I'd keep him safe.

"*As long as he'll be gone, that's music to my ears. I knew you'd be sensible about this. Hope and Faith are a lost cause, but you, no. I can trust you to do the right thing.*"

"*Your tone is far too gleeful.*" I rubbed my chest, hating the ache that the thought of his leaving brought.

"*Lieska, having Davio Loveria and Silas Carver around*

means two protectors too many. Who on earth would want to be soul-bound to the enemy? Not me. Hey, if you need a pep talk, call out. I'll set you back on the straight and narrow in no time. I'll chat to you later, okay? I've got cattle on the move."

"Yep, later." The straight and narrow was looking less straight and narrow by the second.

"Who are you talking to?" Cole flipped his bedroll over top of us, cocooning us in its warmth. Well, he clearly wasn't moving. And now I didn't care to fight him on it. Each hour that passed, was another hour closer to when he'd be gone, and I didn't want to miss a moment of the time we had left.

I stroked his chest, calming at the solid feel of him. "Goldie. She said to remain alert. Between the four of us, we should take a two-hour shift each and keep an eye out."

"Close your eyes and rest. I'll take the first shift. Silas." He called out to him over my head. "I'll wake you for the second shift."

"Great. You do that." He and Hope had bedded down much the same as us.

I hooked my thumb through the belt hoop of Cole's jeans and played my fingers over his hip. "Are you sure you want to go first? I don't—"

"I'll go first." He kissed the tip of my nose. "Sleep well, my mate."

I closed my eyes and relaxed.

So peaceful.

His mate, yes, even though not for much longer.

Chapter 4

Warm breath fluttered across my cheek and Cole's arms banded tightly about me. I stretched my legs and rubbed my feet over his. Each time during the night when I'd stirred, he'd urged me back to sleep. He and Silas had continued taking shifts, one after the other and neither would be denied. Stubborn times two. The night was almost over though, a hint of light along the horizon giving evidence sunrise was close.

I edged up on one elbow and peeked at him. He lay awake, his golden-brown hair a rumpled mess and his chin sharp with a razz of stubble. So cute. Why did he have to be a protector? My soul ached for more. "You're going to be too tired if you don't catch a few more winks."

"I'm good. I slept half the night." He tucked me back against him. "I like having you close."

"Me too." Boy did I like it.

I glanced behind me toward Hope. She was stirring while Silas sat watching her with a smile. He leaned forward and dropped a kiss on her forehead. He murmured to her, so softly I hadn't a chance of catching the words. Half our people were mated. It was what I wished for too, but…

I faced Cole, and then got lost in his beautiful eyes.

"Tell me what you're thinking. I need to know, Lieska."

"I—I—" My throat dried and my eyes misted. I ducked my

head under his chin so he wouldn't see my threatening tears. He was going to leave soon, and I was stronger than this. I wasn't going to cry. I could deal with the decision we'd made.

"Hey, morning you guys," Hope called out.

Oh thank heavens. I blinked rapidly then rolled toward her, beyond glad for the diversion. "Hey back at ya. Did you sleep all right?"

"You know me. I always sleep like a dream when I'm out under the stars." She eased to her feet, tucked one loose violet shirttail into her jeans and stared toward the western bush line. "Hmm, it's hard to tell from this distance what's going on over there." Hand to her forehead, she searched the area south toward the homestead. "And it seems even hazier in that direction. Strange. I wonder what's going on toward home."

I cranked around to look. Why would there be so much smoke near the homestead?

"Silas. Up you get." Hope pulled on her riding boots. "I need you to 'port me into town. Fire Department. Let's go check in with local enforcement and get an update."

"Gotcha." He shoved his boots on then held onto her. The two shimmered and disappeared.

Checking things out was a good idea. I eyed Cole. "I'll do the same. I'll whip home and take a look around, get changed and stuff. Can you hold the fort here while I do?" I wriggled up then found myself flat on my back, Cole above me.

"I can, but let's get one thing straight." The gold flecks in his hunter eyes flared. "If you don't want to end our bond then tell me."

I cupped his face, rubbed his cheeks with my fingertips. "Has anyone ever told you your morning manner needs some improvement? You're far too demanding."

"No one's mentioned it yet, but thanks for the up." He lowered his mouth to mine and kissed me, one very hot morning kiss. My heartbeat thumped out of rhythm. I kissed him back, overwhelmed by the new emotions stirring within me. Oh, why did he have to kiss like a dream? Too soon he pulled away, heaved himself to his feet and lifted me to mine. "I expect you back here in ten minutes."

"Ten minutes? You can't be serious?"

"Very serious."

I grabbed my boots, Stetson and sword. Not prepared to argue further, I 'ported, fast. I needed a break from him. It might clear my head.

I arrived in my room, one Hope and Goldie had insisted I have near theirs instead of outside in the barracks. I adored this space, well, except for the snowy white carpet since I was always getting endless red dust on it. I tramped across it in my socks and tossed my gear onto my queen-sized bed, which took pride of place against one wall. I slipped Cole's jacket off and folded it neatly next to my sword on the golden bedcovers. Goodness, I really liked his jacket. I wasn't looking forward to getting the sweater at all.

At the window, I eased the white lace nets aside. A copse of gum trees near the corral, more brown than green, swayed in the wind. And the smoke. Shoot, it was so thick. It clogged the air. That's why there'd been such a haze in this direction. There had to be fires burning close to here. I shoved open my link to Goldie. *"Hey, I'm at the homestead and—"*

"Great. I need someone there. Hope and Silas just gave me an update. The state firefighters are close to you. They brought teams in a couple of hours ago. They began back-burning in an attempt to snuff this fire out. I wasn't aware of it, but it might mean more smoke your way as their operation spreads back to the west."

"The smoke is thicker. Are you sure the back-burning is heading in the opposite direction?"

"Positive, but as a precautionary measure I want you to 'port the horses to the river. We don't need them suffering from

any fumes. Keep your hunter senses covered up too. I don't want you breathing in anything toxic."

"Okay, gotcha. I've got this covered."

I raced to my dressing room, changed into a pair of skinny red jeans and a bright red blouse. Best to remain a beacon of color with all this smoke about. I added a red and black checked neck-cloth, lugged on my boots, and strapped on my sword belt.

I flashed to the kitchen, dropped bread into the toaster and poured a glass of orange juice. I'd need sustenance to get through today.

"You're a minute late." Cole's deep voice bounced inside my head. *"Don't make me hunt you down."*

"I'm grabbing a bite to eat, but hunt me down if you want." I couldn't keep the longing from my voice. Let the hunter hunt.

"Hope and Silas have returned. They mentioned the back-burning."

"Goldie just told me about it too. I've got to 'port the horses to the river. You keep those cattle in line over there. I'll be back soon enough."

"Silas and Hope can look after the cattle here. Hold on. I won't be a moment."

My toast popped and I slathered it in chocolate spread.

"I'm back in Peacio."

What? He couldn't be. That was a surprise. *"Um, if you've got other things to do, I understand."*

"The only thing I have to do is change then lasso you into line."

"Well, I hate to break it to you, but the lassoing isn't going to happen."

"I'm on my way back."

"Good for you."

"Don't be cheeky."

"Ha. Not possible." I took a bite of my toast then peered out the wooden square-cut window. Along the dusty path from the

stables, Cole stormed toward me. Wow. He cut an impressive figure in dark leathers and belted side-sword. The hem of his white shirt fluttered loose under his tan leather vest.

His gaze clashed with mine through the glass. "Where's the door?" he yelled out.

"Follow the path to the front porch. There's a wide-open foyer. Take the first door on your—"

He leaned against the window pane, got the image and flashed inside.

"Or you could just do that. Impatient much?"

"Like you wouldn't believe." Hands on the metal sink either side of me, he leaned in and breathed deep. If he came any closer, I'd kiss him. "More chocolate. I am going to form an addiction myself if I hang around you much longer."

"Hey, don't sass the chocolate." I ducked under his arm and set more bread in the toaster. After it popped, I spread both pieces with extra chocolate spread and passed him a slice. "You want juice too?"

"Yes, please."

I poured then nudged the glass across the countertop toward him. Outside, the smoke continued to thicken. "That back-burning is certainly close. It better be working."

"Hope said the firefighters know their stuff, and I'm ready to move those horses when you are."

"You're almost ready." I pulled a toweling cloth out of the drawer, draped it over his nose and tied it in place at the back of his head. "Thank you for all your help."

"I wouldn't be anywhere else." He lifted my red and black checked neck-cloth over my nose. "Right. We're all set to go. What's the drill?"

"We have over two-hundred breeding mares, plus foals, and they all need to be moved."

"How do you intend to contain them at the river?"

"Leads. There's a fence line down there, so we'll tie them

to the posts. That should work." I flashed us to the stables. Smoke swirled through the air of the wide central holding room, obliterating the grassy scent of the hay bales stacked to the ceiling. "Use whatever you need from in here. There's plenty of tack hooked on the back wall and tons of rope in the side room." I pointed toward the back door. "Out that way are the fenced yards where we keep the mares and foals."

He caught my hand and squeezed it. "Promise me you'll be careful."

"I will, and you too. No getting hurt on my turf. You take the outside area and I'll move the mares close to birthing from down these corridors. That'll be about half each. Go." I nudged him toward the back door.

"You stay safe, or else we'll be having words." He backed up, his fired gaze on me, and then slowly he turned and disappeared through the door.

Staying safe would be letting him go and living his life, but I couldn't keep denying the strength of our bond. What would it be like if we accepted it as Hope and Silas had done? What was between us would only develop and grow. I closed my eyes as longing swept through me. Damn, I was falling, and fast.

Horses whinnied. Argh, I needed to get them out. I raced to the first stall.

I 'ported each mare, taking extra care to secure them farther away from where Cole tied the mares.

We passed each other going back and forth.

As the hours rolled on, the humidity rose off the charts. Hope and Silas rode the perimeter of the grassy river belt, keeping the cattle contained as more herded cattle arrived. Gee, it was lucky the other warriors were so busy they hadn't yet asked about the two extra hands. It helped Silas had his Stetson low and Cole the cloth over half his face.

At the homestead the smoke continued to blow in, thick with red outback dust swirling within. I scrubbed my eyes with my knuckles. The bitter, choking haze clogged my throat and wiped out my vision. Such a raging, suffocating heat. I groped the walls of the paneled corridor and fumbled along until I reached the end stall. This should be the last one. I unclipped the catch and stumbled inside.

"Where are you, Lieska. I can't see a damn thing. There's more smoke inside these stables now than outside." Cole's voice pounded down our link.

"I'm here. Last mare. I won't be long." I coughed and spluttered. *"Are you keeping the foals calm?"* They fought the foreign restriction, but at least they were safe.

"I've got them sorted, just. I'll head back to the river with this last colt. You better be right behind me."

"Yes, right behind you." I plucked my sweat-soaked shirt from my skin.

I patted the air then knocked into the horse. With my foot. Damn, she was on the ground. On my knees, I stroked the mare's slick neck. She snorted then whinnied as if in pain. Oh hell. One in labor. 'Porting a mare in this condition was asking for trouble.

Gasping for breath, I worked at soothing her first.

A precious minute ticked by. Two.

"Lieska?" Cole's voice echoed in my head, yet as if from a distance.

I coughed and wheezed. I had to get this mare out of here. My throat tightened and constricted.

"Answer me." His tone held a deadly bite.

I fought to get another breath in, managed a pitiful amount of air. Focus. 'Port her. You've done everything you can. She has to go like this.

My lungs burned.

My vision swam, and then nothing.

* * * *

My chest exploded with pain as a crashing weight came down on it.

"Damn it, Lieska. Breathe."

A hot mouth covered mine, pushed air deep inside.

My lungs were on fire.

Another thump over my heart, then another, and another.

Argh, that had to be Cole, and he needed to stop that pounding.

"Breathe. Now."

I wanted to, just so I had enough air to yell at him.

Light flared behind my closed eyelids, shoving away the last of the darkness.

I dragged air in, and it scraped painfully along the sides of my throat.

"That's it, love. Take another breath."

He held me, surrounded me. Everything I wanted.

"Cole?" I croaked his name.

"You truly are the most difficult mate." Hoarse words. "I swear you will never put your life on the line like that again. Do you hear me?"

"Not quite sure." I shoved open my heavy lids, and his beautiful gold-flecked gaze searched mine. I coughed. "Something about hearing you, but I can't do that if you leave me."

"Take a drink. Your voice is far too scratchy." Water dribbled over my lips. Nice. I opened my mouth and more trickled down my scorched throat. "It's just as well you fast-heal. Hurry it up."

Could he get more demanding?

Still, I kept lapping at the cool water, each sip going down easier, smoother, better.

"That's it." Lips pressed to my forehead. "I don't want to leave you either."

"We need to—" I coughed, cleared my throat and tried again. "We need to talk."

He lifted me higher in his lap then brushed his lips over

mine. "I thought I'd lost you."

"As it appears, I'm a little hard to get rid of."

A tear welled in the corner of his eye. "When you were in danger, my soul cried out for yours. I'm sorry, Lieska, but I can't give you up. I think I've known it all along."

"You can't?" I clutched his sooty shirtfront. "I'm struggling too. But how can we make this relationship work?"

"We're hunters. Nothing will truly stop us if we desire it." He smiled, and I'd never seen him look so happy or determined. "Say you'll hunt with me. We'll pursue this bond. You hold the other half of my soul, and I yours. I'll never want anyone other than you. Agree. Say yes."

I wanted him too, so badly. "I do like kissing you. You promise to keep that up?"

"You have my word. So is that a yes?"

I grinned, and unable to help myself, murmured, "Kiss me and find out. I dare you."

He looked deep into my eyes, bent his head and kissed me.

My heart soared and my soul called to his.

Oh, I had my mate, and I'd never let him go.

It was time to live my life, with him.

The hunter had succeeded in the hunt.

Chapter 5

I leaned against Cole's chest as he wrapped his arms around me from behind. We stood at the edge of the mighty river, which pulsed with life. Ducks hidden within the reeds cackled and took flight. Their wings brushed the glistening surface as they swept across the wide expanse to the other side. Above, the skies were a brilliant blue without even a wisp of cloud.

The outback had returned to its most striking, the back-burning operation a huge success. Within days the firefighters had stamped the fires out, more than a fortnight past. Now the cattle, thousands of head, grazed along this green belt and far into the distance.

"I love this place." I wriggled against him, so at peace.

"I noticed." He rubbed his chin over the top of my head. "Though it's still far too hot today. I think I should stick around and make sure none of those fires decide to flare up again."

"Good idea." He wouldn't hear a complaint from me. Whatever time we could steal to be together, was the best. "Did you wanna see CCC. The newborn colt's become quite attached to you."

After Cole had saved me, he'd returned to the stables and rescued the laboring mare. She'd birthed her foal and I'd named the young one Cool Calm Collected after the man who'd saved her.

"I'd rather become more attached to you."

I turned and kissed him, my heart filled with love. How could I have ever wanted to give him up?

"What are you thinking?" His hunter eyes gleamed.

"That you deserve a reward for capturing this warrior."

"What kind of reward?"

"Trust me. You're going to love it." I wriggled out of his hold and stepped back.

"Where are you going, my love?"

I kept moving, one step at a time.

He stalked me.

"Chase me and find out."

Laughing, I 'ported.

He'd catch me. I had no doubt he would.

And his prize?

A lifetime of hunting me.

Love these characters and want more?

Don't miss the rest of this spell-binding series from a *New York Times* and *USA Today* Bestselling Author.

To love and protect…across worlds.

Princesses of Myth

Protector, Book One

Warrior, Book Two

Hunter, (Novella – Book 2.5)

Enchanter, Book Three

Healer, Book Four

Chaser, Book Five

JOANNE WADSWORTH

PROTECTOR

Faith and Davio's Story, Book One

ENCHANTER

Silvie's Story, Book Three

HEALER

Belle's Story, Book Four

WARRIOR

CHASER

Goldie's Story, Book Five

JOANNE WADSWORTH

Joanne Wadsworth is a *New York Times* and *USA Today* Bestselling Author who adores getting lost in the world of romance, no matter what era in time that might be. Hot alpha Highlanders hound her, demanding their stories are told and she's devoted to ensuring they meet their match, whether that be with a feisty lass from the present or far in the past.

Living on a tiny island at the bottom of the world, she calls New Zealand home. Big-dreamer, hoarder of chocolate, and addicted to juicy watermelons since the age of five, she chases after her four energetic children and has her own hunky hubby on the side.

So come and join in all the fun, because this kiwi girl promises to give you her "Hot-Highlander" oath, to bring you a heart-pounding, sexy adventure from the moment you turn the first page. This is where romance meets fantasy and adventure…

To learn more about Joanne and her works, visit:
Website and Blog
http://www.joannewadsworth.com